E.L. RHODES

THE SERIALIZATION OF DISCONTENT

A Novel

THE SERIALIZATION OF DISCONTENT

ISBN: 9782009005781

For Vera

Book Cover By: Walter Brinkley

Author Photo By: Glenn Williams

Edited By: Jean C. Hsu-Lupo & Unice Yeng Hsu

Reviewed by: Marcella Swann, Marjorie Garland, Deshan Mingo

An ASG Publication

Chapter 1 - 1957

The sounds of the huge Hammond B3 organ filled the entire room. Mrs. Davis was tickling the black and white keys and mashing the bass pedals on the floor as she rocked in a back and forth motion. The six-member choir lifted their heads to the heavens as they sang out. "We've come this faaaaar by faith.........leaning on the Loooooooord."

Willam sat quietly on his mother's lap as she bounced him to the beat of the music. This was their weekly ritual.

His mother, Martha Trent, would get up every Sunday morning at 7 am. She'd take her shower, get dressed, have her breakfast, and then do the same for Willam. Willam Trent was her son, her heart, and her joy.

Actually born William Xavier Trent Jr., he was somehow stuck with the first name Willam due to a typographical error on his birth certificate. His parents never could afford to have it corrected. He was small for his age, with caramel colored skin, dark hair, and big brown eyes. He and his mother attended the First Rock Baptist Church of Greater South East. It was a small church located inside a duplex style house on Chaplain Street in South East Washington, D.C. The church consisted only of about forty members, but it had spirit.

Ever since he was placed on this earth seven months ago, Willam and his mom Martha never missed a Sunday. They would attend the eleven o'clock service each Sunday without fail. Although he was too young to really understand what was going on, he'd sit there quietly smiling while his mom clapped his hands together during the choir selections. He would stare into the eyes of the pastor during the sermon as if he understood every word.

It was the spring of 1957, a year of segregation, a year of people of color who still struggled endlessly just to be counted as a people. It was a time when everyone had to do whatever he or she could just to keep their head above water. But not Willam, he had no worries. He had no fears. He was only seven months old and knew nothing about these things.

One particular Sunday morning was different from any other for Willam. It was his first Easter Sunday. The trees and flowers were in bloom and everyone entering the church that day was dapper in their bright and colorful outfits. Women styled some of the most fashionable hats in brilliant colors, while the men would stride closely behind in their fresh, crisp suits. Yes, this was some parade and Willam was enjoying the day. He sat on his mother's lap as he always did every Sunday.

Church went on a little longer than usual. After all, it was Easter. When the choir had finished singing their last selection and the pastor had ended his sermon, dinners were served in the kitchen of the church house. Some of the church folk would get a plate to take home because of the limited space. Others would sit and eat wherever there was room. They would sit on the radiators, the steps, and stools. Folding metal chairs were placed throughout the yard and were occupied quickly. It looked like a family reunion. This was always one of the biggest events of the year and would go on until late evening every year.

Martha gathered Willam up and retrieved a plate from the kitchen. She took Willam out into the front yard. There were no seats available for Martha, but of course one of the young men was eager to give his up. Remember, it was 1957. Martha spread her wide yellow and white cotton dress across the chair. She sat down slowly as not to spill the contents of her plate. She positioned little Willam on her knee by resting his back against her left arm and began eating.

"Would you like a plate for Jimmy, Martha?" Mrs. Gill asked.

"Oh yes please, if it's not too much trouble and thank you." Martha replied.

Jimmy was Willam's daddy and Martha's husband of three years. He was a happy kind of guy who was always laughing, cracking jokes, and dancing, but had the nastiest mean streak if you took him there. Outside of that, he was a very likable guy and Martha loved him. He was a short man, with dark curly hair and dark skin. He also worked a lot, especially on Sundays and Martha hated that.

She'd always tell him, "Sunday is a day for the Lord, Jimmy. Keep the Sabbath holy! You need forgiveness Honey, we all do."

Jimmy would always laugh and joke about it. He would start shaking uncontrollably and roll his eyes around in his head yelling, "I got the spirit! I GOT THE SPIRIT! I'm filled with the Holy Ghost! Yeeeeeeeah!"

Then he'd stop and look at her, all the while smiling. Of course, she saw NO humor in this. She would scold him a little more and storm off into the kitchen. He'd always finish up with something like, "You wanna be holy? Oh yeah, you'll be holy alright; holy shoes, holy blouse, holy everything if I don't make that extra money on Sundays! Just pray for yourself Martha, don't you worry about me. Least I aint like those old hypocrites sittin' over there hoopin' and hollerin' then goin' out doin' God knows what."

You see, Jimmy, like most other men in the neighborhood, had to work more than one job. In fact, Jimmy had more than two. Monday through Friday, he worked as a laborer for a local construction company in the mornings and as a janitor at the D.C. General Hospital in the evenings. On Sundays, he did what most of the other guys did. He hustled. He would make the weekly liquor run down to Calvert County. He and his good buddy Pete Little would drive down to Calvert in a truck owned by the man that Pete worked for, Ira.

Ira owned the neighborhood corner grocery store *"The Food Plaza"*. It was a small store but very expensive for that time. Ira knew that most of the people living in the neighborhood either didn't own automobiles or couldn't afford one. Nor, could they afford a car for hire to take them farther into the city to shop the larger, less expensive grocers, so he took advantage.

Pete worked for Ira making deliveries. Pete, also an enterprising young man, would sneak the keys every Sunday before they closed. Pete and Jimmy would use the truck Sunday night and Pete would return the keys bright and early on Monday morning while Ira got the cash registers ready for business. Ira was Jewish and trusted no one with his money.

Jimmy and Pete would drive down to Calvert Country to meet Hinkly. Hinkly was the biggest white man Jimmy had ever seen. He and Pete used to joke with him all the time about him being so huge. Hinkly would help them load the liquor onto the truck. They'd pay him and he would always leave them with the same warning.

"You boys be careful round these parts. You git caught, you tell on me, you be dead."

He'd smile after saying this, but Jimmy and Pete knew that Hinkly wasn't kidding. The men would always leave without hesitation. The gears of the truck would often scream and squeal as Pete jammed his foot down on the stiff clutch and prematurely shift into gear in his attempt to make a quick exit from the forbidden land. In both directions, they would pass by the small desolate shacks and be given nasty stares from their redneck occupants, giving them even more incentive to keep their swift and steady pace.

"Hey, did you hear that? Sounds like the engine. Sounds like it may have thrown a rod. You'd better pull over and let me check it out." Pete would look over at Jimmy angrily and Jimmy would look out the window and chuckle. "I'd sure hate to break down in these parts," he continued.

Pete never found any amusement in Jimmy's playful comments when it came to their safety down there. He knew that they were flirting with danger every time they crossed over the county line. He'd make sure that just as quickly as they arrived in Calvert, they would depart just as fast. They would load up, pay, and leave without looking back and always made sure to never take the same road twice when exiting.

As soon as the men returned from Calvert, they would pull up to Tyrone Butler's place just off interstate 295. He was the man with all of the connections. Jimmy would follow Pete to Tyrone's house every Sunday to collect his order sheet and money for Hinkly. Tyrone bought and sold the liquor from Hinkly every week and paid Pete and Jimmy handsomely to ride down to get it. Pete was paid more of course, as he was the one who had stolen the truck. They made good money for an evening's work. After Tyrone paid the men, Jimmy would jump in his car that he always left parked in front of Tyrone's house and head straight home.

After finishing her Easter church dinner, Martha made her rounds of hugging and shaking hands with the other members. She had been there for hours. She pulled out the chicken bone that was wedge tightly in Willam's little hand and dropped it into the metal trashcan and they headed home.

Martha opened the front door to her home which was just around the corner from the church. Immediately after stepping in, she switched on the fan. She laid a blanket out on the floor in the living room for Willam to rest on, then picked up Jimmy's plate, took it to the kitchen and placed it into the oven. After fixing a cold drink for herself and a bottle for Willam, she bounced back into the living room where they both consumed their beverages. Shortly after, Martha took Willam upstairs, bathed him and got him ready for the night. They went back downstairs and she turned on the television.

Jimmy and Martha were proud of their television. It was black and white of course, but a TV never the less.

"Plop! Plop! Fizz! Fizz! Oh what a relief it is…" sang out from the television advertisement.

Martha adjusted the coat hanger that was used as a television antenna in hopes of clearing up the fuzziness. After some minor adjustments, the picture became clear.

"*Gunsmoke?* I don't think so young man."

She picked up the pair of pliers lying next to the television, pushed them into the socket and turned the channel.

"*Lassie*, now that's better. You want to watch Lassie Lil Will?"

After fifteen minutes of Lassie, Willam was fast asleep.

As Willam lay sleeping, a knock came from the door. It was Mr. Daniels from the church. Martha placed her index finger to her lips, "Shhhhhhh" then pointed to Willam. She opened the door. Before stepping in, Mr. Daniels looked in both directions to see if anyone was watching. He entered the living room and sat down on the couch. Martha tiptoed into the kitchen to get him a cold drink. She returned with a glass of rum and ice and sat it on the table in front of Mr. Daniels.

Mr. Daniels was a very tall and very well dressed man who always wore sunglasses. Day or night, he could be seen driving through the neighborhood with those dark plastic eye covers on. He was one of only a few men in the neighborhood who drove a Cadillac.

He had a long deep scar on the left side of his face from being cut with a straight razor, but that's the kind of thing you run into when you run numbers.

"Is it cool? I mean, you've got little man right here, and where's Jimmy?"

"It's okay, he's working and my baby's fast asleep. I can take care of you."

Martha leaned over and helped him take off his jacket and his tie. She stood up over him and slipped off her dress. They then stretched out over the couch and he took her.

Most men wanted Martha. She was tall and lean, with just enough meat on her to show her curves. She had light brown eyes, long black wavy hair, and was a very mature woman to be only twenty one years old. Men loved her and she knew how to make them feel good, especially Mr. Daniels.

Martha spoke to him the entire time that she was with him. She knew that's what he liked. She knew how arrogant he was and how he liked his ego stroked.

"That's right baby, stroke it just like that! Oh yeah, yeah that's it!"

With her voice climbing higher, Willam was starting to squirm. Martha placed her hands on both sides of Mr. Daniels' hips to prevent him from moving.

"Wait!" she whispered.

She pushed him upward and he climbed off.

"Why don't you take his little ass upstairs?"

Martha walked over and patted Willam gently on his back until he squirmed no more. She walked back over to Mr. Daniels and mounted him. With her hips thrusting as hard as she could, she leaned over and whispered in his ear.

"Give it to me Daddy, give me all you got. Oh, it's sooooo good! Oh yeah baby!" She continued riding him until he exploded deep inside of her.

He then tried to kiss Martha, but she pulled back. Her kissing was for Jimmy only.

She immediately climbed off of him, reached over and passed him a few napkins, which were lying on the table behind her. She tipped upstairs to the bathroom where she cleaned herself quickly before returning to Willam.

"I left the money on the table, Hon. Thanks again."

That's right, this was a regular occurrence, and Mr. Daniels was one of Martha's regular customers.

He placed his hat on his head and opened the door. He then peeked out of the screen door, slipped on his shades, and made his exit.

Martha had two more similar visits that evening before Jimmy's scheduled arrival. She made a total of thirty dollars that day.

Jimmy would usually get home at about 11 pm. He followed the same routine every night. He would come in the door, kiss Martha, walk upstairs and whisper to Willam as he slept. After about ten minutes, he would make his way back downstairs, grab his plate out of the oven and sit with Martha and watch the "*Honeymooners*".

After putting little Willam down for his slumber, Martha cleaned the kitchen and did some ironing. She folded all of her laundry and put it neatly in its proper place. She then went downstairs and positioned herself on the couch in preparation for Jimmy's entrance. Once more, she looked around the room for anything that could have possibly been left behind by one of her previous guests. Now feeling confident and at ease from not finding anything in her search, she snuggled deep into the cushions of the couch.

She watched midget wrestling and *"The Jack Benny Show"*. She liked the character named *"Rochester"*.

She sat there for over an hour watching the screen until she dozed off.

Hours passed.

The loud constant beep woke Martha from her sleep. It was the sound that followed the playing of the "Star Spangled Banner" every night at the end of the television station's broadcast.

Martha sat there glaring at the large circular black and white object on the television screen. She collected herself and looked over for Jimmy. Not seeing him, she walked upstairs and looked in their bedroom. The bed was unoccupied and the room was without his presence. After searching every room upstairs, she decided to check in front of the house for his car. She tipped down the stairs and quietly opened the front door. She peered up and down both sides of the still and silent street only to see the absence of his car. Jimmy still had not made it home.

"Where is he?" she thought. "He's probably broken down on 295 again or with Pete drinking that devil's water."

She made her way upstairs, not worried, and climbed into bed. She never gave it a second thought because it had happened many times before. Jimmy would constantly breakdown, but

9

would not give up that old *1952 Chevy II*. It was red and shaped just like a little box. He loved that car.

The next morning Martha was awakened by loud banging on her front door. This was the third interruption of her sleep. Willam had awakened her twice during the night. This was unusual for him, but she tended to him, she changed him, patted him lightly on his back until he returned to his slumber.

She looked over for her husband in hopes that he would answer the door, but he was not next to her. She pulled the sheet back and slid into her slippers, put on her bathrobe, and shuffled down the slight incline of stairs leading to the living room.

"Coming, I'll be right there," she yelled down the stairs.

As she approached the door, the loud knocking started again.

"Alright, I'm coming. Next time don't forget your key!"

She gathered her bathrobe then opened the door. Standing on the porch were two D.C. Metropolitan policemen. She looked past the police officers for Jimmy, but he was no where in sight.

"Mrs. Trent?"

"Yes, I'm Mrs. Trent. What's wrong, is my husband in trouble? I told him that one day, one day…"

The blank look on their faces told her that something was wrong. Something was very wrong.

Knowing that Jimmy had not come home last night and now seeing the police at her front door made her nervous. With a trembling voice, Martha forced out the question that she feared to ask.

"My husband, is it my husband? Is he alright?"

Upstairs, Willam began to cry. He was awake and now wanted his mother.

Martha moved away from the door and the officers stepped inside. She sat down on the couch. Now believing that he was probably injured and lying in some hospital, all kinds of thoughts were racing through her mind.

"Where is he?" she yelled out.

The white officer retreated back toward the door and the black officer stepped toward her.

"Mrs. Trent, I'm sorry to inform you that your husband, James, was killed last night in Calvert County."

Martha stared at the wall. Willam was crying louder, but she could not hear him. She had blocked him out completely. She fell to her knees and screamed.

"NO LORD! PLEASE NO, NOT HIM!"

She continued to scream and weep. Mrs. Delaney from next door, already standing on her porch curious as to why the police were at Martha's home, had climbed over the rail which divided the two small houses and rushed in to help.

"Mrs. Trent, we'll do everything that we can to catch whoever did this to your husband."

Martha said nothing.

After the policemen left, like a zombie, Martha dragged herself upstairs and fell across her bed. She wept for hours.

After that dreadful day, there was a short investigation into Jimmy's death. Of course, the murders were never solved. Not Jimmy's, nor Pete's. Rumor has it that that night Jimmy and Pete made their regular run down to Calvert County. Hinkly was there to meet them. He helped them load the truck as usual and they all left. The truck was found ten miles in the opposite direction from their pickup spot, emptied, and set ablaze. Jimmy was found just walking distance from the truck. His face had been severely beaten and charred from the heat produced by the flames and seven of his fingers were broken. His neck had been snapped by the rope which had dug deep into his flesh and his eyes bulged from its tightness. He had swung from that rope all night. His left foot appeared to have been completely blown off by a shotgun blast and several stab wounds ripped through his chest. As for Pete, he was never found.

Jimmy's casket was never opened at his funeral.

Chapter 2 - Willam

Six years had passed and young Willam was growing up to be a handful. Martha, now working as a nurse's aide at D.C. General Hospital, was their only provider. And yes, she still pulled an occasional trick or two. Only when needed though, for special occasions like Christmas and Willam's birthday. Mr. Daniels would still stop by late at night, make both a deposit and a contribution to Willam's Christmas, birthday or school fund, slip on his glasses and then make his exit.

Willam was a happy child. He would run around the yard with his cowboy hat, wearing blue dungarees and his holster, shooting the bad guys. Sometimes while his mom was hanging the laundry out back, he'd tie a towel around his neck and jump off the chain linked fence or swing from the clothes line as if he were flying.

"Look Ma, I'm Mighty Mouse....*Here I come to save the day!*" he'd sing.

Martha would just stand there and laugh at him.

"Boy, get down from there before you break your neck," she'd say, still laughing.

Yes, he was happy. Although he always played by himself, he still had a great time. He had friends at school, but since he always had to stay in the yard while he was at home, he very rarely saw them outside of the playground.

One day while playing with his G.I. Joes in the back yard, he heard a sound from across the alley.

"Dat.dat.dat…dat…dat…dat…dat…dat..dat"

He looked around but did not see anything. Finally, he saw the top of a small forehead and two bright eyes peering at him.

"Hey!" Willam yelled.

The figure slid a stick over the top of the wall leading from the basement as if it were a rifle and began to shoot at Willam once again.

"Dat.dat.dat…..dat…dat!"

"Hey!" the voice yelled back. "I've got a G.I. Joe, too."

"Can you come over?" Willam yelled even louder now, due to his excitement.

"I can ask."

The little boy stood up from behind the wall. He was taller than Willam, but not much older. He ran up the steps and into the house. Moments later he returned with two of his large army action figures and a huge green jeep.

Running down the steps, he yelled to Willam, "She said I could come over. Only for a little while, but she said it's okay. I've got to ask your mom."

The lady from across the alley stepped out of the back door onto the porch and yelled for Martha. Martha stepped outside from the house wiping her hands on her apron.

"Hey Mrs. Jordan, how are you this fine day?"

"I'm fine and you?"

"I'm wonderful. Trying to get this kitchen cleaned. What's up?"

"Is it okay? He wants to come play with little Willam. Is it alright?"

"Of course it is, and besides, Willam could use the company, and it'll keep him out of my hair for a while. It's no trouble, no trouble at all."

The little boy opened the gate which led into the alley and crossed over to where Willam played. He entered the gate smiling.

"Behave yourself," the lady yelled.

"I will Grandma," he yelled back.

The little boy's name was Ralph, Ralph Marshall. He was Mrs. Jordan's grandson. He and his mother were staying with her while his dad was overseas. His dad was in the Army, and Ralph was so proud of that. That's why he loved his G.I. Joes and playing Army so much. He wanted to be just like his dad. That was a concept Willam couldn't grasp.

The boys played for hours. And you know how kids are. They instantly became the best of friends. Everyday was a new adventure for those two.

Ralph and Willam stayed friends for five more summers. When Ralph's dad came home, they moved into the Benning Heights Apartments just around the corner. However, he still went over to his grandmother's house often.

As time passed, they were permitted to play in the alley. Some of the other boys would also come out and they would all play together, with each day becoming more adventurous. They would usually play the standard games that most kids their age played during that time. They would duck and leap from side to side to avoid contact from the hard round rubber ball during an afternoon game of dodge ball. Often, they would play a long enjoyable game of kickball, always using Mrs. Jenkins and Mrs.

Johnson's backyards as "automatic outs". Both yards contained huge, ferocious dogs. The ill tempered dogs were chained, but no matter where the ball landed, it could never be retrieved without assistance from the owner. If no one was home, the ball would become the canine's possession until later that day. The game would be over. This would put a damper in the boys' entire day.

The ball was their treasure. It was more precious than gold to the youngsters. This was not just a kickball. It served multiple purposes: dodge ball, kickball, basketball, soccer ball, football, and ball-tag ball. It was used to play four corners, as a bomb or grenade while playing army, and was passed around and used as a nice comfortable seat during a game break. So you see, this ball meant everything to the boys.

One morning the boys started playing early. It seemed like everybody had the same game on their minds, kickball. They chose teams and started the game. Ralph and Willam were usually always on the same team. Ralph loved to pitch and Willam hovered around second base. They were enjoying a great game. Ralph's eyes lit up when the next kicker stepped up. He turned to the other boys on his team and waved them back. It was Bobby. He was one of the strongest kickers of all the boys and could launch the round rubber ball far and hard. Ralph cocked his arm back then rolled the ball as hard as he could. It didn't phase Bobby one bit. He took two huge steps toward the ball, yanked his leg back then slung it forward with such power that you could almost feel the impact.

A loud boom sounded as he made contact and the ball soared with tremendous force. The ball flew just over Ralph's head bearing in Willam's direction. Willam moved back tensely, trying to judge the ball's course. He raised his hands and jumped as high as he could but was still unable to catch it. After its thunderous impact, the ball quickly rolled down the alley toward the street.

"Get the ball Will! Catch it before it goes into the street, hurry up!" The boys yelled.

Willam ran after the ball. All they needed was for the ball to roll into the street and get run over by a passing car or truck. This happened twice before and both times it shut down game activity for weeks. The first time, Ronnie's ball was crushed by the "Good Humor" man but luckily Bobby's birthday was just two weeks away. He got a new ball for his birthday and the games resumed. That lasted for about a month before Bobby, with his power, did the same thing that he did on this day. The ball was busted by a passing auto and depression had set back in with the boys. Ralph's grandmother bought the next ball out of sympathy, and now it was in jeopardy. Willam ran as fast as he could, but the ball was spinning away even faster.

She appeared from out of nowhere. The young girl stepped over and stopped the ball with her foot. She tapped the ball slightly forward then kicked it as hard as she could. The ball flew over Willam's head back from whence it came. It stopped right in front of Ralph.

"Wow! She's on our side," Ralph shouted.

Willam looked back at Ralph angrily. "No she's not. She's not playing!"

The young girl walked up the alley and the boys met her half way.

"Can I play?"

"Sure!" Ralph replied eagerly.

"No, go home!" Willam shouted.

"Why not? Why can't I play?" she asked.

"Because."

"Because why?"

"Because, we don't know you."

"My name is Cynthia."

"So?"

"So now you know me. What's your name?"

"My name is 'it doesn't matter because you're still not playing so go home' that's my name, so now that we've met, hi and bye!"

"Come on, let me play."

"No, I said."

"Why, 'cause you think that I can kick better than you?"

"No, because I hate girls, NOW GO!"

Cynthia's eyes began to well up. She slowly turned and walked away. Ralph looked over at Willam, "Dang Will, you could have let her play. After all, it's my ball anyway!"

"Well keep your stinkin' ball then!"

Willam too, turned and started down the alley. The boys stood silently and looked at each other before calling Willam back to play. After reaching second base, he turned to Ralph, "Ah, roll the dang ball."

The boys started back playing again. They were back to having a great time until the game was once more interrupted by her tiny voice.

"That's him, that one right there, the one getting ready to kick." It was Cynthia once again, except this time she was accompanied by her mother. They were walking briskly up the alley, with her mother holding her by the hand.

"Young man, I understand that you won't let Cynthia play with you boys, why not?"

Willam looked around at the other boys then at Cynthia and her mom, "She's a girl," he answered.

"And what's that got to do with anything?"

"He says that he hates girls!" Cynthia yelled.

"Well that's 'cause I do!" Willam shouted back.

Cynthia's mother stepped between the two then looked at Willam, "Look young man, you play nice out here or I might just have a word with your mother. I know who you are and where you live and besides, how could you hate girls? Your mother's a girl. You don't hate her now do you?"

"Yep!"

"You hate your mother?"

"Yep, and I hate you, too!"

With that, Cynthia's mom snatched Willam by the ear and marched him home. All the boys chuckled as Willam was put on display. As she walked him down the alley, she called to Martha, "Mrs. Trent! Mrs. Trent!" She walked Willam through the gate with Cynthia trailing close behind.

Martha stepped onto the porch. "What in the world has he done now?"

Cynthia's mother informed Martha of the sequence of their conversation which led to his delivery home. Martha made Willam apologize to Cynthia and her mother then sent him inside for the rest of his punishment. For the remainder of the day he stood in the upstairs window overlooking the alley and watched as Cynthia took his place on the kickball team. She occasionally would look up at him, smile then stick her tongue out at him. Willam was furious, but could not tear himself away from the window. After that day, Willam still never played with Cynthia or any other girl. He would be polite, after all, he did get a thrashing later that night, but would go home anytime a girl was accepted into any of the games by the other boys.

The boys grew up playing and running like boys do. Everything was going great for Willam and Ralph. Life had no ending in sight; it was beautiful and carefree. At least it was, for a while. This particular year was not so kind. It was the year 1968.

It was April 7th. Ralph's mother worked on Connecticut Avenue and was on her way home. Most people hadn't worked that week due to the Martin Luther King riots, but her employer insisted that she report to work. She cared for an elderly lady uptown.

That night, misfortune struck Willam's friend. What happened that night changed things for Ralph forever.

She was found in the backseat of her car, raped and murdered. Her throat had been cut from ear to ear. She had drowned in her own blood and had a cigarette burn in the middle of her forehead. Her murder too, was never solved. Ralph's dad took it really hard. After that night, he hardly spoke a word, not even to Ralph. His only comfort became that of alcohol.

Ralph now spent more time at his grandmother's. He practically lived there. She took care of him while his dad was away or working. Willam felt bad for him, but in some way, he was glad that life had dealt him that hand, because now he could hang out with Ralph more often. There were other kids in the neighborhood that he played with, but they just weren't like Ralph.

This night was a warm one. Willam had just come in from the alley. He was worn out from playing a never-ending game of freeze tag. He walked in the back door and immediately dove into the refrigerator. Although his mom had already cooked and had his meal on the stove, he would always make a sandwich if she wasn't down there. He sat at the small table in the kitchen eating his sandwich. He could hear the squeaking sounds of her bed and his mother calling out for Jesus. He would never leave the kitchen during those times, because he never wanted to see those men's faces. He hated them.

After a while, the high pitched sounds stopped abruptly and the moaning and talking ended. Willam could hear his mother walking in the hallway upstairs and the water in the bathroom run, as usual. When she came out, he could hear mumbling, then the man speaking to her in a loud voice.

"NO! I DON'T HAVE IT!"

"WELL LEAVE ME SOMETHING!" she screamed.

"MOVE OUT OF MY WAY, YOU WHORE!" the man yelled.

Willam could hear them tussling upstairs. Although he was a small scrawny fellow, Willam was not about to have anybody beating on his mother. He was not afraid. As he approached the living room, he could hear the loud footsteps charging down the stairs. As the dark figure approached the front door, Willam could hear his mother crying. The man opened the door for his departure. Just as he stepped outside, the light mounted on the porch ceiling illuminated his face. Willam stopped dead in his tracks. He couldn't move. Although he could still hear the whimpers from his beaten mother from upstairs, he remained motionless. He knew this man. He knew that face all too well. It was Mr. Marshall, Ralph's father.

After the door had slammed shut, Willam slowly made his way up the steps to his mother. She lay in the hallway drenched in tears. Mr. Marshall had beaten her and had paid her nothing.

"Why do you do this Ma? Why do you let these men do this to you?"

"I do this for you son. Only for you would I do such a thing," she replied.

Willam knelt down beside his mother and placed his arms around her. "For me? What do you mean Ma? What do you mean for me?"

Martha slowly rose to her feet with Willam's help. He helped her into her bedroom and eased her down onto her bed. She slowly reached over and pulled the towel hanging over the headboard of her bed and started to wipe the blood from the corner of her mouth.

"I've always wanted you to have nice things Willam, always."

Willam stood tall and looked at his mother. He thought that maybe someday, someone, possibly one of those men, could really hurt her or maybe worse. He gave her the manliest look that he could before speaking. "I can get a job now Ma. Mr. Thompson even said that he'd give me a job passing out flyers for his cleaners on Saturdays, and pay me, too. I don't need anymore stuff. I can work to help out around here now, really I can."

"We'll see, my little man, we'll see."

Willam knew that his mother would never let him work, especially on Saturdays. Willam had choir rehearsal on Saturdays. He was in the church choir named the Sunbeams, and they sang every fourth Sunday.

That following Sunday, Willam and his mom headed to church. As they reached the corner of Chaplain and F Streets, he could see Ralph and his dad entering the alley toward his grandmother's house. Mr. Marshall waved to Martha, but she said nothing. Ralph waved to Willam and he too, looked away. Quickly, Martha gave Willam a smack to the back of his head.

"Boy, what's wrong with you? That's your friend aint it?"

Will nodded his head slowly.

"Then act like it. Don't act ugly Willam. God don't like ugly."

They continued on to church. Willam was still angry, angry with Mr. Marshall for hitting his mom; angry with Ralph for being his son, and angry with his mom for giving him a headache. As far as Mr. Marshall was concerned, all he could think about was revenge. Willam walked into the church with anger still heavy in his heart. He sat in his regular seat next to his mom. When the pastor started his sermon, Willam's eyes lit up. Each word out of his mouth seemed to be directed right at him. The Pastor walked back and forth as he spoke loudly into the small microphone,

"You must feed your spirit. You must feed your spirit with the word of God. You can't live your life and give honor to God obeying just your mind and your body. Saints, we must listen to our spirit man, but in order for him to have any power, we must feed him. Listening to just your mind and your body will have you standing butt naked on Alabama Avenue singing the National Anthem while sippin' on a jar of moonshine, yal don't hear me. Can I get an Amen?! Your mind and body alone can lead you to drugs, can lead you to fornication, it can lead you to evilness and misery."

He went on and on. Willam sat quietly and thought about how his mind and body wanted to knock the hell out of Mr. Marshall.

Later that day, Willam changed out of his church clothes and into his play clothes. He went outside into the alley with his basketball. He dribbled his ball up and down the alley for a while then decided to play bowling. He gathered as many soda pop cans that he could from the trashcans and then lined them up neatly in a row. He'd roll the ball and knock them down and then restack them again. Suddenly, Ralph appeared at the gate.

"Hey Willy, whatcha playin'?"

"What does it look like?" Willam replied.

"Bowling, I guess. Anyway, can I play?"

Listening to his mind and body, Willam yelled out, "NO!"

"Why not?" Ralph asked.

"Because!"

"Because why? I aint do nothin' to you."

"Because your dad's a son of a bitch, that's why!"

With that, Ralph charged out the gate after Willam. Willam hurled his ball at Ralph and hit him flush on the nose. That didn't stop Ralph though, he dove and tackled Willam to the hard concrete ground and they tussled. Martha rushed out of the kitchen wiping her wet soapy hands on her apron. While yelling at both boys, she ran out of the gate into the alley. It took fifteen minutes before she could pull the boys apart and calm them down.

"What is going on with you two? You're supposed to be friends. Why are you fighting?"

Ralph revved back from Martha pointing at Willam, "'Cause he called my daddy a dirty name, that's why."

Martha knew it was true what Ralph spoke. She expected it. She also knew that Willam was still angry with Mr. Marshall. Martha grabbed Willam by the arm and shook him as she asked, "What did you call his father, Willam?"

"Nothing."

"I said, what did you call his father and don't you lie to me boy!"

Martha was getting really angry with Willam. She hated when he lied and Willam knew it. He knew at any minute the beating session would commence. Ralph stepped in closer to Martha. He yanked on her apron between her screaming to get her attention. Martha stopped her yelling and glimpsed over at Ralph.

"He called him a son of a 'B'."

"That's because he is!" Willam yelled out.

Martha snatched Willam by his arm and pulled him into the yard, up the steps, and into the house. She made Willam strip down to his underpants and whipped him. With every hit she screamed out a word, "Don't… you… ever... let… me… hear… of… you... saying… a… noth… er… word… like… that... or… I… will… beat… the… BLACK… OFF… OF… YOU!"

This went on for almost thirty minutes. Ralph sat in the upstairs window of his grandmother's house and listened to Willam's thrashing. He felt sorry for him. Although still angry for the insult that he made against his dad, Willam was still his best friend. Things were never quite the same between the two after that day. Willam seemed to never forgive Ralph for having a father who hit his mom and would often take it out on him. Not one day would pass that Willam didn't lash out at Ralph for any reason at all.

E.L. RHODES

Chapter 3 - Colette

The sun seemed so bright. Willam stepped out onto the front porch. He stood there peeling his orange and observing the neighborhood activities. Mr. Delaney was mowing his grass again. He must have cut his small piece of yard at least three times a week. Mr. Hamilton was working on his car while his son Craig watched closely and Mr. Daniels slowly crept up the street in his new Caddy. He blew the horn and waved and Willam returned the gesture. After finishing up his orange, he gathered all of the peelings into his napkin and wiped the remaining juice from his hands on the side of his faded blue dungarees as he opened the screen door to go inside.

"Hey Willy!"

Willam was just stepping into the living room. He stopped and leaned back behind the door.

"Oh, hey girl, what's up?"

"Nothing, you coming out later?"

"I guess so. Told Rusty I'd come down there and help him with the yard so we could go to the movies later."

"I wanna go," she whined.

"Girl, you're too young."

"NOT TO OTHER BOYS I AINT!" She yelled.

It was Colette. She lived just three houses down from Willam and Martha with her mother and two sisters. They had only been living there for about six years. She was two years younger than Willam and had a crush on him. Willam now sixteen years old, of course, felt that she was too young for him. She was irritating most of the time, but he cared for her and was very protective of her.

Willam straightened up the house in preparation for Martha's return from work. She liked things in a certain order when she got home. Willam would make sure that the dishes were washed and the trash was taken out daily. He kept the bathrooms clean and never sat in the living room. Now that they had television sets in both of their bedrooms, there was no television watching in the living room. Actually, the living room was off limits to Willam and his friends.

Over the years, Martha had refurnished the living room and would not let anyone sit on her new furniture, and could tell if someone had. Willam couldn't see how anyone could damage the fabric, since it was covered in that thick protective plastic. He really didn't like sitting on it anyway. It made a loud gross sounding noise when he sat down, which made him sound pretty flatulent and if he was wearing shorts, it made his thighs sweat. To avoid a long scolding, Willam adhered to her wishes and avoided the room altogether.

He slipped on his old green bottom *Chuck Taylors* that he always wore when he mowed the lawn and headed down to his buddy Rusty's house to help him with the lawn. Rusty was Willam's good friend. His real name was Paul Robinson, but everybody called him Rusty because of a driving incident that occurred years ago.

As a young boy, Rusty was always building things. When he was twelve years old, Rusty had taken a pair of old skates and used them to build two skate boards. He had separated each skate by removing the small screws which held them together. He then nailed the front part of the skate to one end of a piece of board and the remaining end of the skate to the opposite end. He would zoom down Hilltop Terrace onto F Street. He would let anybody who wanted to ride use the extra board that he had built with the additional skate.

Later, still craving the need for speed, Rusty built what he referred to as a race wagon. He used his skates as the front wheels, took two larger wheels and the back axel from an old rusty wagon that he had found and nailed them across a wooden board for the back wheels. He then nailed the front and back boards to a long wooden plank which served as a seat. He tied a piece of rope on both sides of the front board for steering and two small pieces of wood on the front board to use as brakes. Rusty would ride up and down the street all day on that contraption with others watching and cheering him on. Rusty didn't stop there. He later added a top, a door, two empty tin cans for headlights, a backrest, and an old license plate to his vehicle. He even placed an old car battery in back of the seat.

After all his finishing touches were complete, Rusty pushed his masterpiece to the top of Hilltop Terrace. He sat down snuggly on the cushion that was nailed to the master board. He closed the door and placed his feet on the brakes. Willam and Floyd were standing behind waiting for instructions. Rusty stuck his hand through the opening just above his makeshift door and gave the "thumbs up" sign.

"Hit it!" he yelled from the cockpit.

The boys pushed the rolling pile of junk as fast as they could. Rusty was picking up speed by the second. Halfway down the steep hill, Rusty started applying his brakes. The craft was not slowing. The wooden brakes smoked as they were pressed hard against the pavement. The cart began to wobble. Then "Snap!" The right brake had popped loose from the front board. Rusty was now speeding toward E Street. Every time he attempted to press the left brake, the cart would pull to the left toward the parked cars. Rusty started yelling at the top of his lungs.

Willam and Floyd stood there frozen. The cart was now wobbling out of control and flying fast into the intersection. Rusty tried to open the raggedy door, but in his panic, he was pushing on the side that was nailed securely to the back rest. Finally, he pushed the front of the door and in a flash he was falling toward the pavement head first. One of the thick large rear rubber wheel smashed him in the face which then caused his head to slam into the car battery. After being thrown free, he tumbled about three feet and landed with the back of his head smacking solidly on the driver's side door of Mr. Howard's brand new Ford Station Wagon.

Willam and Floyd rushed down the hill to help him. They found him laying on his back and holding the back of his head. His toes were curled up abnormally through his shoes. They were curled up so much that they made his sneakers resemble a pair of Dutch clogs. The boys helped Rusty up. He was bleeding from the head, mouth, and knees, and he was crying.

"My racer! Did the cars smash it?" Rusty whined out.

Neither Willam nor Floyd had the heart to tell him that as he dove for his life, in fear of getting run over by a car, bus or maybe even a truck, that no traffic had passed, not even a scooter. They were in no particular hurry to let him know that he had prematurely risked his life for no reason at all.

They walked down the hill to retrieve his death cart from the curb. It had slammed into a lamp post and turned over on its side. One of the tin can headlights lay next to a big maple tree, and the car battery was knocked loose and had landed in the middle of the street. The boys righted the cart and picked up the dislodged items from the ground and stacked them back on the vehicle. That's when Floyd noticed the yellow and tan object wedged deeply inside one of the hard rear rubber wheel. It was one of Rusty's front teeth. His entire face was covered with rust from the contraption tumbling over him. He even had rust marks on the back of his head. Of course after he was feeling better, the boys in the neighborhood laughed and gave him all sorts of nick names, but the one that stuck was "Rusty One", which was later shortened to just plain old "Rusty".

The boys worked in the yard for over an hour. Rusty mowed the grass while Willam edged up the lawn around the wall which completely surrounded the yard. After they were done, Willam trotted back home to wash up. He changed his shirt and put on his good sneakers and left Martha a note on the dining room table as to his whereabouts. He stepped back out onto the front porch and sat on the rail waiting for Rusty. About ten minutes had passed and Willam started getting restless.

"What are y'all going to see?" said the voice from the distance.

Colette was standing in the doorway of her house. Willam lifted himself off the railing and looked over in her direction.

"I think *Shaft in Africa* why?"

"I still want to go. I like Richard Roundtree. Who else is going?"

"Nobody, I told you, just me and Rusty. And no, you can't go."

"Well, maybe I'll see you up there."

Just as Willam was about to respond, he could see the top of Rusty's head bouncing just above the hedges. He turned and headed down the front steps. He met Rusty at the gate.

"You ready to go man?"

"Yeah, I asked my mother if she could drop us off, but she told me to go to hell. You think that meant no?"

"Nah man, that's more like a HELL NO!"

The boys laughed as they headed up Chaplain Street toward Coral Hills.

The movie theater line was long. It wrapped all the way around the building and onto Southern Avenue. Everybody wanted to see smooth Shaft stick it to the man one more time. The boys stood in line and rested from their long walk. It had taken them almost an hour to get there. It seemed like forever, too. The walk consisted of cutting through two alleys, across the elementary school playground, and then up hill for about three miles. It wasn't an easy walk either, especially in a pair of *Chuck Taylor AllStars*. The soles on those sneakers were as thin as *PlayDoh*; if you stepped on a quarter you'd find a print of George Washington engraved on the bottom of your foot. It was like walking in a pair of bedroom slippers, but they looked cool.

The long line moved quickly and the boys finally reached the ticket counter. The clerk looked over the top of her black rimmed glasses at the boys. She was an old, cranky looking woman who seemed as if she really didn't quite feel like sitting in that crammed little box. She was partially encased by glass, but by no means did she have the appearance of a Barbie Doll. Old movie posters covered the back wall, with one narrow door just behind her. She blew out her cigarette smoke then mashed the filter deeply into the ashtray before she spoke.

"How many?"

"Uh, two please," Rusty replied, clearing his throat.

"Are you seventeen or over?"

"Yeah, I'm eighteen and uh, so is he."

The clerk stared at Rusty for a minute then at Willam. Then she spoke those words, the words that can make any young boy trying to get in an R rated movie crumble. Those words that have shattered the dreams of many.

"Do you have any ID?"

Rusty looked at Willam then back at the clerk.

"ID? Uh no, but we're both eighteen. Why do we need ID?"

"Sir...."

Just as the clerk was about to speak, a voice from behind the boys yelled out. "Ah just let them in. You're gonna make all of us miss the movie."

The clerk rose to her feet and peered out at the crowd through the glass window that surrounded her. Other voices soon joined in, sounding frustrated and annoyed.

"Yeah, let them in. If they need to be with a parent, then they're both my sons. Now let them in, damn!"

The lady sat back down in her seat and spoke into the round opening of the glass.

"That'll be two dollars a piece."

The boys pushed their dollars and coins through the small opening under the glass then watched the clerk push the little button to dispense their tickets. She stared at the boys for a brief second then slid the two small tickets through the opening.

"Enjoy the show." She said sarcastically.

The boys didn't care. They rushed through the revolving door and into the lobby. They handed their tickets to the short fat man standing in the center of the red velvet ropes. He ripped the small paper tickets in half. He handed both boys the bottom half of the printed paper and also extended a warm greeting. After stepping beyond the ropes, they ran over to the concession stand. Willam rested both of his forearms across the warm thick glass and marveled at all the assorted boxed candies. He asked for a box of "Rasinettes" and a soda, while Rusty was set on some popcorn. The attendant filled the small paper sack with some of the warm kernels and poured hot liquid butter over the top. Rusty scraped along the bottom of his pocket and retrieved the remaining coins and dumped them on the glass counter.

After counting them and realizing that he had just enough to get a small soda too, he ordered one. After everything was laid out on the counter, the attendant punched the keys on the bulky cash register and told them their total. They both paid for their goodies and headed for the stairs that lead to the balcony.

The lights were just beginning to fade as the boys made their way through the comfortably situated patrons. They excused themselves and inched their way to the two vacant seats of the fourth row. As soon as the lights were completely out, the projector lit up the back row of the balcony and the scratchy sound of the reel was distributed around the theater. The boys sat back in their seats and started in on their snacks and refreshments.

As Willam munched on his food and peered at the movie preview on the screen, Rusty sat up and nudged Willam with his elbow. Willam too, leaned forward in his seat. Rusty motioned his long pointy head in the direction of the couple sitting in the corner of the front row. They hadn't even waited for the movie to start before they were engrossed in their physical activity. That was part of the reason the boys loved sitting in the balcony: the free show.

After the movie was underway, other couples soon joined in. There was heavy panting and moaning throughout the balcony, but the boys couldn't tear their eyes away from the first couple that they had noticed. The girl was all over the guy. He had a big bright yellow afro bush pick stuck in the back of his hair which was all that they could really make out. Everything else was in shadow. Now twenty minutes into the featured film, the girl had taken her right leg and laid it along the railing of the balcony and of course the young man did what any young red blooded male, under the age of eighty five, would have done. He slid his hand between her legs for the prize.

The boys were now sitting on the edge of their seats. Neither of them moved much, for they had put themselves in the young man's place and was now both producing steel in their trousers. The young girl was now rocking in a back and forth motion and grunting and moaning with every movement of his hand. This went on for over twenty more minutes and then everyone returned to their upright positions in their seats.

The small circular light illuminated every area it touched. It was blinding to Willam when it ran across his face, catching his eyes. The usher walked up and down the steps sweeping the light of his flashlight across every row. Willam glanced down at the heated couple. They sat in their seats still and lifeless. It was hard to believe that they were the same two that were running a sexual marathon just moments ago. The usher parked himself on the railing just below the projector booth. Everyone knew that he was not leaving anytime soon. To Willam, that seemed to be a more than appropriate time to go and release some of the grape soda from his full bladder.

"Be right back man, gotta take a wiz." He whispered to Rusty.

Rusty nodded then took another sip from his drink. Willam stood up and made his way down the row. The usher shined the bright light down on him then quickly shut it off. As Willam headed down the stairs, he could see the young horny girl inching her way down the front row. He giggled to himself thinking, "She probably needs to go change her panties or at least go dry herself off."

He made his way to the bottom of the steps and down the hall to the men's room. He too, needed to cool himself down. After urinating what felt like all of Lake Michigan, Willam stopped at the dirty sink and washed his hands. With nothing in sight to dry his hands, he wiped them on the back of his dungarees and headed out the door. Willam started for the balcony stairs, but suddenly detoured back to the concession stand. He wasn't planning to buy anything; he had decided to wait and see what Miss Nasty actually looked like since he would be using the image of her face during his next private "happy time" session. He was already planning to lube up as soon as he got home and play her moans, grunts, and pants back in his mind. He was getting excited just thinking about it again.

Disrupting his daydream was the slamming of the door to the ladies room. He could see the small framed silhouette making its way down the dim hall. Willam leaned against the warm glass of the concession stand counter as if he were looking to purchase something. Just before she reached the bright lights of the lobby area, he looked over in her direction.

"May I help you sir?" The concession attendant asked.

"Uh, no that's okay. I was just looking." Willam swung his head back in the direction of the attendant and casually walked away. He headed for the stairs leading to the balcony. He paused after reaching the landing and looked back to see if the young woman was following. She did not appear. He could hear the concession attendant speaking to someone. It was her. Willam knew that he couldn't stand in the stairwell like some weirdo waiting for her, so he decided to return to his seat. Shortly after, the dark silhouette returned and slid by the other viewers to her seat. William was upset with himself for missing the opportunity to see her. The usher never left the balcony and everyone remained on their best behavior.

During the love scene, Shaft was really giving it to his lady. At least that's how it appeared to the boys. That was their real reason for wanting to see the movie, the sex scene. They knew that Shaft would be stroking some woman and she would be digging her fingernails into his back. This was more than sexy to them, it was orgasmic! After the movie was over, the boys rose from their seats. The movie credits were still rolling while everyone was exiting, except for those who were planning to watch the next running. Willam looked back to see if the young couple was leaving. They were. He and Rusty walked slowly down the stairs leading to the lobby. After reaching the lobby, they stood by the stairs to see her as she made her descent.

"You boys move along, you're causing a fire hazard. Come on, keep it moving. Exit to your left folks."

"Damn!" Rusty whispered.

The boys followed the crowd around the opposite side of the stairs and then out the side exit door. Willam kept looking back but still didn't see them. "Damn, I wanted to see what that little hot fine thing looked like. She was hot as fire. And main man was all over that. She probably would have let him tag it, if it wasn't for Mr. Flashlight. I think they're trained for that. They must go to 'Cockblocking -101' classes or something."

Rusty looked at Willam and started laughing. The oncoming traffic had just stopped and the green light was illuminated for the boys to cross the street. Just as Willam stepped off the curb, Rusty grabbed him by the arm.

"I think you're gonna get that chance after all brotha."

Willam looked back at the door. He could see the big yellow afro pick sticking out of the back of his hair. He had his back toward them but they both knew that that was the pick. The guy held the door open for his date. Rusty and Willam stood there frozen but tried not to be too obvious. Finally, the young girl appeared. She walked through the door looking as sexy as anything they had ever seen. The guy released the door and placed his arm around her neck and they headed toward the boys' direction. The boys, now pretending to read the up and coming feature from the theater marquee, both wanted a closer look. Just when Willam was about to slowly lower his eyes to get a glimpse, her high pitched voice projected in his direction.

"Hey! Did y'all enjoy the movie? It was good, wasn't it?"

Realizing that she was speaking to them, the boys smiled and turned to answer and to get a good look at her. She was now close enough for them to see her in all of her splendor. They both avoided eye contact with the guy and smiled hoping to look attractive to her. Upon making eye contact with her, their eyes widened and both of their mouths flung open. They both stood there, shocked and in disbelief.

"What in the hell are you doing here?" Willam asked.

It was Colette! She had gone to the movie with Ralph. Willam was so angry that he couldn't think straight. He also realized that it was her who looked too good to him. It was her that he found to be so sexy. It was her who had him aroused.

The young girl smiled shyly then looked at her date, who was looking away as if he had committed a crime. "I told you that I would see you up here. You said I couldn't go with y'all."

"How did you get up here?"

"My mother brought us, but we're gonna walk back."

"So your mother thinks it's okay for you to go to the movies with a guy at your age? And an 'R' rated movie at that!"

"You're the only one who looks at me like I'm a baby, Willam."

"That's because you are a baby! You're only fourteen!"

"You know I'm your favorite girl." Colette said trying to display her sexiest smile.

"Sorry, my favorite girl's spot has been taken. That's my mom's spot. You're more like a sister and that's why, as a brother, I DON'T WANT TO SEE YOU UP HERE AGAIN WITH SOME GUY!"

"Well, he's not some guy, he's Ralph!"

"Well, him neither!"

Willam now realized that Colette was growing up. He had always protected her and watched over her, ever since she was a little girl. Looking at her for the first time, he also realized that she wasn't so little anymore. She was a very mature looking fourteen year old. Although very petite, she had curves throughout her small framed body. She was a pretty girl with nice size breasts and the prettiest legs, and her butt was her signature asset. It was round and firm. All the guys in the neighborhood would always kid with Willam, saying things about her and what they were going to do to her after she was a little older. They knew how protective he was over her, too. Willam never paid her any mind, at least not like that. This was the first time and he felt somewhat embarrassed about it.

"You always act like you're somebody's daddy." Colette continued.

Willam turned and looked at them both. He was now showing his anger. Ralph knew that Willam would be upset if he knew that he was after Colette so he had never mentioned it to him. He and Colette had been seeing each other for over three months. He told her that he would be her boyfriend but she could never tell anyone. The only other person that knew about them was Colette's mother, but she felt that Ralph was a nice little fellow, and besides, she was attracted to Ralph's dad. Ralph knew if he said anything Willam would be ready for a fight so he tried to be as humble as he could while showing Colette that he wasn't afraid at the same time.

Ralph turned and looked at Willam. "She'll be alright, I got her. I'll make sure she gets home ok."

"Yeah, I saw how much you had her up in that balcony. Oh hell naw, I'm walking you home girl."

All four crossed the street. Willam lectured Colette all the way home. He didn't speak to Ralph the entire time.

After the long tense walk home, all three of the young men walked Colette to her gate. She quickly trotted up the stairs of her front yard then looked back at them.

"See you later Ralph," she said as she held up her hand.

Ralph waved back but said nothing. She smiled and made her way up the next short set of steps which led to the porch. She opened the screen door of the house then yelled down to the boys once more. "See you Rusty. Bye Willy."

"See ya Colette." Rusty replied and Willam just grunted.

She slowly turned and unlocked the front door and stepped inside. The door let out a muffled thud and the darkness quickly filled the porch after she had switched the light off. Shortly after, the window curtains from Colette's room were overflowing with light. Now knowing that she was safely inside and in her room, Willam turned from the house and looked at Ralph. Still feeling the anger, Willam looked at him with hatred in his eyes. Ralph didn't want to deal with Willam and decided that he'd be better off going home. Avoiding eye contact with Willam, Ralph closed the gate to Colette's house and looked at Rusty.

"Well, guess I'll call it a day. I told my grandmother I'd help her do something when I got back from the movies."

"She's just a kid man, that's all, just a kid." Willam grunted.

Ralph knew that Willam wasn't going to let it go and dug himself in for the argument or maybe even worse. He replied as calmly as he could. "Maybe she is to you Will, but not to me. I like her and she likes me. What's wrong with that?"

"What's wrong? What do you mean what's wrong? Look at her, she's..."

"I know she's only fourteen, but have you looked at her lately? I mean, have you really looked at her man? She may be fourteen in numbers, but she is mature for her age. She looks older than most sixteen year olds. Her mom is cool with it so why do you have to be so hard on us? You should be happy that it's me and not some other crazy guy that you don't know. Or....or is it that you want her?"

With that statement Willam balled his tongue up inside of his mouth and pressed his teeth down tightly against it. This was something that he did every time he got extremely angry. He balled up his fist and looked at Ralph as if he were ready to kill him.

"FINE, see her then. You'd better not do anything to hurt her either, GOT IT?"

Willam stormed off for home. Rusty and Ralph stood there silent for a moment then disbursed. The curtain to Colette's bedroom window slowly closed.

The next morning Willam was still upset and it showed. He walked into the kitchen where Martha stood in front of the stove, frying an egg in a big black cast iron skillet.

"Morning Will, you hungry?"

"Nah, not really, think I'll just eat a bowl of cereal."

Martha looked at him strangely. She knew her son. She knew him better than he knew himself most of the time. She said nothing. Willam walked over to the refrigerator and grabbed the large box of cornflakes from the top. He then pulled the handle of the huge box and the door opened. He reached in and pulled the small can of "Katydids" out of the fridge and placed them on the kitchen table while grunting the entire time. Martha looked over at him then went back to her cooking. He placed his head inside the cold box and pulled the bottle of milk that was resting deep in the back of the top rack then pushed the door closed. Martha looked over at him again.

"Hold on young man, put my Katydids back where you got them from. By the way, don't think that I haven't noticed that a few are missing from the bottom. You're not gonna get me this time with that. You know I don't like you sneaking my Katydids now don't you? You know, you're not too big for me to go upside your head boy, now put them back in there and don't let me catch you in them either."

"Okaaaaay! I heard you Ma. They're too sweet for me anyway."

"Well just when did you find that out, after you ate the first one or the fourth one? Don't hand me that mess, just stay out of them. And what's going on with you today? You've been walking around here like you're mad at the world. Huh, what's the problem?"

"Nothing Ma, I'm just tired, that's all."

"Well, you seem a bit upset to me. You lying to me boy, 'cause you know I don't play that."

"No Ma, just got some things to sort out."

"Ok, since you're grown, you can sort out all you need to while you're digging out that old clothes line pole out of the backyard."

"Aw Ma, do I have to do it today?"

"That's what I said isn't it? Today. I don't care when you do it, as long as it starts with a 't' and ends with a 'y' and has 'oda' in between."

Willam sat down at the table. He slammed his bowl down and grabbed the box of cereal and poured it into the bowl until it overflowed. He dipped his spoon in the glass sugar bowl and then sprinkled the white substance over the crisp flakes. The milk splashed onto the printed table cloth as he poured it over his breakfast. He jabbed his spoon into the bowl and raised a spoon full of cereal and milk to his mouth.

Just as the shiny spoon was about to enter his more than ready mouth, Martha yelled over at him. "Grace! Where's your home training? Act like you know."

Willam looked over at his mom who was now standing in the doorway between the kitchen and dining room. He closed his eyes and slowly bowed his head and gave thanks for his meal. He could hear her walking away as he mumbled to his creator. Willam gobbled up his breakfast and washed his utensils. He brushed by his mother and went outside to collect the shovel and pickaxe from under the porch.

He began digging a small ditch around what used to be his and Ralph's super hero launcher, the old clothes line pole. He had so many fond memories of that thing. He thought back to when he and Ralph would swing on that old "T" shaped piece of metal and then let go and fly through the air. They were flying. He dug and picked for about an hour. There was so much concrete around the base of the metal and it was buried deep into the ground.

"Need some help?"

Willam look up and over in the direction from where the voice came. It was Ralph. He was letting Willam know that he was not angry about what happened the night before.

"Nah man, I've got it." Willam mumbled.

Martha stood in the doorway watching. Ralph turned and headed back up the steps to his grandmother's back door.

"I asked you earlier what was going on with you, boy. Why are you treating that boy so mean? Get in here."

Willam kept on digging and tugging on the metal pole.

Martha opened the screen door and yelled, "I said GET IN HERE!"

Willam threw down the shovel and stepped inside. Martha pointed to the chair positioned in front of the kitchen table.

"Put your butt in that chair."

Willam sat down and placed his hands on his knees after wiping them down his thighs. Martha walked up to him and looked down on her angry son.

"What's going on with you two? You'd better tell me and I mean right now."

Willam looked up at his mom. He knew that she would rain down on his head if he tried to act like he was grown and he'd probably get punished as well. He would never disrespect Martha. She had been through too much for and with him. She was his all. Martha had now stepped closer. "Well, young man?"

Willam lifted his head and told her about the night before. He told her how he thought Colette was too young to be involved with boys yet, and how he didn't trust Ralph, not with her. Martha stepped back and leaned against the stove.

"Boy, you aint that girl's daddy! It's up to her mother, what she can and can not do. Although admirable, sometimes you just gotta let things be. Ralph's a nice boy. He's been your friend for years. He won't do anything disrespectful or hurt your precious little Colette. If anybody, it's probably her that you need to be watching. Has he ever let you down? No, he's been nothing but a friend to you, a true friend. Now his daddy, that's another story; now he's a real son of a bitch. Oh forgive me Lord! That man still brings out the worst in me."

Martha began to smile but could see that Willam was not satisfied with her words of wisdom. She stepped back over to Willam. He now had his head down, staring at the tile floor. Martha took her hand and reached under his chin and raised his head. "Is that what you're worried about? You think that Ralph's gonna turn out like his daddy don't you? Oh don't you worry about that. He's nothing like that dad of his. Shoot, that boy doesn't have a bad bone in his body. He's always been such a sweet and kind boy. All boys don't take after the dads you know. Look at you, you have some of your dad's traits, but you're really not that much like him. He was wild and crazy acting. Now you, you're more of the strong silent type. Just do like you've always done in the past, just trust your friend. Don't judge him on his daddy's accounts, they're two different people. You know I'm right too, don't you? You don't have anything to worry about. Your Colette is safe with him."

Willam looked at his mom. He actually felt better about things. He knew she was right. Ralph has always been a good friend. Even when he would beat him up when they were kids, he'd be back over to play the very next day. Willam forgave him.

Willam went back out to complete his work. He was per-spiring and winded from trying to pry the pole from its resting place. He heard the door of Ralph's grandmother's door shut. He looked up and saw Ralph coming down the stairs carrying a large bag of trash and his basketball. Ralph dropped the ball near the wire gate and lifted the metal top of the trashcan by the handle. He tossed the trash filled bag into the container then replaced the lid. Willam released the metal pole and dropped to one knee. Wiping the sweat from his forehead, he yelled over to Ralph.

"So I guess you're just gonna let me break my back off, huh?"

Ralph looked puzzled, but he knew that was Willam's way of making up. He bent over and slowly picked up his ball from its resting place then reached down and lifted the latch of the gate. He stepped into the alley and began bouncing his ball. He passed it through his legs and then around his waist. After shoot-ing the ball into the air and catching it, he walked over to the fence where Willam still sat quietly.

"You seemed to be doing just fine earlier, oh so now you need help?"

"Okay, that was my fault man. I mean, I was still just a lit-tle mad I guess."

"So you aint mad no more?"

"Nah, I know you're cool and besides, I aint her daddy!"

Ralph inched closer. He opened the gate and stepped into the yard. He rolled his basketball up to the concrete sidewalk. It bounced against the steps that led to the backdoor where he could see Martha in the kitchen preparing dinner. He bent over and grabbed the center of the rusty pole. Willam remained on his knee and gripped tightly near the bottom and they both pulled. They pulled as hard as they could until the concrete based pole was pried loose from the tight soil. Both boys dropped to the ground in relief. Willam pulled a patch of grass from the turf and threw it over at Ralph.

"Thanks man. I was about to break my back over here."

"I figured that's the only reason you decided to become so friendly again."

Willam chuckled. "Nah, I just realized how stupid I was acting. I mean, we boys right?"

Ralph started climbing to his feet. "Yeah, we boys, especially when there's back breaking work to do and you need help, but yeah we're cool. Now that we got that all established and you're sitting over there feeling like Abe Lincoln and all, why don't you go ask your mom to make us some 'Kool Aid'? I mean, we did just finish up some Jim Thorpe type stuff. We're men. As a matter of fact, just go tell her to stop with dinner and make us two hard working men some Kool Aid and not too much sugar."

"Oh so you want me to commit suicide, huh? So I guess you're still pissed at me huh? Wait, let me make sure I've got this right. You want me to go in there and ask her to stop making dinner to make YOU some Kool Aid? Did you bump your head on that pole? No, maybe you swallowed some of that rust from the pole because something has made you crazy. Heck no, you'd better go stick your lips on that water hose over there."

"Make US some Kool Aid, I said. I thought we were boys man."

"Apparently not, since you're trying to get me killed!"

The boys broke out into laughter. Martha poked her head around the door and began to smile. She was happy to see that the boys had made up and were friends again.

E.L. RHODES

Chapter 4 - Lessons

Months had passed. School was now back in session and the fellows were checking out all the new prospects. The new freshman ladies were looking better than last year. For some reason they didn't look like the little girls that had just walked out of junior high school earlier in the summer, they looked like little women.

Eastern High School was known for good looking women and everybody always dressed to impress. Many referred to the school as the *Fashion Show*. The guys would wear three piece suits and carry empty briefcases and the ladies would always look so fine with their slacks and high heeled shoes. You had your small groups that didn't quite fit into the upper echelon, you know, the common folk. They wore blue jeans and sneakers. They couldn't afford to wear suits and buy new shoes all the time. They could barely afford to buy lunch everyday. That's where Willam and his friends dwelled, in the heart of *Broke City*.

After the first few weeks of school and everyone had migrated into their categories, the hunt began. You had your *"Stuck ups"*, girls who thought they were high sidity, and the *"Season Girls"*, who only dated football or basketball players. There were *"The Cheerleaders"*, who wouldn't want to be seen with you if you didn't look as good as they thought you should, and were almost impossible to date. There were the *"Intellects"*, girls who most of the guys were intimidated by because they always made most guys feel stupid. Besides, most of them seemed pretty boring to date anyway. Then there were the *"Rejects"*. These girls were the bottom of the barrel; the leftovers. Most of the guys started with these girls since they were just as hard up. *Rejects*, too, had to deal with the same type of standards from the opposite sex. Most of them had been put down by the jocks, ignored by the intellects and were fishing down in the bottom of the barrel as well.

Ralph, although supposedly so in love with Colette, was the biggest flirt of all while away from her. Since she was not yet in high school, he didn't feel the need to worry about her catching him at his wrong doings and besides, high school girls were ready to explore young boys and try new things that Colette was not yet ready to explore and definitely not ready to try.

Several months had passed and Willam was now dating his new girlfriend, Kathy. They met during track team tryouts. They both ran cross country and worked out together. She was a mild mannered girl who too, wasn't in a rush to lose her virginity. That was just fine for Willam. He didn't like those fast girls that the other boys chased and most times would eventually catch. Kathy was a plain and simple girl who was serious about her studies and running track. She also had very strict parents who watched her every move. Willam could come by and sit on the porch with her, but he had to leave before the street lights were illuminated. If not, Kathy's dad would turn on the porch light as a warning that the opening of the door was soon to follow, and that meant punishment. This happened once before. Her father had switched on the light and Willam had hopped up, but took too long to collect all of his books from the porch. When the door opened, Kathy's father mumble two words, all the while he was giving Willam the most evil look that he could muster.

"Kathy, inside."

As she stepped inside, she clenched on to her books and looked back at Willam as though she would never see his face again. Kathy was grounded for a month. Since that day, Willam has never let the porch light shine on him. He would leave promptly after the street lights began humming.

Ralph too, had met a young freshman named Dana. She wasn't a very attractive girl, but had everything else that every hot vibrant young man was longing for. She had very dark skin and the body of a twenty-five year old. She had thick lips and legs and a full round bottom. Her breasts were like two large, perfectly round grapefruits and her stomach was as flat as a board and she was fast. She had been with several boys at the school and Ralph had been with her several times since meeting her just two months prior. They would sneak over to her house during lunch period and return after they scented up her room. He never went to her house after school, that was Colette's time and Colette never knew any difference.

The nocuous smelling fumes filled the entire rear section of the D.C. Metro bus. Everybody was laughing and talking as the bus traveled at a high speed across the East Capital Street Bridge. Willam sat on the long back seat next to Blue and gazed out of the window thinking about Kathy. She was punished again for not washing the dishes before talking on the phone.

Blue was a good friend of Willam's who used to go to Catholic school but was not able to return because of his poor grades. He was given the nickname "Blue" because of his deep dark complexion. The kids used to call him "Blue Black" then they shortened it to Blue. He was a guy who could always make you laugh. He was also the fastest runner in the neighborhood and was on the track team with Willam.

Rusty was sitting comfortably in the seat in front of him talking to Ronnie. And Ralph was sitting next to a girl that he had been trying to get since the first day of school, Wilma. Wilma was probably the best looking girl in the entire school. She had a face and a body that had been hand delivered personally from the Man upstairs Himself. We all knew for sure that she had a tag stamped on the back of her neck that read: *"Made in Heaven"*.

This particular day, Ralph was making some lead way. He was sitting next to her pouring it on. Willam watched for a while, her giggling and smiling at Ralph, but couldn't stand to watch for long, as it made him increasingly angry with Ralph. No, Willam didn't want Wilma, he just hated how Ralph treated Colette. Willam still felt very protective over her.

As the bus moved along its scheduled stops, Ralph moved even closer to Wilma. He slid his arm around her neck and started whispering in her ear. Willam could see her write her phone number inside one of Ralph's books. As the bus turned the corner for the boys' stop, Willam could see Colette standing there talking to a couple of girls near the stop sign on the corner. She was waiting for Ralph.

Every now and again she would walk down to Texas Avenue to meet him and walk back home with him. Ralph, so busy staring into Wilma's eyes, didn't even see Colette. He had decided to ride with Wilma to her stop then walk back home. The bus stopped and everybody scheduled to get off headed for the door except for Ralph. He and Wilma were still deeply engrossed in conversation. As the students piled off the bus, Willam could see Colette standing in the distance through the large front window of the bus. She stood quietly on the corner staring at Ralph, who was still oblivious to her. Willam stepped off the bus and walked up to her.

"Where is Ralph going, Will? And who is he sitting with? Who is she?"

"Oh, she's nobody Coley, don't worry about it."

Even though he hated what Ralph was doing, he didn't want to see Colette hurt. He walked her up F Street and up to her gate.

"I'm not stupid, Will. He thinks that I am, but I'm not. He said he could wait - wait until I'm ready, but I see he can't."

"Girl, stop talking crazy. It's not that. It's.... it's... girl, he'll explain when he gets here, and you'll see. You'll see that it's nothing to worry about, nothing at all."

Willam headed for home. He didn't want Colette to see his anger. He always knew that someday Ralph would do this to her. He wanted to go back and remind his mother of the day that she said what a good guy Ralph was. He wanted to tell her what he knew all along, that Ralph WAS just like his father.

As Willam headed up the hill still filled with anger, he could hear Rusty just ahead shouting. As he reached the corner of Hilltop Terrace, he could see Rusty arguing with three other boys. He didn't know the boys but he knew the girl who was leaning against Mr. Morgan's cab weeping. It was Sheila Rollins. She lived just a few houses up from Rusty. Willam watched from the corner. Just as he called out to Rusty, one of the boys punched Rusty across the face and the remaining two moved in. In a flash, Willam ran up the hill to help his friend who was now swinging wildly against the onslaught of punches being thrown at him.

Willam rushed up and grabbed one of the boys and slammed him into Mr. Morgan's cab, next to Sheila. She jumped away screaming and fled to the sidewalk. Willam began pounding the young man's face. He was swinging like a mad man. One of the other boys rushed over, only to be greeted by Willam's fist. He too, was beginning to receive his whipping.

Willam alternated his pounding on both boys while Rusty wrestled with the other. Willam beat the two boys so badly that they both fell to the pavement, battered and lifeless. He then walked over and pulled Rusty off the other boy. Raising his foot high over the boy's face, he looked down smirking. He wedged his foot just under the chin of the boy and pressed down hard on his throat causing the boy's eyes to bulge. The boy grabbed hold of and held on to Willam's leg. He squirmed wildly attempting to release the relentless Willam's foot. He pried and pulled, but Willam was determined to cause as much damage as he could. Each attempt to release himself caused Willam to push down harder. Finally, the boy's body went limp.

"You're gonna kill him!" Shiela screamed.

"He'll know next time. Won't you?" he said to the boy as he looked down upon his weakening face. Willam only smiled as if he was really enjoying administering such pain to the helpless young man. Rusty walked over and began tugging on Willam's arm.

"C'mon man, that's enough. He can't breathe."

Willam looked at Rusty strangely. He continued applying pressure to the young man's throat.

"Willam, Willam Trent! Let that boy up from there!" yelled Mr. Morgan from his living room window. He was reading the newspaper when he heard all of the yelling and screaming from in front of his house. "You'd better quit all that fighting out there! Act like you've got some home training. Do I need to call your mother?"

Willam released his foot from the boy's neck. He looked down at the boy smiling, "You're lucky. If I were you, I'd never come around here again. And that goes for the rest of you, too!"

The crowd watched as the boys slowly rose to their feet and hobbled down the hill. Willam watched until they were out of sight. After they were gone, Willam noticed that every eye was on him. "What are you looking at?" He asked as he looked around to the faces in the crowd. The crowd quickly disassembled. They had never seen Willam act like that before.

"What was that all about?" Willam asked Rusty.

"I came up the hill and saw that punk slap Sheila. I couldn't stand that."

Willam shook his head while frowning. He could hear her voice over his right shoulder.

"Thanks Will, and thank you too, Rusty."

Without looking back at her, Willam said, "I didn't do it for you. I did what I did for Rusty. As for you, you can go to hell. If you weren't walking around here acting like some kind of slut, they wouldn't come around here acting like they own you."

Sheila said nothing. After seeing what Willam had done to the boy, she thought that it would be in her best interest to just walk away. She picked up her books from off of Mr. Morgan's cab and walked home, still wiping away her tears. Willam walked back down to the corner and gathered his books. As he bent over to pick up his stack, he noticed a small feather rustling just behind the concrete wall. He stepped behind the wall and discovered a small injured sparrow. It was tangled in some small twigs and grass and was barely able to move.

"Watcha got over there Will?" Rusty yelled over.

Willam didn't answer. He reached down and untangled the small bird and gently lowered it from the wall. Rusty walked over still rubbing his face from his beating.

"Poor thing." Willam whispered.

"What happened?"

"I think it was hit by a car or something. I'm not quite sure."

"What are you going to do Will?"

"I'm going to help it."

"Are you taking it home? Your mother won't let you do that." Rusty said while looking at Willam strangely. He was really puzzled. He had just finished witnessing Willam's ability to take a life in one moment and now this strange demonstration of compassion to save a life in another.

"No, it needs help now." Willam reached down in his pants pocket and pulled out his pocket knife. He opened it up and locked the short thin sharp blade in place. Grabbing the bird and holding it firmly in his left hand, he pressed it against the concrete and steadied its resistance. With slow steady movements, Willam sawed the head from the defenseless bird until it moved no more.

"Aw man that's sick!" Rusty grunted.

Willam only smiled. "No, I helped it. It won't have to suffer any more now."

He took the blade and wiped the remaining blood off in the grass then placed the knife back in his pocket. Using only his thumb and forefingers, he gathered and placed both severed sections of the dead animal into the sewer then returned to the grassy area to wipe his hands. He went back to where his books were, bent over, picked them up and headed home. He acted as if nothing had happened. Smiling, he looked over at Rusty. "Bye Rusty, I'll see you after dinner!" Then he trotted up the hill.

Willam walked into the house and dropped his books down on the dining room table. He went into the kitchen and made himself a sandwich, poured a glass of milk and returned to the dining room. He sat down with his food and milk and prepared to do his math homework. That's when he heard the yelling. It was Colette.

"WHY RALPH!? Why did you do this to me?" She yelled.

Ralph stood quietly at first, looking as if he were the victim.

"I wasn't doing anything. She had a lot of books and I was just helping her out. That's all! Anyway, she's my cousin. We just found that out last week. I wasn't doing anything wrong and if you think I did, then you're wrong, dead wrong."

Colette stood there with her arms folded and started crying. A small crowd started to form as people heard her yelling. Willam stood up and walked over to the front door. He could see Colette, Ralph, Rusty, Ronnie and now others gathered around. This was alarming to Ralph. He didn't want anybody to know that he and Colette were seeing each other. Nor did he want them to see Colette chew him out and he definitely couldn't have her break up with him in front of all these people. He folded his arms and spoke calmly to her, but was still trying to be stern.

"Look, let's talk about this later."

"LATER MY ASS!" She yelled. "So what is it Ralph, is it that she does all the things that I won't do? Well is it? I told you that I'm just not ready yet. I thought you said that it didn't matter and that you could wait!"

Ralph was beginning to get angry. He could hear the low giggles and mumbling throughout the crowd. Then he too, lashed out. "Damn right she does. I told you a long time ago that I needed a woman, not some little girl. And I told you that if you didn't, I'd find somebody else who would."

Colette just stood there crying. The crowd was getting even larger now and Willam knew that Ralph would do anything, including cursing her to make himself not look bad in front of the others. He stepped out onto the porch and watched. He wanted Ralph to see him standing there in hopes of keeping him from doing anything stupid to her. It didn't help. Ralph started in again.

"What makes you think that I'm going to stand around and wait on you? I thought that you were mature, but you're not. You're still a little girl and I can't do nothing with a little girl."

Colette continued to cry. Willam stepped from his porch and went down the stairs. He rushed into the crowd and grabbed Colette by the arm. Some of the bystanders were laughing at her and some felt bad and mumbled obscenities at Ralph. Either way,

Colette was hurt. Willam walked her up the stairs to her front door. He opened the screen door for her and she stepped into the house. She looked back at Willam and spoke in a crackly voice.

"Thanks Willy. You tried to warn me. You did. You tried to tell me that this would happen." Colette turned and closed the door.

The next morning, Willam didn't know how to feel. He despised Ralph for what he did to Colette, but he also felt relief for her. She was no longer with a guy like Ralph. He got up and showered, quickly ate a bowl of cereal and grabbed his lunch money that Martha had left for him, from off of the dining room table.

Rusty, Ralph, and Blue were always out front waiting on Willam. He was always late. Willam would burst out of the front door every morning and the boys would run as fast as they could to the bus stop, just barely making it every time. This morning was different. For the first time, Willam was not late and Ralph was not with Rusty and Blue.

"Where's Ralph?" Willam asked.

Rusty shrugged his shoulders then turned to Blue. Blue stood there for a second then shrugged his shoulders, too. Willam walked back into the house and straight through to the kitchen. He looked out of the kitchen door window and saw Ralph standing in the alley talking to Colette. She kept trying to hug him and he kept pushing her back.

"I'm sorry Ralph, really I am." she cried.

"I'm sorry too Colette, but it's time for me to move on." Ralph responded, as cold as he could.

Willam's first instinct was to open the door and scold her for being stupid but then he realized that Ralph wasn't giving in to her. Ralph was still doing his job for him, getting Colette out of his life.

Ralph turned quickly from her and walked down the alley. Willam could still see her body shake as she cried uncontrollably. He quickly ran through the house and out the door to his awaiting buddies as if nothing had happened. They hurried down the walk, meeting Ralph on the corner and rushed up to the bus stop. Ralph acted as if nothing had happened. He rode on the bus laughing and talking to everybody like he did everyday. He had no remorse. Willam could only sit in his seat quietly, picturing Colette walking to school late, lonely, and crying. Once again, he began to stare at Ralph with rage in his heart. Finally he couldn't hold it any longer. Willam yelled loudly over the other voices on the bus.

"Hey Ralph, what was up with you and Colette yesterday? She looked really pissed at you. Did she break it off with you?"

After he spoke, everyone turned their attention to Ralph.

Ralph stopped laughing. He knew that Willam was putting him on the spot. He also knew that deep inside, Willam was angry at what he had said and done to Colette. He looked around at all the waiting faces on the bus. He sat back slowly in his seat and placed both of his hands on the metal bar which straddled the top of the backrest of the seat in front of him.

William spoke up again. "Well Ralph? Inquiring minds would like to know. Did she quit you?"

Ralph could now hear the faint chuckles emitting from the rear of the bus. This made his blood boil. He couldn't have anybody think that any girl would ever break it off with him. He was too arrogant for that. Ralph leaned forward and turned in Willam's direction. He jabbed his thumb deeply into his chest and screamed out, "No, I cut her back! I don't need some little girl, I need a woman."

"Oh, I see." Willam said calmly then sat back in his seat and smiled.

This question led to many from the other travelers and Ralph obliged them all with answers. He wanted them all to know how she begged and pleaded with him. How she cried and how now he would be with Dana.

After school, Willam rushed home and grabbed a bite to eat. It was Friday and time for work. When he was first offered the job, he knew that Martha would never approve. He was in complete shock when she told him that it would be alright with her. He had finally obtained approval to work from Martha. Actually, it was Martha who had spoken to his employer and secured his employment.

On Fridays after his studies, Willam did what he loved most, he drove. He would drive Mr. Daniels wherever he needed to go. Mr. Daniels was not in the best of health these days but still tried to do whatever he could for Martha and Willam. Neither of the two would ever be satisfied with a handout so Mr. Daniels offered Willam work.

Willam is the only person, other than Mr. Daniels, to sit behind the wheel of any of the five Cadillacs that he owned. Mr. Daniels and Willam had a special bond. Despite all those years of secretly crossing Martha's threshold, he knew that Willam was aware of their doings. Yet Willam never said a word, not even after he was older and had come face to face with Mr. Daniels on several occasions. He never treated Mr. Daniels with any disrespect or rude behavior even though he knew that he was having sexual relations with the woman whom he honored and adored. Sometimes they would even hold long conversations in the house prior to Willam's departure for school. However, when their paths crossed in the neighborhood, they only spoke casually to each other.

Mr. Daniels trusted him and for some strange unknown reason, Willam respected Mr. Daniels, too. After hiring Willam, their bond and respect grew for each other. Willam drove him on weekdays and Saturdays as well, but never on Sundays.

Sunday was still Martha's day. It was a day for church. Mr. Daniels paid Willam handsomely for his services. He paid more than Willam thought he would, but he figured that Mr. Daniels was only trying to help him and his mother Martha. He knew that Mr. Daniels secretly cared for his mother but had a family of his own. Willam never wanted to dwell on that subject for too long and would always quickly dismiss it.

One fine Saturday afternoon, Willam was making his rounds with Mr. Daniels. They stopped by the barbershop on Benning Road where Mr. Daniels would get his hair cut and spend hours just talking, mostly about the old days. Willam would sometimes get his afro shaped up, but on most days he'd just listen to the long and funny stories the men told. They all called Mr. Daniels, "D" and after several visits to the shop with him, Willam soon followed suit. "Mr. D." is how he now referred to Mr. Daniels. Martha scolded him at first, telling him that he was being disrespectful, but Mr. Daniels assured her that it was alright. Martha could see that their relationship was getting closer and Willam was learning a lot from him, too. Mr. Daniels would go in the back with the owner of the shop and return after thirty minutes or so and then would be ready to go. Willam never knew what went on back there and never asked.

Later, he'd drive Mr. Daniels over to the tourist home that he owned. Willam hated that place. It had all sorts staying there. Willam would sit and quietly watch the people as they entered and exited the small building. There were all types. Willam would sit there for the longest time while Mr. Daniels spoke with the manager, checked the books, and walked around. That was his legitimate hustle. Willam would wait patiently. After all, he was on the clock. He would often play a mind game with himself, trying to guess each patron's occupation. He'd sit there, looking up at each person as they passed, thinking quietly without expression, "Hooker... junkie... homosexual... asshole..."

He'd label each person that crossed his path until Mr. Daniels was ready to go.

Mr. Daniels would step from behind the counter with a stack of mail, pass it over to Willam and mumble, "Let's roll man."

Willam would jump to his feet, grab the mail from him and open the door for him. Mr. Daniels would step out slowly and on most days, someone would be waiting to come in. After Mr. Daniels was through the door, Willam was soon to follow. He'd hold the door for the awaiting person and after they were inside Willam would always mumble what he thought.

"Pothead."

Mr. Daniels would look over at Willam and chuckle. After reaching the car, he would stand and wait patiently for Willam to open his door, then climb slowly into the huge custom made automobile.

This particular day wasn't a good day for Mr. Daniels. Willam had to pull over and stop several times so that Mr. Daniels could open his car door and spit out the yellowish substance from his mouth. Once again, Willam didn't know what his ailment was nor did he ask. He drove Mr. Daniels to his house early that day and then walked home.

As Willam approached his block, he was met by Rusty and Ralph. They were talking about hanging out that night. Willam, though still secretly hating Ralph, continued to tolerate him and agreed. They walked up the stairs to Willam's house. Just as Willam stepped inside he could hear Ralph mumbling.

"Who in the hell is that?"

"Don't know, but he's not from around here." Rusty replied.

Willam stepped out through the door. He looked over to where the guys were locked in, and there standing on the front porch for all to see, was Colette and her new boyfriend. They were standing there hugging and kissing passionately. Willam looked over at Ralph who was desperately trying to conceal his rage. Rusty was standing there fondling himself and mumbling.

"Damn boy, he's handling that like he's already had it. Damn that girl's got a body on her. Woooo, they're making me hot over here."

Ralph looked over at Rusty with an angry face.

"Shut the hell up man. She's not giving up a thing. I'll still be the first one to hit that."

"Doesn't look like it from here, my man. Looks like you've been replaced and he's going for the gusto!"

"Damn slut!" Ralph grunted.

Willam stood there taking it all in. He was laughing at Ralph secretly inside his mind. His hatred for Ralph was now gone. Unknowingly, Colette had gotten her revenge and Willam was glad.

Willam placed his hand on Ralph's shoulder and decided to rub a little salt into his wound. "Well buddy, I guess what they say is true, what goes around comes around."

Ralph yanked his shoulder from Willam's hand. "We'll see." He continued to stand there boiling with rage. He couldn't stand to see Colette with someone else. He stood staring at the two of them but they never looked up. Finally, Colette backed away from the young man. She wiped her lips with her hand and then smiled shyly at the boy. He giggled in return. They talked briefly until they both noticed the audience that they had been entertaining.

"I'll see you tomorrow baby." The young man yelled as he trotted down the porch stairs.

"Not if I see you first." She replied. "And don't forget to call me tonight," she continued.

Colette stood on the porch waving to her new boyfriend until he was out of sight. She then looked over at the guys still standing there watching. She peered directly into Ralph's eyes as she opened the screen door, paused for a second then yelled, "Take a picture why don't you? It'll last longer."

She smiled and then stepped inside. Ralph stuffed his hands deeply into his faded Levi's and walked over to the wall of the house and leaned against the red brick. He looked over at Willam, who was now smiling. Ralph smiled too, then poked out his chest.

"She's just trying to piss me off, that's all. I'm still the man. She's just trying to make me jealous so I'll get back with her. Jealous of that clown? I don't think so." He boasted.

Even during his lowest time, he was still a bastard. He stood there thinking to himself for a moment and then down the stairs he went. "I'm gonna settle this once and for all. She's not going to make a fool out of me."

With this, Ralph rushed out of the gate and down the walkway toward Colette's. As he headed up the stairs, the curtains from the window of her room opened slightly. Before he could get to the front door, she was there to open it. She spoke softly and Willam and Rusty were unable to hear what was being said. They spoke for a while and the boys could see Ralph waving his hands and gesturing to her. Soon after, the door closed. Willam smiled once again to himself but before he could bask in his satisfaction, Colette's door opened once again. She slowly stepped outside and Colette and Ralph walked hand in hand down the steps and out into the yard.

"Damn that brotha's smooth. I guess he is the man." Rusty whispered.

Willam leaned back against the wall. He was no longer smiling inside or out. His sweet Colette was about to be conned even more by the biggest con man in the neighborhood. He felt his bitterness return. It had moved right back into his heart like an unwanted in-law.

The cab sped up the hill and slowed just before reaching the house. The brakes squealed and the rear door opened quickly. The driver opened his door, pulled himself out of the vehicle and slid along side of the dirty dull yellow painted car to avoid the oncoming traffic. After making his way around the car, he popped open the trunk. A thin figure climbed out from the back of the automobile and gently closed the door. Meeting the driver at the rear of the vehicle, the street lamp which had just illuminated, partially produced an image of her face. It was Martha. She was digging in her handbag to retrieve her purse. While doing so, she yelled up to the boys.

"Well don't just stand there, you boys come on down here and help me with these groceries."

Willam and Rusty both rushed down the steps and out the gate to assist her.

After paying the driver, Martha limped across the street, up the stairs and into the house. She pushed her shoes off, one at a time, and sat back on the sofa. Willam and Rusty continued the round trips to the cab, retrieving the multiple bags of necessities, after which, Willam put them away while Rusty stood around talking his ear off about Ralph and Colette. After hearing Rusty's continuous loud comments, Martha although tired, managed to make some inquiries of her own about their latest situation.

"Those two still having problems?" Martha asked.

"Yep Ms. Trent, but it looks like they're going to get back together now." Rusty yelled out.

"After all that boy has done to her."

"Yes Mama, after all that and he's not even sorry for any of it, either. He's not as nice as you think." Willam interjected.

Willam continued putting away the groceries while Rusty continued the discussion on Ralph and Colette with Martha. Soon after Willam was done, he stepped into the living room and sat down on the bottom step of the staircase. The interrogation began.

"So Willam, has Ralph and Colette.....you know, have they?"

"Have they what, Ma? You mean have they had sex? That would be a no. She's not like that. She's a good girl and I think that's what makes Ralph so mad."

"You mean he's trying to get her to do something like that? I need to talk to that boy. I know that he knows…."

Just when Martha was about to lecture the boys, a loud bang rang out from the screen door. Martha leaned forward to see who it was and Willam raised himself up from the soft carpet and opened the door.

"Boy, get in here!" Martha said while leaning back on the sofa. "I was just talking about you. So what's going on with you and Colette? I heard you the other night yelling at her in front of all those people. Showing off is what you were doing. Now you know your mother would turn over in her grave if she knew that you were mistreating somebody and you know your grandmother would have a fit, too. Why are you being so mean to her? She's a nice girl and you weren't raised that way."

Ralph stood there shrugging his shoulders and looking down at the floor. He glanced only once at Rusty, who was giggling, and then quickly back at the stitched fabric of the woven rug. He said nothing else. Martha realized that she wasn't going to get any kind of response from him and decided to let it go. She also knew that Willam would let her know all she wanted after he was informed. Martha pulled her foot up across her knee and began massaging her foot. She looked around the room at the boys who were now completely speechless then began to yawn. Between moans and sighs of exhaustion, she mumbled. "You boys get on outside and let me get some rest."

Willam stood up from the step that he had returned to after Ralph's entrance and looked over at her strangely.

"You want something to eat before I go Mama?" he asked.

"No baby, but if I'm asleep when you get back, wake me."

Willam knew what that meant. She wanted information when he returned.

Willam acknowledged his mother and off they went. They trotted down the steps, out the gate and down the walkway toward Rusty's house. As they passed Colette's, they could see the curtain open and then draw close after they were beyond her front yard.

"Ok man, what happened? Are you guys back on? Is she going to break up with Mr. Hushpuppies?" Rusty asked.

He kept jumping around Ralph like a little hyper miniature Poodle. When he wasn't talking, he was slapping on his chest and thigh as he walked. This was a daily ritual of Rusty's. He always walked while beating out rhythms on his chest and thigh. He looked silly, but he was actually pretty talented.

"Come on Ralph, what gives man?" Rusty continued.

"Nothing gives! No, she gives!"

"Huh? What in the hell does that mean? Are you two getting back together or what?'

"Hell no, I don't want to be going with some young slut!"

"Slut? Come on man, all she did was kiss the guy. I've seen you and her do much more than that. Oh, so just because it wasn't you with a half of yard of tongue down her throat on her porch, now she's qualified as a slut. Am I a slut, too? 'Cause I damn sure aint letting you put your nasty ass tongue in my mouth. Man, I don't get you, I don't get you at all."

Ralph stopped and looked back at Colette's house then over to Rusty, who was still standing, staring at him very attentively and mumbled, "I just thought I'd be her first, that's all."

Ralph turned and walked away. Willam and Rusty both stood there with their mouths sagging like the breasts of an eighty five year old woman without implants.

"No way!" Rusty yelled and then quickly followed in pursuit of the already fast walking Ralph. Willam trotted up from behind. The conversation now really interested him.

"Ralph, are you saying what I think you're saying?"

Ralph kept up his high speed strides. After reaching the wall in front of Rusty's house, he headed up the steps toward the front porch. He passed through the marijuana smoke filled gauntlet that Rusty's brother and friends had established and coughed his way through. This is something that Rusty's brother Joe and his friends did on a daily basis. They would gather in front or on the side of the house and smoke their hand-rolled cigarettes just prior to Rusty's mother's return from work. Rusty's mom was hardly ever there. She worked two jobs and was always too tired when she got home to really even care. He also had an older sister, Marjorie who stayed at her boyfriend's house most of the time. The young guys often referred to her as "Kabuby" after the camel on the cartoon "Shazam" because of her long, thick lips, but only behind her back. She was as mean as a snake and gave Rusty and his friends a hard time whenever she could.

Rusty and Willam followed Ralph to the porch. After reaching the door, Rusty opened it and they stepped inside.

"Hey, anybody want a beer? They won't know and besides, Ralph, you probably need a drink."

Ralph opened the door leading to the basement and started down the steps. Rusty yanked one of the cold Budweiser cans from the connective plastic rings which held the six pack securely and he and Willam followed. They sat downstairs in Rusty's basement which they referred to as "the Apartment" and took turns sipping the cold brew. Rusty was still bouncing off the walls with excitement.

"Ok Ralph, how do you know? I mean, did she tell you that she did it?"

"Yeah, she told me that she's no longer a virgin, that she was just as good as my new girlfriend. She said that she was glad that it wasn't me because I didn't deserve to be her first. She's nothing but a slut."

Rusty continued his questioning and Ralph ignored him. Willam sat still on the foam covered bench, staring at the floor. He couldn't believe that she would do such a thing. Finally Ralph walked over and grabbed the half empty can of beer from Rusty and downed the remaining liquid. He unlocked the back door and left.

Three days had passed. The huge metal public transport was moving like a compact automobile up the steep hill of Ridge Road. Blue and Ronnie sat snuggly in the back of the "V4" Metro bus heading home from their part-time job. They both worked at the McDonald's fast food restaurant just off of South Capital and "M" streets. It was almost 10 o'clock and had gotten breezy and chilly. The bus had made its regular turn onto "G" Street, then onto Burns Street. As it made its final turn onto Texas Avenue, the boys stood up and headed for the back door of the carriage. They both reeked of grease and sour pasteurized milk. The boys stepped off the bus and the inside lights immediately went dark.

The dark figure moved across the open field and into the wooded lot which had only caught the boys' attention for a second. Papers blew out into the street and had already covered part of the corner of the small wooded area which led down to the huge drainage tunnel. Just as they were about to cross the street, they both heard the faint moans and cries for help. They looked at each other at first then slowly turned and walked cautiously toward the voice. Ronnie picked up a large stick and Blue pulled out his knife. The papers continued blowing up the hill and the boys advanced slowly back in the same direction from where they came.

Upon reaching the bottom of the hill, Blue jumped down onto the large cement platform that led to the tunnel. It was dark. He waved Ronnie over and the moans grew louder.

"Who's in there? Are you ok?" Blue yelled.

Ronnie then joined Blue on the platform. Both boys walked over to the thick barred metal gate that led to the tunnel, which was always half open. The boys knew the tunnel well. On several occasions they had walked through it all the way up to Coral Hills, Maryland. The only things that scared them were the voice and the darkness, not the tunnel.

"Help me, please help me," the voice whimpered.

"Are you hurt?" Ronnie asked.

"Yes."

"Where are you? We can't see you."

There was no answer. The boys walked through the gate. The scent of urine filled the dark, cold burrow. They remained very close to each other until Ronnie disappeared. Blue held his hand out reaching for him, but could not find him. Ronnie had fallen. He had tripped over the young girl's body. She began to gurgle as if she were drowning then started to moan again and

Blue followed the sounds. He found the girl and placed his hands under her shoulders and started dragging her back toward the exit. He could hear Ronnie fumbling in the darkness, then felt her legs rise as Ronnie helped him carry her. They placed her gently on the cement and Ronnie took off to get help. Blue knelt down and stayed beside her, still unable to see her face.

The light moved from left to right until it was directly upon them. Ronnie had ran to one of the homes on Burns Street and called the police. The owner of the house followed Ronnie back to the tunnel with a flashlight and for the first time Blue was out of the dark.

"It's Colette!" Ronnie yelled as he lifted one of the papers that had blown from her notebook into the wooded lot.

Blue looked down at her beaten, blood drenched face. She was naked and her neck had been cut. Luckily, her attacker missed her carotid artery.

The lights bounced off of every house, tree, and car on the street. The paramedics tended to her as best they could, then placed her on the stretcher and carried her up the hill to the awaiting red and white van. Once she was securely inside, one of the attendants climbed in back and closed both doors behind him. The siren blared out as they turned onto Texas Avenue, heading for D.C. General Hospital.

The police officers walked the boys over to the squad car and continued to question them.

"What were you boys doing down there and why did you take her down there?"

"We didn't take her anywhere. We had just gotten off the bus. Ask the bus driver." Ronnie replied.

"You didn't see anybody?"

"Just some guy walking across the field."

"That's all for now. We may need to ask you some more questions later. We've got your information and know how to contact you, so you can go. You know you guys just saved that girl's life, don't you?"

The boys said nothing and headed for home.

Martha and most of the other neighbors stood on their porches while the police squad car was parked in front of Colette's home. After the police had returned to their car and drove off, Colette's mom also rushed out, climbed into her car and sped off. Willam stepped out onto the porch and inquired as to what was going on.

"I think something happened to Colette. The police just left."

Willam stood there with a blank look on his face. He sat down on the porch steps and placed his head into both of his hands.

"Are you OK, Will?"

Willam said nothing, he just shook his head.

Just then, the phone rang. Martha opened the screen door and walked in. Shortly after, she returned to the front door.

"Will, it's for you, I think its Paul. And come inside before you catch your death."

Willam gathered himself and went inside. He picked up the phone receiver and placed it to his ear.

"Hello."

"Will, it's me, Rusty. Did you hear? Did you hear about Colette? They found her naked and beaten in the tunnel. She got beat real bad and I heard she got raped, too."

"What? How is she? Is she OK? Damn! I can't believe it! Who did it? Do they know? Ralph…have you seen Ralph today?

I haven't seen him at all today. Was she with him, does anybody know if she was with him today?"

"I don't know, but we can check tomorrow."

"Right on man, let's do that. I don't trust him and I wouldn't put nothing past him, either."

A week had passed. Neither Willam nor anybody else in the neighborhood had seen Ralph. Willam went to Ralph's grandmother's house and she said what she always said.

"He's around here somewhere."

Colette had been home for two days but no one had seen or heard from her either. It was crazy. Willam had stood in front of her house on the night that she came home, hoping to see the curtains open then slowly close. That would at least let him know that she was alright.

Later that night, Willam was awakened by faint voices in the distance. He rose to his feet and walked over to his window. He looked out and saw the familiar face of the fat guy who made the best hamburgers on a grill. He was Colette's uncle. Willam had met him many times at Colette's cookouts and birthday parties.

He stood in front of his car like a Secret Service Agent. Shortly after, he could see Colette being escorted by her mom. They walked over to the car and stopped at the rear. The fat man met them at the rear of the car and grabbed the suitcase from Colette's mom and placed it into the trunk. He walked around and opened the passenger side door.

Just before climbing in, Colette turned to her mother and gave her a long, lingering hug then slid in the car seat. Willam rushed down the stairs to the front door. He turned on the porch light and stood in the door for her to notice. Colette saw Willam and they glued their eyes to each other. Her uncle crammed himself into the driver's seat of the vehicle and started the engine.

Colette kept her eyes on Willam until the car drifted out of sight. Willam knew that he would never see her again.

The next morning, Willam got up early. He stood at the back door and stared at Ralph's grandmother's house for over an hour. The phone rang. Willam lifted the receiver from the cradle where it rested and spoke calmly.

"Hello…..uh huh…..OK…..thanks."

He placed the phone back to its original position and continued his staring.

Martha walked into the kitchen and noticed him. "Morning Will. What are you doing?"

Willam said nothing for a few seconds then answered his mother. "What's good about it Mom?"

"Everything! This is a day that the Lord has made, so boy, you'd better be glad in it."

"Colette's gone."

"Gone? Gone where? They done shipped her off haven't they?"

That was a common thing back then. Anytime a woman had gotten raped or pregnant, they were sent away to keep the family from embarrassment or shame.

"Yes ma'am. I just found out she was sent to Waterloo, Iowa to live with her grandmother."

"How'd you find that out?"

"Rusty just called and told me."

"Rusty? How does he know? Who is he, the neighborhood Rona Barrett?"

"I don't know. He just hears things I guess. I wonder where Ralph is, I haven't seen him in days."

"Surely you don't think?"

"Like I said before Mom, he's not as nice as you think."

Chapter 5 - Livingstone

"Will, get up! You'll be late for class."

The light leaked through and into the cracks of his eyelids and now he could hear the faint sound of the alarm clock's beeping. After a heavy night of drinking, his head felt like he was wearing a football helmet filled with cement. His mouth was dry and his breath reeked of a terrible mixture of alcohol and something truly disgusting. Willam slowly crawled out of his small twin sized bed and reached down to the foot of his mattress and retrieved his sweat pants. He slipped one leg in at a time and stood up slowly.

After covering himself, he made his way down to the fourth floor bathroom. He disrobed and climbed into the shower, washed up and then hurried out. He was now awake. With his towel folded neatly upon his shoulder, Willam stood in front of the long mirror which spanned across the multi sink counter and brushed his teeth. This was his morning ritual ever since he had first arrived in Salisbury, North Carolina. He was living in his temporary new home. He was starting his first year at Livingstone College.

Willam began the fall semester in August. He and Rusty had decided to attend the same school until Rusty was later informed that he had been denied acceptance into Livingstone. Although his grades were acceptable, his SAT scores were not very impressive. This discouraged Rusty so much that he gave up on the whole college thing and immediately enrolled in the U.S. Navy. Willam felt bad about going on without him, but Rusty encouraged him to do something they both wanted, attending college.

Willam arrived green, fresh, inexperienced, and alone. He met several other freshmen during the orientation, but none who seemed to be compatible with his personality. Shortly after moving into the dormitory, Willam was surrounded with new friends, and not all were of the sort that Martha would be comfortable with associating with her son. It was a pretty diverse group. There were guys from New York, Philly, Charlotte, Baltimore, and other areas, all with the same thing on their minds, partying and girls. Willam wasn't there for that. He knew that he had to buckle down and concentrate on his studies. He didn't hang out with them much, but would occasionally have a beer or five when they gathered with his roommate Alfonso in their room.

Alfonso was the lady's man and the party guy. It only took him three days after arriving on campus to sleep with four girls. Three of them lived on campus and the other one was just some local girl that he had met at the grocery store. He was always trying to match Willam up with one girl or another on campus. Willam just wasn't the type. He wasn't like Alfonso at all; he was more of a home body.

Now, even after he was used to his new environment, Willam still didn't venture out too far. He stayed close to the dorm where he now lived. Even on weekends, you would find him in his room watching television or reading. Not Alfonso, though. He went home every weekend and he always told Willam that he had to go home to check up on his women. He always bragged about all the girlfriends he had back home. He went on about how fine looking they all were. He was a pretty arrogant fellow, but that never seemed to bother Willam. As Alfonso talked, Willam would listen for as long as he could stand it. He would only smile when Alfonzo finished with his story or until he would fall asleep from boredom. A few times Alfonso would talk Willam to sleep. Willam would wake back up only to find him still talking. Alfonso didn't care who or if anybody listened at all to his trash talking, he just loved to talk.

Friday nights were always full of activity around the campus. Young college students were dying to release some of the stress still piled on their shoulders from the long and heavy study week. Most Fridays or Saturdays or both, at least one of the school organizations would be hosting some type of function either on or off campus. They'd have big parties, dances, and other social events.

Willam never attended any of them. He was never interested. He was there to study only. This particular night, Willam had decided to stay up and watch movies all night; his own personal movie marathon. After he had showered and looked over a couple chapters of accounting, he turned on the television. He surfed through the channels until he was able to find a movie. It was an old Boris Korloff horror. It was just after 10:00 pm and he was more than ready to kick back and relax. Just as he had fluffed his pillow to perfection and eased down onto his thin twin sized mattress to assume his viewing position, the pounding started.

The knocks were rapid in succession and grew louder with each strike.

"Will, you in there? Hey Willy! Will, open up!"

Willam eased himself up off the bed and walked over toward the door. As he opened the door he also used it to shield

himself from his visitor's view. Now peeking around from behind the door, he could see the young men standing in the hallway impatiently. One was Vic, Alfonso's buddy who also stayed
in the same dorm. He was always in their room. Willam often
thought of offering to switch roommates, so that Alfonso and Vic
would not have to interrupt his studies with all the noise that they
made daily. Also standing in the hall with Vic was Daryl and his
brother Syd. Syd didn't attend Livingstone, but it often seemed
so since he was there most weekends.

"Hey guys, what's happening?" Willam asked.

"Willy, Willy, Willy, what are you doing man? We were just
in my room discussing community service and we thought of you.
So tell me, are you really planning on staying here in this drab
little room all weekend? You do know that it's Friday don't you?
I mean, what's with you? Every weekend you glue yourself to this
room like a hermit. You never go anywhere," said Vic. "Daryl
came up with a bright idea earlier, he said, 'Why don't we ask Will
if he wants to hang out with us tonight?' I said right on, that's a
great idea. So you see, you have been chosen to be our community service for the night. So come on, get out of those shorts, slip
on some pants and a shirt and let's see what the night has in
store!"

Willam moved over in front of the doorway and Vic
brushed by him. Daryl and his brother followed.

"As you can see, I already have some plans for the night."
Willam replied.

Vic looked around the room then over to Daryl and Syd.
"Do you see her? How about you Syd, do you see her?"

"See who?" Syd asked.

"Will's date…his plans? C'mon Will, where is she? Is she
in here hiding or is she coming over?"

"It's not like that. I was just going to hang out here and
check out some movies."

"Oh hell no! C'mon man, change up!"

Daryl and Syd both chimed in with Vic trying to convince Willam to leave with them. Willam knew that they would not let up and if they had to, would hound him all night about going. Finally, Willam gave in to the boys and changed his clothes.

The boys laughed and talked strategy for the night's events. Of course, their strategy topic was nothing more than how to get girls. They continued toward the old historical building located near the center of the campus. There was a big party there that night and they were not going to miss it. It was being hosted by the Delta Sorority and was sure to be a big bash.

The party was in full swing by the time the boys arrived. Kegs of beer lined the table tops and music filled the Student Union Multi-Purpose Room. This was the room where most of the organizations held their social events which was just another name for "party". Vic had disappeared for a brief moment but returned to the pack toting four cups of beer. He extended one of the thin plastic cups of sudsy liquid toward Willam.

"Drink up my friend and there's plenty more where this came from."

Willam took the cup and turned it up to his mouth. He gulped the beer until only suds remained at the bottom of his cup.

"Man, you sure can put it away!" Syd yelled over the loud music.

Willam walked over to the table where one of the kegs was located and refilled his cup. He stood there watching as Vic and the others stood gawking at the young ladies on the dance floor. He decided to stay clear of them for a while. He headed over to the nearest secluded corner and watched as the wild college students danced, laughed, and drank. He stood in the same spot with one hand stuffed deep into one of his pants pockets and the other cradling his half filled cup.

Vic and the other boys were now out on the floor dancing and having a good time with girls that they knew. They called out to Willam a few times to come over and join them, but he did not move from what was now his safe haven. No one bothered him and no one cared that he was standing there watching. Every time one of the boys called to him, he would only raise his cup just above his head, smile and nod. He was happy to be just observing the festivities.

Willam leaned his head over to his left then tried moving it to his right. She was obstructing his view. Willam took a step over to his left then resumed his observation as his viewing path to the dance floor was clear once again. Her slow, sexual dance moves and gyrations shortly positioned her back in his line of sight. She looked back at Willam and smiled. Willam took a sip of his beer, nodded his head then stepped back over from behind her. He returned to bouncing his head and tapping his foot to the music. He could still see her watching as she danced slowly toward him. After reaching his side, she tapped Willam on his arm.

"Do you go here?" She asked loudly trying to carry her voice over the music.

Willam looked at her and simply nodded once more then continued watching the dancers.

"I haven't seen you on campus."

Only wanting to be left alone, Willam shrugged his shoulders as he looked on.

"You know, that's pretty rude."

"What's rude?" Willam yelled back.

"I'm trying to talk to you!"

Willam turned and looked at the girl and produced a semi-smile on his face. "Yeah?"

"Yeah what?"

"Uh yeah, I go here."

"Do you stay here on campus?"

"Yep."

"Yeah? What dorm?"

"Harris."

"I know some guys who live in Harris. Who's your room-mate?"

"Alfonso...."

"Not Mr. Pretty Boy Alfonso? He thinks that he is the finest man on the planet," she said chuckling.

"I guess." Willam said without laughter.

"I stay over in Goler. I'm surprised that I haven't seen you before. I'm sure I would have remembered seeing you."

Willam said nothing. He turned and resumed watching and bouncing his head.

"So you like this song, huh?" She asked. "You wanna dance?"

"Nah."

"Ah c'mon, one little dance won't hurt."

"No, and besides, the song's just about over anyway."

"Well, how about the next song then?"

Now irritated, Willam looked over at her sternly. "No, I don't dance. Now can't you find somebody else to dance with?"

"Sure I could, but I'd rather dance with you. What's your name anyway?"

"LOOK! I DON'T WANNA DANCE, NOW LEAVE ME ALONE!" Willam yelled.

The entire room went silent. Willam had yelled at the young woman failing to realize that the song had finished and the music had stopped. Now, all eyes were on the two of them. Willam looked around at the many eyes which stared at him then back over at the girl. Muffled snickers seeped out from the crowd and the girl lowered her head in embarrassment. She turned and walked through the crowd and out the double doors into the lobby of the building. Vic forced his way through the crowd and rushed over to Willam. The brothers quickly followed. Vic grabbed Willam by the arm and leaned closer to talk.

"Man, are you crazy? Do you know who that was? That was Donna Jefferson, the hottest girl on campus. What were you thinking about? She asked you to dance and you said no? I don't believe it. Why you, better yet, why not me? I've been chasing after that girl since I've been here. Wait until Alfonso hears about this. He can't even get her to go out with him. Man, he might just throw you out of the room, no, make that out of the dorm when he hears about this."

Willam stood there looking as nonchalant as ever, just as he always did and said, "I don't dance."

"Then I suggest you learn and learn quickly. You don't turn down a Donna Jefferson, man. Are you going after her? You know, to apologize or something? I mean, that girl is a goddess!"

"She's just a girl."

"Wait, just a girl? Is that what you said? Look man, I've only got one question for you, just one question. It's a multiple choice, so you can take a second to think about it before answering. Are you homosexual or just plain insane? I gotta know!"

Willam frowned up his face and shook his head as he walked away from the boys. He walked through the doors where he saw Donna sitting out there with her girlfriends. Willam continued toward the door leading outside. As he pushed the door open to exit, he heard her make reference to him.

"Asshole!"

He never looked back. He walked back to the dormitory. He rushed up the stairs and down the hall to his room. He changed back into his t-shirt and shorts and flopped back down on his bed just in time to catch a few remaining minutes of the

Boris Karloff movie he had abandoned for the party. He lay there vowing to God, that he would never attend another campus party. He had enough trouble avoiding all of the young ladies that Alfonzo pushed on him already. Alfonso was relentless and he too had made a vow, but his was quite different from Willam's. Alfonso had promised himself that he would get Willam with a girl before the school year was out and every week without fail, he would go to extreme measures to carry out his promise.

Once he had brought two girls up to the room and told Willam that one of the girls, Debra, was for him. Willam wasn't interested; he would never cheat on Kathy. Instead, he told Debra that he respected her too much to take advantage of her and they spent the rest of the evening talking about Kathy. Alfonso on the other hand was kissing and fondling the other girl until she began to feel cheap when she noticed that Willam and her girlfriend hadn't followed suit.

Debra enjoyed their conversation and Willam's honesty. She thought he was gay at first, but soon realized that he was just a genuine gentleman. Debra appreciated him and they became the best of friends. He told Kathy all about Debra and couldn't wait for them to meet.

Debra was from Greensboro, North Carolina. She was majoring in Theology. Her father was a Southern Baptist Minister and her mother never worked a day in her life. She was a sweet girl, but associated with the wrong crowd occasionally. Debra was chunky but had a very attractive face. She was also very nice and Willam liked talking with her. He felt very comfortable around her. Willam often thought of how he would have pursued her if the circumstances were different. They did most things together, studying, watching television and attending games. Most people who didn't know them thought that they were a couple, yet they were nothing more than good friends.

Willam focused on nothing but school. He was there to get an education so that he could get a good paying job and take care of his mother. She had been through so much over the years. He majored in Computer Science and wanted to become a programmer. He figured that it was an up and coming industry that would have plenty of high paying jobs by the time he graduated.

Martha was now working two jobs to pay for him to go to school along with his grants and financial aid. He also worked part-time at the Roy Rogers fast food restaurant and continued to work for Mr. Daniels anytime that he was home for extra money, so you see, Willam had his hands full.

While at school, Willam's thoughts were mostly of Kathy. He missed her very much and felt so lonely without her. He often thought about how he used to hang out with his friends, Rusty, Ronnie, Blue and even Ralph, but that still couldn't compare to the times that he spent with Kathy. Although they had never been sexual in any way, they had a deep and committed relationship that only few could understand. Ralph had often called him a fool for holding on to his virginity, but Willam didn't care. He loved Kathy. She was his heart.

Kathy was currently attending Wilberforce University in Ohio. They wrote to each other often and vowed to stay true to each other despite the distance. They agreed that they would get together during the holidays and school breaks.

As for Ralph, after their graduation, he vanished without a trace. Some say that he moved out of state with his aunt and others say that he moved with his dad, but it wasn't until Thanksgiving that Willam found out that Ralph had joined the Marine Corps. He and Ralph hadn't really spoken much since the Colette incident. Ralph had always felt under suspicion by Willam after that night. He stayed to himself, finished up high school, and left without telling anyone.

After returning to his dorm room, Willam yanked his towel from around his waist. He slipped on his underpants and t-shirt that he had retrieved from the small wooden chest which rested against the wall next to his desk. He pulled up his Levi's jeans and slowly buttoned the fly. After placing his feet into his white crew socks, he jammed them both into his size twelve, beige colored "Wallabee" boots. Now standing and peering at his red blood shot eyes in the small mirror which hung neatly between the two small beds, Willam began picking out his afro with his huge bush pick.

The short rapid succession of knocks quickly caught Willam's attention. He walked over to the door and leisurely opened it. The gentlemen stood staring at Willam with their shiny badges held up at eye level.

"Willam Trent?" One of the guys asked.

"Yes, I'm Willam Trent, uh, what is this about?"

"I'm Detective Morgan, DC homicide and this is Deputy Torrence from the Salisbury Sheriff's department. We just need to ask you a few questions."

"Why? About what? I haven't done anything and I'm kind of already late for my class. Can we do this after my class?"

"No son, I think you might want to do this now."

Willam walked over to his bed and sat down. The two men followed. Deputy Torrence stood and leaned against the chest while detective Morgan pulled the small wooden chair from under the desk and placed it next to Willam's bed. He sat down and pulled his pad and pen from his coat pocket then tossed his coat onto the opposite bed. Detective Morgan crossed his right leg over his opposite knee and started in on Willam.

"Willam, do you want to tell us about your relationship with Kathy Williams?"

"She's my girlfriend. Well, I guess she still is. We've sort of lost contact with each other. She's stopped writing me. I don't know what I've done to make her angry with me. Why?"

"When is the last time you heard from her?"

"Right before I came back to school from the holiday break, why? Has something happened to Kathy?"

"Where were you on the night of January 6th?"

"I was here. Classes started on the eighth and I needed to get in some study time. My roommate was here as well."

"Where can I find him?"

"What is this about? I'm not saying anything else until you tell me what this is about. I know my rights. And why are you asking questions about Kathy? Is she ok?"

"Mr. Trent, I'm afraid that's all I can discuss with you at this time. We'll be in touch."

The detective stood up, reached over and picked up his coat. He slung it over his arm and motioned the deputy toward the door. They walked out and Willam closed the door behind them. Willam sat quiet and still on his bed but he had an on-slaught of questions racing through his mind. He jumped to his feet and rushed over to the desk and yanked open the small left drawer. He gathered all the coins that lay at the bottom of the drawer and headed for the pay phone. After reaching the phone, Willam lifted the receiver and depressed the button marked "0". After only one ring, the voice answered.

"Operator, how may I help you?"

"Yes operator, can you please connect me to 202-555-1704?"

"One moment please…."

After a short pause, the voice returned. "That will be $1.80 please."

Willam began slamming the coins into the metal opening. After a succession of beeps, the operator returned.

"Thank you, your call is being connected."

The phone rang several times before he finally heard her sweet voice.

"Hello?" It was Martha.

"Hey Ma, how are you?"

"Willam, is that you Willam? Is everything alright? I've been trying to reach you all week. Why has it taken you so long to call? I've been worried sick...."

"Sorry Ma, I've been pretty busy here. I didn't get the message that you had called until last night. One of the guys pinned my message on somebody else's door. Anyway, I'm fine Ma."

"Well what's going on Will? Are you really alright? The police came by looking for you."

"Yes, I know...."

"So why were they looking for you Will, are you in trouble?"

"No, I'm not in any trouble; none that I'm aware of. They were here today asking me a bunch of questions about Kathy. Have you heard anything about her, is she ok?"

"Oh my, is that what this is about? When they came by and asked for you earlier this week, I told them that you were away at school. Then they asked me where and I told them. I asked what it was about, but they wouldn't tell me. I haven't heard anything about Kathy though."

"Well have you seen Rusty? He'd know."

"No, I haven't. He stops by occasionally on his way home from work, but I haven't seen him in a few days, either."

The voice interrupted their conversation abruptly, "Please enter seventy five cents for an additional minute."

"Willam!" Martha yelled.

"Yes Ma'am, I'm still here. I'll call you back as soon as I find out anything."

"Okay sweetheart, I'll….."

Before Martha could complete her departing words of wisdom, a loud click followed by deep silence replaced the sound of Willam's voice. The phone call was disconnected.

Willam had spent the remainder of the day trying to contact Rusty. He knew if anyone had information about Kathy it would be Rusty. Willam wanted to know just what he knew.

He also tried calling Kathy's home, but there was no answer. He had no way to reach her at school except by letter. Willam wondered to himself what could have happened, but in his heart he already knew that it was something dreadful.

The train pulled into the station promptly at 7:15 pm. Willam climbed down the short but steep steps of the passenger car onto the platform. He looked in both directions only to see a familiar but unexpected face. It was Mr. Daniels. Willam slung his small duffle bag over his shoulder and advanced toward him. Mr. Daniels walked up to him and placed his hand on Willam's shoulder and stared at him through the dark lenses of his eye wear.

"Smooth trip?"

"Yeah, I guess. Is there any word on Kathy? I can't get a hold of Rusty, either. I've been calling him since yesterday but he doesn't answer."

"Your mom is waiting for you. She couldn't make it so she sent me. She didn't want you to have to catch a cab. Here, take the keys, it was hard enough on me driving down here."

Mr. Daniels held out his car keys and Willam stood there staring at them for a brief second. He had realized that Mr. Daniels had not answered any of his questions. Willam took the keys from Mr. Daniels and they proceeded through the terminal and into the parking garage. Mr. Daniels reached up and pulled the small ticket that was wedged between the sun visor and the ceiling of the car and handed it to Willam.

The car pulled up slowly and Willam inched his way into the parking spot just in front of Colette's mom's house. The men climbed out of the car. Mr. Daniels walked to the back of the car and held his hand out for the keys.

"This is as far as I go son, you be careful and tell your mother I said I'll catch her later."

Willam nodded his head while thinking, "Be careful? What does he mean by that?"

Mr. Daniels slid back into the big Caddy and pulled off.

Willam slung his bag over his shoulder and headed for the house. He looked up briefly at Colette's window wishing that the curtains would open and she would appear, smiling and waving to him. He hurried down the walk to the gate. As he flung open the gate, he could see Rusty exiting out of the front door to meet him. He was standing on the porch with a brand new military style crew cut and missing his thin piece of mustache that he cherished. As Willam made his way on to the porch, Rusty placed his arm around his neck, opened the screen door and escorted him inside.

Martha was standing in the living room. As he approached her, she opened her arms wide and embraced him. She held him so tight and so long that it seemed as if time itself had stood still. After she had finally released her son, Martha smiled at him and turned for the kitchen.

"Let me fix you something to eat."

As she slowly made her way to the kitchen, Willam looked over at Rusty. Rusty motioned him over to the steps. Willam followed and sat down in his usual spot, third step from the bottom and looked up at him.

"Well, what's going on man?"

Rusty looked at Willam with the most solemn look on his face. He placed his hand on Willam's shoulder and began to whisper.

"I just found out that Kathy has been missing for weeks. Actually, it turns out that she had been missing since the day you left to go back to school."

"Had been missing? What do you mean had been, is she back home now? And where in the hell have you been? I've been calling you for days."

"Will, I just got back from basic training yesterday. I leave in five days to go to my 'A' school." Rusty paused and then leaned in closer. "Will, I need you to be strong man. Kathy was missing, missing for weeks. Everybody knew. It had been on the news and everything. Your mother should have known. They….they uh…..they uh found her yesterday. They found her over at Sandman's cave in Fort Dupont. She was…..uh….she was raped and um……and her throat….her throat was slit. I'm sorry Will, but she's dead. Kathy's dead."

Willam sat there still and quiet. He could feel his heart sink into his stomach and the bucket of tears flow like waterfalls down the sides of his face. He placed his head inside the palms of his hands and wept. He looked up at Rusty while wiping the running snot from his nose.

"Why? Who would do this Rusty, who? She never bothered anybody. You've got to help me find out who did this man."

"You know I'll do whatever you need. I have to leave in five days so that's all the time we've got. I've called my uncle and he should be here any minute. He told me that he'd come by and speak with us and share as much information as he could. He's also going to want to ask you some questions too, Will. Are you up for that?"

Willam couldn't answer. With tears gushing down his face, he walked upstairs to his room and closed his door.

Moments later, a knock on the door forced Martha out of the kitchen. It was Rusty's uncle, Ray. He was on the D.C. police department but not a detective. He has known Willam and Martha since Willam was a young boy and wanted to help. Willam and some of Rusty's other friends called Ray, "Uncle Ray" and Ray treated them like they were his nephews. He would always gather a group of the boys together and take them down to compete in the city 'pass, punt, and catch' competition and some-times to watch the Cherry Blossom Parade. He was a good guy.

Martha stood smiling as she wiped her hands on her apron. "Hey Ray, how you doing? You hungry?"

Ray, standing there in his blue uniform raised his hand up to the brim of his hat and tilted it as he spoke to Martha.

"Oh no thanks Martha, how have you been? Wish I were here under different circumstances."

"We appreciate anything you can do to help Ray."

Martha smiled and nodded her head then returned to her frying food.

"Lil' Paul, is he alright?"

Uncle Ray always called Rusty, Lil' Paul. Rusty was named after Uncle Ray's brother Paul and most of his older relatives referred to him as Lil' Paul.

"Will's up in his room. Let me go get him."

Rusty headed up to Will's room and knocked on the door.

"Will, Uncle Ray's here. You cool man? Are you up to talking to him?"

After a few moments, Will opened his door. His face was ruddy and his eyes were beginning to swell and were red. Other than that, he had himself pretty together. Will looked at Rusty and nodded his head. They went back downstairs.

Uncle Ray greeted Will and gave him a hug. "You alright son?"

"I'll make it. Thanks for coming out. Tell me Uncle Ray, tell me everything you know. Who found her?"

"Ok. Well, I did speak to one of the guys working the case. He told me that they received an anonymous call telling them where they could find her. He said that she had been beaten severely with a blunt object, raped, urinated on, and her throat slit. He also said that she was pushed close to the cave opening. Strangely, no semen was found on the scene but they did find traces of latex indicating that her attacker wore a condom during the assault. The traces of urine are being analyzed to see if we can find anything that might be helpful."

"RALPH DID THIS! I JUST KNOW HE DID IT, THE BASTARD!"

Willam, now yelling at the top of his lungs, forced Martha to return to the living room to calm him down. She tried to embrace him but Will pulled away and charged back up the stairs to his room.

"I'll do everything that I can Martha. I'll keep an eye on him. I'm gonna head back to the station. Come on Lil' Paul, I'll drop you off on the way."

"Thanks Ray." Martha whispered.

"It's not a problem. I'll let you know when I have more."

"I'll be back in the morning Ms. Trent. Let Will know that I'll see him in the morning," said Rusty.

Martha walked the men to the door. As they exited her home they stopped on the porch and she continued to whisper to them.

"Yes, he's strong, but just give him some time to pull himself together. I just couldn't bring myself to tell him about Kathy. I'm glad you were here, Paul."

Rusty gave Martha a hug and Ray tipped his hat and the men left.

The next morning, as his vision had not yet been restored to full clarity, Willam could see the outline of what appeared to be a large boulder. As he began to regain his complete vision, the jagged beige and white image became identifiable. It then became smaller as it retreated from his view and disappeared as he spoke. It was Rusty's front tooth.

"Morning Will, you up?"

"I am now. Look man, why do you have to get so close when you're trying to wake somebody? You look like a rabid dog or something. How would you like to wake up to a huge moon rock in your face? Looks like you just got finished gnawing on a chew toy or something. Actually that's the first time I've ever seen dusty teeth. How does dust get a chance to settle on one's teeth? And they're still jagged, won't Uncle SAM fix those? I mean you are in the U.S. Navy aren't you?"

"Whatever! I was just thinking if you were down there in college and all, they could at least teach you how not to talk with your breath smelling like death. Shut up with that man. What do you want to do first? I thought we'd go over to Sandman's Cave and see if we can find anything."

"Yeah, that's good thinking, but first I'd like to at least go over to see Mr. and Mrs. Davis."

"You sure that's a good idea? After all, you are a suspect Will."

"A suspect, that's how the police have me labeled. I don't think her parents do. They know I could never have harmed

Kathy in any way, but maybe you're right. We'll head up to the cave first and see what we can find, then maybe stop by her parent's house on the way back."

Willam got dressed. He ate a quick breakfast with Martha and he and Rusty left.

Sandman's Cave was just as the boys remembered it from years ago. They used to go up there when they were kids and jump from the high hill into the soft dirt below. They would play there for hours on end and leave at dusk to get home in time for dinner. Not many people knew about the spot so deep in the woods of Fort Dupont Park.

They walked around and pushed branches and kicked leaves around trying and hoping to find some evidence that the police maybe had overlooked. The bright yellow tape lay there on the ground along with other evidence that the police had been there and worked it as a crime scene. The area where Kathy was found was marked but was now very faded along with a faint stain from her blood.

"Why here, Rusty? Who would have thought to bring her here?"

"I don't know Will, it seems kind of weird doesn't it? She didn't know about this place, did she?"

"I told her about how we used to play here, but never told her where this place was actually located. Whoever brought her here knew about it already."

"Maybe we should talk to Uncle Ray about this."

The boys looked around for several more minutes but didn't find anything helpful at all. Will plopped down on a log and stared at the blood stained stone that lead to the small entrance of the cave. The cave opening was just wide enough for a small animal to possibly fit inside.

"It looks like he tried to stuff her inside the cave. The bastard! He's a coward bastard, that's what he is, whoever did this and without reason, too."

Rusty had climbed up to the top of the hill and was now yelling down to Willam. "How do you know he had no reason? Maybe he knew her. Maybe he felt something for her or didn't like the way she acted toward him. Maybe he saw her do something and decided to hurt her for something that she had done. And maybe...."

"Shut up Rusty, you didn't know anything about her and you definitely don't know anything about that murdering bastard!"

"I'm just saying we do have to weigh all the options. You have to think like a murderer to catch one and I say that he had been watching her. He probably saw her talking to someone or doing something that he thought that she shouldn't. Something that made him upset or maybe turned him on. That's it. She probably turned him on in some strange way and he wanted to treat her like a whore or maybe she did something to make him think she was a whore; it could have been something that she was wearing."

"SHE WASN'T A WHORE! You forget, she was my girl!" Willam yelled back up at him.

"Maybe he didn't know that. Maybe he saw you two doing something and didn't like it and thought he was protecting you. Maybe he just thought she should be punished. Don't you think whores should be punished? If a whore from uptown was murdered, don't you think she would have it coming to her? Those nasty sluts who walk around selling themselves and give nice men diseases to take home to their wives. They break up happy homes and care nothing of it. Colette had the makings of a whore and look what happened to her. Maybe she got what she deserved.

Maybe the guy is doing what he considered to be something just. Maybe it's the same guy."

"Who's up there? What are you boys doing up here? This is a crime scene, you have to leave, and you young man, come down from there." said the officer as he approached the boys.

Rusty jumped to the bottom of the hill and giggled.

"Wow! Still a rush, you should try it one time."

As Rusty walked toward Willam and he noticed the officer's stern look, his smiled slowly dropped. Willam approached the officer and began explaining their interest, but the officer was not interested in hearing anything that Willam had to say.

"This area is restricted. Didn't you boys see the tape and what did you do, pull it down? You can't be here."

The officer escorted the boys down to the path toward the road.

"You boys know anything about what happened here?"

The boys looked at each other. Willam was trying to hide his anger from the police officer, but was doing a poor job of it. He cleared his throat then answered calmly, "No sir."

The policeman looked into Willam's eyes then leaned toward him.

"If you know something, I think you two had better tell me."

Rusty stepped in front of Willam and grabbed his arm and pulled away from the officer. He looked back at the policeman as they walked off. "Like he said, we don't know anything."

The boys walked down the road and walked out of the park without uttering a word. Willam was still angry at Rusty for all the remarks that he had made about Kathy and Colette. It was as if he hated them both.

The boys walked down Texas Avenue onto Adrian Street where Kathy lived. Willam walked up the steps and onto the porch. Rusty waited by the gate. Willam could see the thin dark silhouette approaching the door. After reaching the door, Willam could see the figure raise one of the thin metal panels of the mini blinds. Willam waved to the figure and the blind was quickly release.

"Go away! We don't want to see you," said the voice from behind the door.

"Mrs. Davis! Mrs. Davis! It's me, Willam"

"I know who you are and I don't want to see you. Why did you do it? Why did you kill my little girl?"

The woman was beginning to scream at Willam as she cried. Suddenly the door opened and the figure standing before Willam was not that of Mrs. Davis but Mr. Davis. He bolted out of the door and grabbed Willam by the arm and forcefully removed him from their porch. Rusty ran into the yard and Mr. Davis pushed Willam toward him. Mrs. Davis continued to cry as she stood in the doorway. Mr. Davis was now pointing at the gate and yelling at the boys.

"You boys get off my property and don't come back here. If you do, I'm calling the police, and I'm sure they'd like to talk to you Willam."

Rusty grabbed Willam by the arm.

"Let's go Will, it looks like they think you're a monster, too. I told you this wasn't a good idea."

Willam was no longer angry with Rusty, he was now so upset by what Mr. and Mrs. Davis had said to him.

"They think I'm a killer. They think I killed Kathy." Willam mumbled.

"Don't worry about them, I know you didn't do it and we'll prove it," Rusty replied.

The intoxicating fog blocked the walkway as the guys moved aside so that Rusty and Willam could enter the yard. Rusty's brother Joe and his friends were back in their usual spot doing their usual thing, getting high. Rusty and Willam had just walked back to Rusty's. Willam was emotionally worn out already and it was only 12:30 in the afternoon. As they walked in the door, Rusty stopped at the refrigerator and pulled two of the cold aluminum cans of beer from the plastic ring.

"You'd better not be fooling with my beer you little Punk! Don't make me have to come in there and kick your ass! I don't care what kind of training you've been to," yelled Joe from the wall where the guys sat.

Rusty looked out the window to see if Joe was coming in the house. He felt grown since he had graduated high school, but didn't feel that grown. He knew that Joe could still give him a pretty good beating. He watched him light another marijuana stick and begin to inhale. Rusty placed one of the beers back in its original plastic ring then stuffed the other down in his pant pocket and headed downstairs to the apartment.

Willam sat quietly on the small padded bench staring at the floor. Rusty walked over to him and retrieved the can from his pocket and pried the small metal ring up and pulled the tab off. As the foamy liquid rushed out from the can, Rusty offered it to Willam. Willam normally wouldn't accept it but this was not the old Willam. He took the can from Rusty and placed it to his mouth. He turned the can up and gulped down every drop.

"What's next Will?" Rusty wanted to know.

"I'm not sure. I don't even know what I can do. I guess I'll just go back to school and wait. I can't afford to miss many classes you know."

"So when you heading back?"

"What's today?"

"It's Friday."

"Well, I guess I'll head back Sunday night then. I'll spend some more time with my mother and hang around as long as I can just in case something else comes up."

"Yeah, I have to head back Sunday morning myself."

Willam turned the empty can up to his mouth once more and shook it in hopes of retrieving a few more drops. He stood up and went back up the stairs. Rusty opened the screen door for him and Willam left. After making his way through the refer cloud, he held his fist up in the air and Rusty returned the gesture.

"You better not had drank any of my beer, boy, and I know you've been driving my car, too! Let me find out you did, you hear me?" Joe yelled at Rusty again.

Rusty flipped Joe the finger and went back inside. Willam disappeared from sight.

The days passed quickly and Martha enjoyed Willam's company. Mr. Daniels stopped by a few times, but Willam didn't drive him this time. He just didn't have it in him to go anywhere. He just hung around the house, watched television, and ate. He didn't even call or go down to Rusty's. Blue and Ronnie had dropped by to see if Willam wanted to hang out but he decided not to. They sat and talked with Willam for a while and then left.

On Sunday after church, Willam ate dinner with Martha and then headed back to the train station to return to school. Willam drove Mr. Daniels' car with Mr. Daniels seated comfortably in the passenger seat. Mr. Daniels was to drive solo on his return after dropping Willam off. After reaching the station, Willam climbed from behind the steering wheel. He grabbed his bag from the back seat and headed around the back of the car. Mr. Daniels met him on the curb.

"Look Will, try not to worry about what's going on up here and concentrate on your studies. I'll check in on your mom from time to time. If anything comes up I'll contact you, ok?"

Willam nodded. The men embraced and off Willam went into Union Station.

The light from the ceiling lamps that hung in the long hallway illuminated the dull cheap floor tile of his room. Willam pushed the door open and after switching on the light, stepped inside. After a quick look around, he decided that Alfonzo had not yet returned to the campus from his routine weekend commute home. He went home every weekend without fail.

Willam tossed his bag on the floor and noticed a large piece of green paper with writing and pictures printed on it. Willam bent over and picked up the paper. The AKA Sorority was hosting a party. Willam balled up the paper and threw it toward the trashcan by the desk. He missed the trashcan and the paper fell to the floor and began to absorb the thick red fluid. Willam peered at the fluid, but was not quite sure what to make of it.

"What has that crazy Alfonzo been up to now?" he thought.

The river of blood flowed from the side of his bed to the wall beyond the desk. Now realizing that it was in fact blood, he leaned toward it for a closer look. He looked over and saw the blood stained hand that hung just above the floor. The blood still continued to drip from the finger tips as he stood there. The sheets that covered the lifeless body were completely drenched with blood. Willam couldn't move. He was terrified but yet he could not dismiss the horrific sight from his vision. This was not happening, not to him. It was as if he was someone else looking at him from a distance. He felt numb.

"Alfonso!" he called out. "Alfonso! Are you alright man?"

Willam inched his way over to the body. He had to look. He stood in the large puddle of blood by his bedside and leaned over the body. He lowered his hand hesitantly to the sheet and gently grabbed it. He slowly slid it away from the face. Willam froze. He stood there trembling and started sobbing.

The eyes were piercing as they stared at the ceiling. The mouth was wide open but shifted in a strange manner, as if the jaw bone had been broken or fractured and the dried blood line began at the deep cut in the lower lip and dissipated just before the bottom edge of the right ear. Bloody flesh hung out from the long gash which started from just under the left side of the jaw and ended just under the left ear. The left hand rested on the side of the mattress as if it had been clenched to the side of the bed tightly and the nail of the right index finger had been ripped off from the tense grip that was applied to the bed.

After a few minutes, Willam managed to pull himself away from the gory sight. He backed away from the body and walked down the hall to the phone, leaving a blood stained trail behind him. He called campus security and then Martha.

"Hello," she answered.

"Mama, help me. She's dead Mama."

"I know baby. It'll be okay. They will find who's responsible."

"No Mama, not Kathy. My friend, my friend Debra, somebody killed her Mama. They're gonna think that I did it."

Silence filled the phone as Willam pressed his ear firmly against it before speaking. "Mama? Are you there?"

Martha never answered and soon the phone went dead, she had fainted.

Campus security officers arrived quickly on the scene followed by deputies from the Salisbury Sheriff's Department. One of the deputies took Willam downstairs and began asking him an onslaught of questions. Willam answered all of his questions as best he could. After over an hour of interrogation,

Willam was asked to accompany the deputy to the station. Will obliged.

After spending half the night being questioned by two more deputies, Willam was driven back to campus and dropped off at one of the fraternity houses. The dean, along with a counselor, had spoken to Willam and he had agreed to stay in the frat house until things could be sorted out. Earlier, when Alfonso returned to the campus dormitory, surrounded by the flashing lights from the patrol cars and the ambulance, they had brought him over to the frat house also.

Willam walked into the door of the frat house to an awaiting group of young men, all with solemn looks on their faces. One of the guys brought him a towel and a wash cloth and offered to show him to his sleeping quarters. No one spoke of the horrible incident. The young man was escorting Willam toward the back of the house when the loud voice from the top of the stairs rang out.

"What in the hell happened in there, Will?"

It was Alfonso. He had been drinking heavily and was now standing at the top of the stairs in his slippers and boxer shorts. Willam looked up at him, tired and not really feeling like talking about it anymore, shook his head and shrugged his shoulders.

"And what in the hell was she doing in our room. Wait, is anything missing? Hope my new stereo wasn't stolen. You know who did this, don't you? It's probably some jealous woman who wants you," he slurred out. "I told you that you two had gotten a little too close. Looks like you made somebody pretty jealous."

"Look man, can we talk about this in the morning?" Willam yelled back up the stairs.

"Talk in the morning? Yeah right, in the morning."

Alfonso turned his glass up to his mouth and drank all of what remained of the brown liquid. He looked down at Willam as he began chomping down on the ice cube which he had also dumped into his mouth. He held up his glass and pointed it at Willam yelling, "Willam Trent ladies and gentlemen, Willam Trent."

Willam followed the young man to a small room toward the back of the house. He curled up on the undersized bed and stared at the wall until daybreak.

Will remained on the campus of Livingstone for only two weeks after Debra's murder. It seemed that everywhere he went and everything he did on campus reminded him of Debra, not to mention the presence of police officers wherever he went. He knew that he was under suspicion, but tried to continue his everyday routines without intimidation.

Willam was sinking fast. He couldn't study, didn't attend class, and stopped reporting to his part-time job. He just could not function and began to question his presence at Livingstone. He often thought of Kathy and Debra and still could not make sense of it all. Realizing that he had fallen behind in all of his classes, Willam decided to leave Livingstone and return home.

Chapter 6 - Homecoming

Upon Willam's return home, the train station seemed almost desolate. He told no one that he was leaving school, especially his mother. He knew that she would have tried everything in her power to convince him to stay and continue with his studies, something that he knew that he just couldn't do. He collected his luggage and waved one of the porters over to assist him with the large trunk that he had managed to drag from the luggage compartment. The porter positioned the large black metal box onto his dolly and placed Willam's other luggage on top and proceeded to exit with Willam trailing close behind.

Once outside, the porter directed him to an awaiting cab. The driver, who was already leaning against the rear of his car, slung his dreadlocks over his shoulder and assisted the porter in placing the chest and bags into the large trunk of his cab. Willam handed the porter four one dollar bills and climbed into the back seat of the cab.

The driver climbed into the car and started the ignition before looking back at Willam, "Where to, young mon?"

Willam placed his hand on the back of the driver's seat and pulled himself forward. "4360 F Street Southeast, please."

The driver nodded his head, turned and proceded into traffic. He picked up the handset to his two-way radio and spoke loudly into the black plastic device. "Dispatch….this is 182 on call."

He placed the handset back onto the squealing metal box, lifted the lever of the meter, and drove quickly and without caution through the traffic. He drove and hummed along to the sounds of 'Bob Marley' which blared from the small transistor radio which sat on his dash. Now yelling, he looked over his right shoulder, only catching a glimpse of Willam. "So Mon, did you have fun?"

"What do you mean?" Willam asked.

"You know, wherever you be comin' from. Was everding cool dere Mon?"

"Uh, not really."

"Lotta pretty womon I bet?"

"I was at school."

"Wait Mon, and you be home already? School's not done yet mon. What brings ya home? Somebody gettin' wed or somebody die, ay? You don't do wrong to somebody huh?"

"You sure ask a lot of questions."

"Aye Mon, I do but I only ask you tree question and I get no answer dough. So, was it a lady Mon, I bet you be havin' lady problems? A lady who run you off?"

"No, I don't have a lady."

"You got no lady! Wait Mon, you be not a little batty boy, ay? Let we go back to the station if you be dread Mon?"

"No, I'm not that, whatever that is so you can keep driving."

"So if you be not dread, why you got no lady den Mon?"

"She died."

Just as Willam had made this statement, the cab swerved to avoid contact with another passing car. The driver of the vehicle yelled several obscenities at the driver of the cab then displayed more rude gestures through his window.

"Ah, stoppin' your blood clot cryin'!" The cabby yelled. "Sorry Mon, and sorry to hear bout your lady. How long she been gone? Was she sick?

"No."

"Accident?"

"I don't want to talk about it."

"C'mon Mon, it'll do you good to get it off you chest."

"No, I don't want to talk about it. Can you just drive?"

"Mon, If you don't get it out, it's gone eat you up whole Mon, like a barracuda. It's already cookin' ya head Mon. Back home, when I had heavy problems, you know what I do den?"

"Nope, but I know you're gonna tell me."

"Ah Mon, I sit down to a nice big bowl of fish soup and a Red Stripe beer or maybe some oxtails. I'd eat 'til the belly was bustin'. If dat didn't do it, I'd roll a huge splif of gonja Mon, tote it 'til my head was in the sky while drownin' my sorrows with a nice Jamaican rum. Ah yes, dat would do it Mon, ah yeeeessss."

"Yeah, I guess that fixes all of your problems!"

"Wait Mon, ya smart talking me? I'm only tryin' to help you Mon. Only sayin' how ya can drown you sorrows, you know? Ya don't have to take my help if you don't want it." The cab driver discontinued his conversation and Willam welcomed his silence. Just as he grew comfortable in the quiet, the driver grunted once more at him. "Did you say the farty tree hundred block of F?"

"Yes." Willam replied.

The car sped up directly in front of the house then stopped abruptly. The cab driver lowered the meter box lever then grabbed the clipboard that lay on the seat next to him. "That'll be $8.25, young man."

Willam handed the dread haired man a ten dollar bill and sat quietly. The driver paused for a second and realizing that Willam was not going let him keep the change for his tip, he dug into his pocket and retrieved a thick wad of folded bills. He pulled the rubber band from the stack releasing them from its bind. He peeled off a one dollar bill then dug in the small pouch that was attached to his belt and retrieved three quarters and handed the change to Willam.

"Tanks Mon!" He said.

Willam just looked at the man as he climbed out of the cab. The driver opened his door and walked to the back of the car and popped the trunk open. The driver helped Willam heave his luggage and chest from the deep compartment. He slammed the trunk door and hopped back into the car and drove off leaving Willam and his luggage on the street.

Willam managed to drag his things over to the steps before the van pulled up.

"What in the hell are you doing here?" the voice yelled.

Blue and Ronnie jumped out of the van and helped Willam carry his bags up to the house.

"So Will, looks like you're planning on staying for a while. You had enough schooling already?" asked Blue.

"I don't know, it's been kind of hard with Kathy and all, you know?"

Blue looked over at Ronnie. Wondering why Blue had such a strange look on his face, Willam also turned and looked at Ronnie. Ronnie looked down at the floor then back over to Blue. "Look man, we'd better get going."

Blue looked back over to Willam. "Uh yeah, we gotta get going Will, but we'll get together and catch up real soon."

Willam nodded and the boys left.

After Willam had gotten settled in, he sat quietly in his room thinking about Kathy and Debra and what he was going to say to Martha when she arrived home. He went downstairs and threw two chicken potpies into the oven. He sat in the dining room and wrote down as many things as he could think of related to the murders. After the chicken aroma had filled the entire downstairs, Willam pulled the hot foiled pies from the oven. He let them cool for a while then devoured one of them. He placed the other pie back into the cool oven for Martha's return. He left a note on the dining room table for her and went back upstairs and stretched out across his bed.

Willam was awakened by the faint sound of her voice. "Thanks again girl, I'll see you tomorrow."

It was Martha returning from her part-time job. Ms. Hollis, her girlfriend who had gotten her the job, would drop her off at home when they got off from work. Martha would share on the gas and Ms. Hollis would have company on the way home.

Martha waved to Ms. Hollis as she pulled off then slid her key into the door lock. She turned the knob and pushed the door open slowly. After stepping in she threw her coat across the arm of the sofa and sat her bag on top of the coffee table. As she walked into the kitchen, she noticed that things were not as she had left them before leaving for work. She looked around the kitchen then stepped in the dining room where she discovered the note.

Martha didn't know how to feel. She knew that Willam was hurt by all that had happened, yet she didn't want him to throw his life away for something and someone that he could never bring back. At the same time though, she felt a feeling of joy come over her. She was happy to have him home.

Martha returned to the kitchen and opened the oven door only to find the small covered tin foil pan. Just as she began to pull it out she felt a presence in the room with her. She looked over, and there stood Willam in the doorway.

"Sorry mom, I tried, I really did," he said looking down at the floor.

Martha placed the pie on top of the stove and closed the oven door then rushed over to him. She wrapped her arms around her son and squeezed him tight. "I know son, I know you did. I can understand how you feel and I know it's hard. Don't worry, the pain may not go away, but you'll learn to deal with it and life will and can go on. I too, felt that kind of pain when your dad was taken from me. I still feel it every time I think of him. It just doesn't hurt as bad. I still miss him, too. Life has to go on Will, it has to."

"I know, but it's just so hard. Everything that I do reminds me of them. And what makes it even worse is.......I just don't understand any of it."

"You take your time son. We'll figure this thing out together. Maybe you can enroll in school here when you're feeling up to it."

Willam nodded, then led his mother to the dining room table and sat her down. He pried the meat pie from its foil container and placed it on a plate and warmed her food in the microwave oven. After the oven began beeping, Willam popped open the door of the small oven and pulled out the heated pie. He grabbed a fork from the utensil drawer and carried the plate of food over to his mother. They sat and talked while she ate. After she was finished, they retired to their rooms.

Several months had passed and not much had changed. Willam was not working or attending school and didn't socialize much with anybody. Mr. Daniels managed to get him out occasionally when he needed to get a hair cut or run one of his other errands, but that was about the extent of his life. Martha was beginning to think that he would never snap out of his slump.

As time passed, there had been no updates or encouraging information on the capture of any of the murderers. Uncle Ray would stop by on occasion but would never have anything new to report.

With his life at a standstill, Willam finally decided that it was time for him to do something, anything. He knew that both Kathy and Debra would not want him wasting his life away, so he decided to go back to school, but not Livingstone. He didn't want to leave Martha again and didn't want her to have to worry about how they were going to pay school tuition every semester. Willam decided to attend a school nearby. He enrolled at the Washington Technical Institute in D.C.

It was the summer quarter at Washington Tech. Willam had to start in the summer to try and catch up with classes from which he had withdrawn and get at least one of his electives out of the way. Attending Washington Tech was a lot easier for him. With his grant and financial aid money, Willam hardly paid anything for school and with the money Martha had saved up over the months from her part-time job, she was able to purchase an old used car for Willam, a 1972 Chevrolet Impala. It was light green with a dark green vinyl roof.

Willam was ecstatic. He loved that car. Although the passenger side of the long bench seat had a busted spring and rocked every time the brakes were applied, it was perfect.

After the first couple of months of school, Willam found himself a new job. He began working at the Dart Drug Warehouse in Landover, Maryland. Now with a car, he was able to venture out to where the decent jobs were and the pay was much better than at the fast food restaurants.

Willam enjoyed his new life. He enjoyed his new school, although not as prestigious as Livingstone, he liked it nevertheless. The new job was great, too. He drove a fork lift and used motorized hand trucks to load and unload tractor trailer trucks at the docking bays. It was a fun job.

Willam got along with everyone at the warehouse. Tony Roberts was the first person that he had met to whom he was assigned. Tony had shown him around and had introduced him to everybody working on his shift.

Mr. Nesbitt was the shift supervisor, an ex-military guy who worked and ran his shift as if it were the Marine Corps. During Willam's orientation and initial tour, he met his section supervisor Wallace Cotton, whom everyone referred to as "Cotton". He also met the two ladies who worked across from him, Beverly and Diane.

Willam had now been working at the warehouse for almost a full month. Beverly began her subtle propositioning after his second night there. She would walk over to Willam's section and open her smock and "innocently" expose her protruding breast through her tight blouse to him. Meanwhile her girlfriend Diane reminded him constantly of how Beverly wanted to go out with him. Willam never said anything ungentlemanly to her. He only showed her respect. She didn't know his past. She didn't know about all that had happened to him and how he got to where he was in his life on that particular day. She didn't know that getting too close to him could cost Beverly her life. She didn't know that he was afraid to get close to another woman again, yet he would converse with her daily.

Eventually Willam and Beverly did become friends. During their break, Willam would go out back with Beverly while she enjoyed a cigarette. They would talk and laugh then return back to work and later would have lunch together. This was a daily occurrence.

The fall semester of school was different. Washington Tech had merged with Federal City College and D.C. Teachers College to form the University of the District of Columbia.

Willam registered for school. He had successfully registered for three computer courses and one elective, Introduction to Music Theory. Willam figured this would be an easy course and decided to take it only two days a week, Tuesdays and Thursdays.

Without ever realizing it, the music class became very interesting to him. There was also a young lady in the class that somehow despite everything that had happened to him, he found attracted. Her name was Lynn. She was also a Computer Science major, but was taking the music class because she played the saxophone and thought that the class would provide her with a better understanding of music in general. Willam tried to ignore the feelings that he had for her for as long as he could but it didn't last. Then he fought the feelings that he had for Lynn every time he thought of her. He didn't want to take a chance of having something happen to anybody else that he knew because of him.

Lynn was a very attractive, young woman. Several of the guys on campus had made advances toward her, but they were always unsuccessful. She was a short girl with thick legs and short curly hair. She walked with her back arched and her shoulders pinned back. She was truly adorable to Willam.

After several weeks of interaction, Lynn asked Willam out. He declined. Vick, one of the students in the class, pulled Willam to the side away from the other students to talk to him.

"Is she your girl?" he asked.

"No, we're just friends." Willam replied.

"Cool, I didn't want to be stepping on anybody's toes, you know?"

"I mean, we might, I mean, she wants to go out with me, but I don't know."

"You don't know? As fine as she is, you don't know? What's wrong with you bro? I mean, you do like women don't you?"

"Yeah, of course, but…."

"But what? Man you need to make up your mind quick. If you don't, I'll make it up for you. I'll tell you what, you decide what you're gonna do by the end of this week. If I see that you guys have gotten it together, then cool, but if not by next week, I've gotta make my move man."

The guy turned and then walked back to his seat as the instructor and some of the other students entered. Willam stood there and watched Lynn as she entered the room and took her seat. She looked up and smiled at him. Willam smiled back.

The next week had come and Willam had not spoken to Lynn. He thought about her the entire weekend, but could not muster up enough courage to call her. After class that Tuesday, Lynn was heading out the door and was met by Vick. He motioned her over and started talking with her. Lynn was smiling. As Willam passed the two, she seemed so engrossed in their conversation. Vick glanced over at Willam and produced an arrogant smirk on his face for Willam to see. With this, Willam headed for the door.

"Hey Will, wait up!" It was Lynn.

Willam turned and she ran toward him. Willam looked at Vick and smiled. Vick frowned up his face and walked back into the classroom. Lynn rushed up and took Willam by the arm and they left.

Willam realized that there's more than one way to lose someone. He didn't want to lose Lynn either way. They began to date from that day forward.

Willam's new girlfriend Lynn was very attentive to him. She would come over and watch television with him, but only while Martha was at work. They would go to concerts together and would catch almost every movie that came out. She was truly a good mate for him. During work nights, Willam would leave his big Impala car doors unlocked and Lynn would drive up during his dinner break and sit out in the car with him as he ate whatever she would bring. They would sit and talk and kiss. Beverly was a bit jealous at first, but soon became happy and relieved that he wasn't gay.

One Saturday evening, Willam had arrived early for work. He normally didn't work on Saturday but had and opportunity to work some overtime. This was a rare occurrence for the new guys. Dan Barkley, an old timer with the company couldn't make it in due to illness and Willam was called to take his shift. Willam usually hung out with Lynn on Saturday and told her that he would decline the overtime, but she insisted that he go.

The phone rang and was answered promptly by Mr. Nesbit's secretary. "Hello. Yes, he is. He's in the bay right now. I can take a message or you can call him back at 10:00 pm, during his break. Ok, uh huh, ok, I'll make sure he gets the message."

The secretary hung the phone up and scribbled on a square note pad. She ripped the paper off the pad and folded it in half. Just as she was about to place it in Willam's message box Beverly walked by.

The secretary handed the small piece of paper to Beverly and asked her if she could pass it on to Willam on her way to the bays. Beverly agreed and proceeded toward her work section.

Beverly and Willam stood outside and talked until she finished her cigarette. Just as they started inside, Beverly took Willam by the arm. "What's wrong with me Will?"

Willam looked at Beverly in puzzlement. "What do you mean Bev?"

"I mean, I'm not a bad looking girl, am I?"

"Of course not, you're very attractive. Any guy would be crazy not to want to be with you."

"Well do you consider yourself crazy?"

"Bev, when I first started working here, I was going through a lot."

"A lot like what?"

"C'mon Bev, I was just going through some things, that's all, nothing that you would want to hear about."

"Oh, I see, it's something that has destroyed my self esteem and ego, but nothing of interest to me. You know I'm still attracted to you Will. I pretend like I'm not, but I am and always have been."

"Look Bev, when I first got here, I was just returning from school. My girlfriend was murdered and my friend in school was murdered, too. I just didn't want anybody else to get hurt that's all. I just wasn't sure if whoever did those things was gone and that it was over."

"I see. You felt safer and were willing to take that chance with Lynn though? Will, you should have given me that chance. You still should."

"But Bev, I can't because….."

"Our time's up Will. We'd better get back in before Cotton comes looking for us."

Willam and Beverly dropped their discussion and returned to work, but Willam knew that it wasn't the end of it.

Willam and Beverly continued to work through their shift. She smiled and waved to him every time they made eye contact across their work sections. This flirting went on throughout the evening.

The dinner whistle blew and Willam hurried to park his forklift in anticipation of seeing Lynn. He unbuckled himself and rushed to the restroom to wash up. He walked up to the clock box mounted on the wall near the front office and punched his time card. He was buzzed out by the security officer then stepped in full stride to the employees' side of the parking lot.

The blood slowly dripped from the bottom of the passenger side door of Willam's Impala and onto the pavement. Willam stopped in his tracks. He grabbed both sides of his head with his hands, shaking uncontrollably. He couldn't believe what he was seeing. He slowly approached the car. After he was close enough, he looked away. He was afraid to look inside. He began to cry and began screaming as loud as he could over and over as he backed away from the vehicle.

Cotton was walking to his car to have a drink when he heard Willam's screams. He ran over to where Willam was standing and grabbed him, trying to calm him down. Others started walking over, too. Cotton, not noticing the red stained pavement, began questioning Willam. "What's wrong Will? Calm down and tell me what's wrong."

Finally Willam stopped yelling and began staring at the car. He never spoke a word. He couldn't.

Cotton repeated, "Will, what's wrong man?"

Diane rushed past the crowd and looked inside the Impala. She began screaming as she pointed to Willam. "He killed her! He killed her! She's dead!"

Everybody moved closer and Willam fell to the ground. He fell right in the puddle of her blood. He sat there lifeless, holding himself up with only one arm.

Cotton made his way through the crowd then looked back at Diane. "Killed who? Nobody's dead."

Willam finally spoke, "Lynn, I killed Lynn, I must have. I just don't remember. I'm sorry baby, I'm sorry. I'm sick that's all. I need help." Willam turned to the crowd and yelled out. "I NEED HELP!"

Cotton walked up to the car. The passenger side door was ajar. He placed his boot against the small opening and pushed the door completely opened. The gasp from everyone who could see her was almost in unison. Some of the people quickly turned their heads and others rushed off. Cotton backed up, yelling to the fleeing spectators. "Somebody dial 911, call the police!"

She was slumped over onto the seat. Her eyes and mouth were wide open. The look of shock still remained plastered across her face. The blood seeped out from the long opened gash across her throat and dripped onto the floor and pavement now that the door was opened. Her left hand draped across her lap and the other lay in the puddle of thick red blood soaked into the carpet and was still clenching the thin worn fabric. There was a large bald spot left from where her hair had been ripped from its tough surface and the hair below the missing plug was tangled and matted. The inside of the vehicle reeked of death and defecation, as the young woman had lost her bowels after her unsuccessful struggle for her life.

The police arrived quickly on the scene. Willam was still sitting motionless on the concrete pavement staring off into space. He was in shock and unaware of anyone around him. The paramedics arrived shortly after the police. They rushed over to the woman's body and check her vital statistics. She was dead.

The paramedics attended to Willam while the police officers cleared the area and spoke into their walkie-talkies. Willam was escorted over to the ambulance and a blanket was wrapped around his shoulders. One of the paramedics shined a small flashlight into his eyes, but Willam was still very unaware.

As the detectives pulled up to the scene, they waved the spectators out of the way. They slowly stepped out of the solid colored brown Ford and advanced toward the other officers. They walked over to the car and pulled out their small notebooks. One of the detectives was fat and had crammed himself into the snug brown suit that he wore. The other detective was tall and thin, wearing a blue suit and dark shades. They asked the officers if anyone had seen anything. The officers briefed the detectives on all of the information that they had obtained from Cotton and Diane. The detectives continued looking around, then they both pulled out a pair of latex gloves from their jacket pockets and slipped them on to their hands.

The heavyset detective walked around the car and opened the driver's side door and started scanning that area. The other one examined the dead girl's fingernails and swabbed them with a Q-tip then placed the Q-tip into a plastic bag. With a pair of tweezers, the detective pulled hair samples and other small pieces of evidence from her body.

"Whoever did this was either pretty strong or full of rage." Said the heavyset detective.

The blue and white van pulled up and several men piled out and they too, began inspecting the site. One of the men took pictures while the others were dusting the car for fingerprints and taking blood samples.

The two detectives tried speaking to Willam, but again he was inattentive. Getting nowhere with Willam, the detectives released him to the paramedics to be transported to the Prince Georges County Community Hospital for treatment. They directed an officer to accompany him and to stay with him until he could be questioned.

The following day, Willam was visited by the two detectives. He was feeling better, but was still sedated. They introduced themselves to him as Detective Lindsey and Jones. The heavyset detective Lindsey, sat in the chair next to him. He pulled out his notebook and began to question Willam.

"How well did you know the young lady that was in your car?"

Willam struggled to swallow then tried to raise himself up but failed at his attempt. He licked his lips and tried to speak. His voice was raspy and at a whisper. "She's …I mean, she was…my….she was my girlfri…."

"Is he a suspect detective?" Asked the voice from the hallway. Martha stepped into the room and both detectives stood up.

"And you are?" Asked Detective Lindsey.

"I'm his mother," Martha replied.

Willam looked over at Martha. He could see that she was tired and worn out. She had been at the hospital all night. Willam licked his lips again before speaking, "Mom, Lynn…, Lynn, she's…"

"Yes baby, she's here. She's right outside."

Just as Martha was finishing her statement, Lynn stepped into the room.

Willam opened his eyes wide in disbelief. He could hardly speak, but continued trying until he was able to get his words out.

"I thought, I thought you were…but I don't understand, if not you who was….?"

"I know, everyone told us how you two would usually eat in the car on your break. You probably thought that it was Lynn in your car, but it was your co-worker, Beverly Jenkins. It seems the secretary gave her a message for you to notify you that Lynn was not able to make it last night. Beverly failed to give you the message. Her girlfriend Diane told us that she went out to meet you in your car hoping that you were still expecting Lynn. She told me that Beverly had a crush on you. Somebody was expecting her to be you, Lynn. Is there any reason why anybody would want to harm you?"

Lynn looked over at Willam.

"Nobody wanted to hurt her, they wanted to hurt me," said Willam.

"Why you Willam, why would anybody want to hurt you?" The large detective asked.

"I'm not sure."

"Do you know if you have any enemies?"

Willam shook his head and dozed off.

Willam slept for the rest of the day and all through the night. Detective Lindsey continued asking Martha and Lynn questions about Willam's acquaintances and about school. Both of the ladies answered his questions as best as they could.

The detectives hung around for about an hour after Willam had fallen asleep, but after realizing that he would be out for sometime, they collected their things and made their exit.

The next morning Willam went home from the hospital. Martha and Mr. Daniels had driven him home. His car had been impounded by the police as evidence.

While sitting in the dining room, they all turned, startled by the loud knocks on the door. Martha leisurely walked over to the door and opened it. She spoke softly through the screened opening of the door for a second then slowly backed away.

The gentlemen stepped inside. Detective Lindsey pulled out a paper from his suit jacket pocket and began to read while Detective Jones advanced toward Willam as he retrieved the solid, shiny bracelets from their compartment attached to the rear of his belt.

"Willam Trent, you are under arrest for the murder of Ms. Beverly Jenkins. You have the right to remain silent. Anything you say may be used against you in a court of law. You are entitled to an attorney. If you can't afford an attorney, one will be appointed to you. Do you understand these rights?"

Willam nodded his head as the detective placed the handcuffs on his wrists.

Martha stood crying next to him then Mr. Daniels walked over and hugged her. The detectives escorted Willam toward the door. Just before stepping out, he looked back at his mother. "I didn't do this Ma, I didn't."

Martha continued to weep. "I know Willam, I know you couldn't have done any of it. It's all a mistake, they'll see."

The detectives walked Willam to the car and detective Jones placed his hand on the top of Willam's head as he assisted him inside the back of the car. The men climbed into the car and pulled off. Martha immediately rushed over to the phone and dialed Uncle Ray. They spoke briefly. Martha thanked him then hung up.

"He's going to see what he can find out and go check on him." Martha stated.

Mr. Daniels nodded and sat back down at the dining room table. Martha paced back and forth from the dining room to the front door talking aloud.

"Lord Jesus, help my son. Help him Lord. They're wrong, they know they are. That boy wouldn't harm a fly. Lord Jesus, help him."

Chapter 7 - Arraignment

After his transport to the precinct, Willam was led over to a small metal bench and one side of his handcuffs was removed from one of his narrow wrists. It was connected to the solid metal rod that was coupled to the arm of the bench. After only a few minutes, a large police officer stepped out from the room across from where he sat and once again, his constraints were removed.

The officer escorted Willam back into the room from which he came and walked Willam over to the counter of the well lit room. The officer then slid the white, thin cardboard paper into the metal holder and clamped it down with the metal bars attached to the contraption. He took hold of Willam's left hand and pressed each finger one at a time across the black ink box then rolled each finger individually onto the assigned finger square printed on the cardboard paper. He repeated this process with the opposite hand before walking Willam over to the wall and positioning him in front of a camera. He grabbed the small rectangular shaped sign which had Willam's name type set and embedded in it and handed it to Willam. Willam was then positioned to the front, left, and right and photos were taken of him at each of the positions. Willam was being booked.

After his booking was complete, Willam was led to a holding area. It wasn't quite what you would call a cell, but he felt exactly how they wanted him to feel, like a prisoner.

Willam sat on the small cot and placed his head in his hands. He thought over and over about everything that had happened the past year. He ran down the list of people that he knew and still could not come up with anyone who would do such a thing. He lay on the cot and looked up at the ceiling for hours just thinking. His eyes welled up as he thought about how badly things could possibly turn out and how all of this was affecting his mother. He reflected about everyone who now thought that he was guilty: Mr. and Mrs. Davis, the students and faculty at Livingstone and UDC, his co-workers and boss at his job, his neighbors, and now everyone who watched the evening news. Realizing that his life was destroyed, Willam wept.

Willam was awakened at 5:45 am by one of the officers. He opened the door to the holding cell and motioned for Willam to follow. Willam was taken to a small room with a table and two chairs, one on each side of the table. The drab, gray walls and bright hanging lamp reminded him of an interrogation room from an old Dick Tracy movie. After only a few minutes, the door opened. A man in a poorly fitting gray suit carrying a brown briefcase stepped into the room. "Mr. Trent?" he asked.

"Yes, yes sir, I'm Willam Trent," Willam answered in a trembling voice.

The man walked over and placed his briefcase on top of the table then extended his hand over to Willam. "Hi Willam, Sam Fisher, Attorney at Law. I've been assigned to represent you. We need to get started right away. Your arraignment is in two hours."

"My what?"

"Your arraignment; that's where we plead your case. You do understand the crime that you have been accused of, right? Did they read you your rights when they arrested you? How are going to plead, guilty or not guilty?"

"Yes. I know why they arrested me and read me my rights. Mr. Fisher, I didn't hurt anyone. I wouldn't have ever done that to Beverly. I'm not a killer."

"So I guess that'll be a not guilty, huh?" Mr. Fisher smiled at Willam and began scribbling on his pad of paper before continuing. "Willam, I must inform you that if this case is tried in court and you're found guilty, you're looking at a lot of jail time. Now, we could plead guilty and possibly get the charges reduced down to manslaughter with a lesser sentence. That's just something to think about. I've reviewed this case and I must say....it doesn't look very promising, but it's your choice. You'll also get a chance to speak briefly to your mother about this, but we have to make a decision really soon."

Willam looked over at Mr. Fisher and nodded. The attorney stood up and began placing his pad and pen back into his briefcase. He pushed the latches shut then extended his hand once again toward Willam. "Don't worry son, it'll all work out."

Willam stood as he saw the officer enter the room. He looked at Mr. Fisher strangely before mumbling, "You never said if you believe me."

Mr. Fisher looked at the officer then back at Willam. "Son, it doesn't matter if I believe you or not. We may need to get twelve people who know nothing about you to believe you. My job is to help you in any way that I can with this case and to convince those twelve strangers that you didn't do anything wrong. I plan to do just that."

Willam then extended his arm toward the man and shook his hand. Mr. Fisher smiled at Willam before making his exit.

Willam was escorted back to the holding cell where he was given a towel, a bar of soap, toothpaste and toothbrush and deodorant. He was allowed a short time to wash up and collect himself. He returned to his cot, placed his head in his hands and began to pray silently.

It seemed like forever had passed before the irritating sound of the cluster of keys caught Willam's attention. He slowly lifted his head and opened his eyes and there before him stood the massive policeman along with Mr. Fisher standing in the distance.

Willam rose to his feet and immediately extended his arms and the officer stepped forward. He placed the chained metal bracelets around both of Willam's wrists then took him by the back of the arm and escorted him back to the small room where he and Mr. Fisher were left alone.

Mr. Fisher discussed Willam's options with him once more. He had spoken with Willam's mother briefly and relayed her messages to him. He went over the courtroom procedures and informed him on what to expect. "This case has received a lot of media attention Willam so try not to say anything to anybody about the case, understood?"

Willam nodded his head.

Moments later the door was opened and the officer reappeared. He led Willam and Mr. Fisher out to the back of the building into the awaiting mob of reporters and photographers. Willam was terrified.

"Willam, are you innocent? Just give us a statement Willam," was yelled at him by some of the members of the crowd.

As he stepped into the blue and white transport van, Mr. Fisher walked up to him and placed his hand on his shoulder. "Don't worry son, I'll be right behind you."

Willam stepped inside the van and looked out through the metal mesh covered windows surrounding him. The advancing crowd continued snapping photos of him and yelling out questions even up to the moment the vehicle sped off.

The van pulled up quickly from the short drive to the rear of the courthouse. The officers climbed out of the front of the vehicle. They disappeared for a brief second then the side doors were opened. Willam stood and slid out from the short gray leather bench seat and made his way over to the side with the assistance of one of the officers. Before he could exit the van, Willam could see them. They were standing as if they were positioned at the starting line of a marathon race awaiting the sound of the pistol. They were like scavengers waiting to feed off of his flesh.

Willam stepped down onto the pavement. The volume increased as they neared the reporters. Cameras flashed and an onslaught of questions blared out from the crowd as they made their way inside.

The inside of the courthouse was dim and old looking, an historical building from the seventeen hundreds. It was Willam's first time there and he wished the he wasn't there now. He was led down the long hallway and into a small room. His handcuffs were removed. He and Mr. Fisher met with the bailiff for a short while before being led into the courtroom. Willam was seated near the front of the courtroom with others who were also awaiting their judgment. Indistinguishable mumblings filled the courtroom. There were police officers, accused criminals of all sorts, and a host of lawyers.

As he looked down the row, he could see others sitting as nervously as he did, while some looked on as if this was nothing new to them. Willam felt ashamed to be there, but that feeling was hidden behind another, fear. For the first time ever, he felt totally out of control. He was now solely dependant on someone else, someone who he didn't even know and someone who didn't know him. He was scared. He now wore the face of fear and everyone saw it and for those who could not see him, they smelled the fear seep from his pores. He looked around the room for Mr. Fisher, who had vanished without notice. While scanning the courtroom, he saw her.

He sat quiet and still. He watched her as she entered. Martha, Mr. Daniels and Lynn hurried into the courtroom and sat on the opposite side of the room near the front. Martha waved to Willam and he produced as much of a smile as he could. Lynn smiled and waved, then wiped away the tear that was just beginning to make its way down her cheek.

Suddenly the bailiff yelled out as the side door opened. "All rise. This Court of Justice is now in session, the Honorable Judge Samuel Diggs presiding."

Everyone in the court room stood as the short round figure in a dark robe entered the room and sat in the large, high-backed, leather chair behind the freshly polished wooden enclosure. The preceding had begun.

Willam sat quietly as he watched case after case being called before his. He watched as the "first timers" stood before the judge solely at his mercy while the "seasoned criminals" stood before him nonchalantly and full of boredom. They would speak with attitude and with total disrespect to the judge. One young lady yelled and screamed until she was restrained and escorted out of the courtroom. Even with all of this, all eyes were still on Willam and all ears were awaiting his plea.

Finally, the bailiff stepped forward and shouted, "The case before the court, Case Number 82160 in the matter concerning murder in the first degree, the parties are the State of Maryland versus Willam Xavier Trent. The Applicant and the Respondent are each allocated 45 minutes to present their pleadings."

The bailiff returned to his seat. The judge took a moment while he read through some papers in front of him. He lowered his head and looked above the top of his eye glasses. "Counselor, what plead do you enter?"

Mr. Fisher stood and buttoned the top button of his suit jacket. "We plead not guilty your Honor."

The judge looked back down at the papers before him and began to scribble. He looked over at the District Attorney, "Any objection Counselor?"

The tall thin man who sat at the other table also stood. "No objection your honor, we're only asking that no bail be set for the defendant, sir."

Mr. Fisher rose to his feet and interrupted. "Your Honor, my client is an upstanding young man who has never been in any kind of trouble. He is enrolled in college and is currently employed. He has a strong backing from his family and….."

"Your Honor, we feel that, because of several reasons outside of this case, the defendant could possibly try to flea the state, sir", interrupted the prosecutor.

Judge Diggs knew exactly what reasons the prosecutor was talking about. He knew that Willam was currently being investigated for the other murders. He looked down at his pad then scribbled. He glanced over at Willam who was looking over at his mother and Lynn. "Bail is set for one hundred thousand dollars. Counsel will be notified of the trial dates." He shouted then slammed down his gavel, "Next case!"

Mr. Fisher looked down at Willam then over to Martha. She was smiling at Willam with her hands lifted to the heavens. Willam turned to Mr. Fisher with a somber look on his face. "Where are we going to get a hundred thousand dollars? We don't have that kind of money."

"Don't worry son, we'll figure something out. We'll get you out of here."

Willam was escorted back through the side door and Mr. Fisher walked over to Martha. She hugged him as she wept. "Thank you for all of your help."

"It's no problem, no problem at all. Just keep in mind, this is only the beginning. It's going to get pretty rough from here."

"I know, but we will fight this for as long as we have breath in our bodies. My son is innocent; Mr. Fisher and God will protect him. He will answer my prayers and send him back home to me."

"You just keep praying Ms. Trent. All of you keep praying, because we'll need all the help that we can get. Now let's go get your son out of here."

Mr. Fisher escorted Martha through the side door and down the hall to a small office which displayed the words "RECORDS" just above the door. They stepped inside and were greeted by a young lady standing behind a long wooden counter.

"May I help you?"

"Yes, we're here seeking bail for Willam Trent, Case Number 82160. We wish to post by way of property bond." Mr. Fisher laid his briefcase down on the counter and retrieved several papers and handed them to the young lady.

"Okay, who's the property owner?"

Martha stepped forward hesitantly then raised her hand slightly. The young lady gathered several papers together and handed them to Martha. "I'll need you to fill these out then sign here, here, and here."

Martha nodded then pulled her ink pen from her handbag and began filling out the papers. After she had completed the forms she signed them and passed them back to the young lady. She separated them, then looked over each one of the forms. After her review was complete, she looked up at Martha and smiled, "I'll need to make a copy of your identification please."

Martha pulled her wallet from her bag and slid her driver's license from the tight leather slot. She handed her driving credentials to the lady who walked toward the back of the office to the XEROX machine to make a copy of the small plastic document. She quickly returned. "Thank you," she said as she handed the license back to Martha. She began pounding the forms with a rubber stamp, stapled them together then placed them neatly in a metal tray labeled "Property Bonds". She pulled another short form from the third slot of the multi-compartment tray and began scribbling on it. She signed her name, then placed it in the electric time stamping machine before handing it to Mr. Fisher. "Take this down to the holding area and they will release him."

"Thank you," Mr. Fisher replied.

Martha smiled and nodded. The young lady smiled back at her and off they went.

After following the young lady's instructions, Willam was released. He rushed over to his mother and embraced her as tight as he could. He gave Lynn a hug and gently touched her face. She smiled at him and placed her hand on top of his. Willam kept his arm around Lynn until they had reached the car. Mr. Daniels had been waiting for them in the parking lot. He hopped out and walked around the car to open the door for Martha. She placed her hand on top of his shoulder and smiled at him. "Thank you."

Mr. Daniels looked at Willam, "You want to take us in?" Willam declined and slid in the back seat with Lynn. Mr. Daniels climbed back into the driver's seat, backed the car out of its resting place then headed for home.

THE SERIALIZATION OF DISCONTENT

Chapter 8 - Betrayal

The aroma floated throughout the house. Willam, just stepping out of the shower, could smell the feast that his mother was preparing downstairs. He could smell the collard greens, macaroni and cheese and the fried chicken as he strolled through the hall toward his room. Lynn was still downstairs listening to the radio. She offered to help Martha, but Martha wasn't letting anyone in her kitchen that day. She wanted everything to be perfect. Will quickly changed into his blue jeans and tee-shirt. He slipped on his socks and shoes and rushed downstairs. He smiled at Lynn as he passed her and headed for the kitchen.

"Smells great Ma, and I'm starving." Willam reached over and removed the lid from the pot of greens cooking on the back of the stove. He picked up the long fork and stabbed into the greens and Martha smacked his hand.

"Just hold on, it'll be ready soon enough."

Willam placed the lid back on the pot and walked back into the living room. Lynn stood up as he entered the room. "Will, can I talk to you for a minute?"

"Sure, are you alright?"

"Can we talk outside?"

"Sure," Willam answered, looking at her strangely.

Lynn walked over to the front door and stepped onto the porch. She placed both of her hands on the rail and leaned forward to look below at the small evergreen bushes that were surrounded by the brick edging. "Will, should I be scared? I mean, am I safe? It seems like every girl that you've been associated with has....."

"You don't think that I hurt them do you?"

"Of course not! I'm just saying that you should have told me."

"Nobody's gonna hurt you, I pro....."

"Don't say you promise Will. How do you know that he won't come for me, too? They seem to want to hurt everybody that you care about. Please don't make any promises that you're not sure that you can keep, especially when it comes to my life."

Lynn turned and faced Willam. Her face was somber and she began to cry. Willam stepped over and embraced her. "Lynn, I promise, I won't let anything happen to you, not ever."

The door flung open and Martha stuck her head through the door. "Dinner's ready, so come on and eat!" she said and then quickly returned to the kitchen. She began placing the plates on the dining room table followed by the silverware and glasses. Willam and Lynn returned inside and Lynn walked upstairs to wash up. "She seems upset," Martha whispered.

"Can you blame her? Everybody thinks I killed them, everybody! She's probably having doubts, too."

"Not everybody thinks you did such a thing Will. I know you didn't, you're a good boy. And besides, if she thinks that, just how much does she really care about you?"

"What kind of question is that?"

"I'm just saying that maybe she should be a little more trusting, that's all."

"She trusts me Mother and I know she cares about me, too."

"How do you know, how? Just because she's always coming around here and calling you on the phone doesn't mean that she's in love, boy. That's infatuation. All kids go through that! Or is it more than that? I know one thing, she'd better not be popping up over here when I'm not home!"

"We like being around each other, that's all. She's a nice girl."

"Yeah, right Willy. There are a lot of nice girls around here. Most of them are walking around here with babies under their arms. They pretend to be so sweet and innocent when in reality they're sneaky and just plain fast. Before you know what hit you, you'll be a daddy. But that's not going to happen with her, now is it?"

"Ma, she's not like that."

"Boy, you're just too trusting but you can trust this, if she turns up pregnant because you couldn't keep your little pecker in your pants, then there's gonna be some consequences. You can believe that! I've told you time and time again, NEVER TRUST THOSE FAST LITTLE TRAMPS!"

"She's not a tramp Ma, and don't say that about her!"

"Well we shall see, won't we?"

Now hearing Lynn return downstairs, Will and Martha ended their discussion and sat down at their places. Lynn joined them and smiled at Willam to let him know that she was alright. Willam looked over at Martha who quickly looked away.

"Bless the food young man," said Martha.

They all closed their eyes and bowed their heads and Willam began saying Grace over the food as he did with every meal. They ate in silence. Willam ate three full plates of Martha's wonderfully prepared dishes. Lynn hardly ate anything at all.

Finally, Martha looked over at Lynn and asked, "Lynn, you've hardly touched your food, are you alright?"

"Yes ma'am, I'm fine. I guess I'm still just a little worried about Will, that's all. This whole thing is just so stressful. Excuse me for not eating; I'm sure everything tastes wonderful."

"Yes it does!" Willam shouted.

Martha started laughing. "You should know, it doesn't look like you're planning on leaving anything for anybody. You might wanna leave a little room for some chocolate cake, that's your favorite." Martha stood and collected both her and Lynn's plate. "I know times like these can kill your appetite. Well, everybody's except old Will's over there. Yep, there are two things that can always destroy a woman's appetite, stress and babies. I know yours is stress alright, because we all know that you sure aint carrying no baby, isn't that right?" Martha slyly asked while smiling at Lynn.

"Ma!" Willam shouted. He looked at Martha angrily and once again, she turned and looked off to the distance. She folded her arms across her chest then stared at Lynn awaiting an answer. Lynn looked very uncomfortable while answering.

"Of course not Mrs. Trent, how could I be pregnant……oh, you think…..Oh no Ma'am!"

Martha looked at Willam then back over to Lynn. "Sorry if I embarrassed you sweetie, I was only kidding, besides, it doesn't hurt to ask. You do want children some day don't you?"

"Well yeah, I guess, but I'm afraid you're gonna have to wait until Will and I are married, if that ever happens. Then you can have some grandchildren." Lynn replied while looking embarrassed.

"Ah sweetie, trust me, I'm in no hurry and neither is Will, right son?"

Will looked up at his mother as sternly as he could before answering. "When Lynn and I decide that the time is right, then and only then will we have children, Mother."

"Relax Will, your mother's just kidding around. She's just trying to take everybody's mind off of what's been going on, that's all. There's no need to act rude," piped Lynn.

"Oh is that what he was doing?" Martha began wiping her hands with her napkin. "Let me know if that's what you were doing because I want to make sure that I fully understand why I'm slapping the taste out of your mouth! Boy, don't show off and make me embarrass you in front of your company. You know I don't play that!"

"No ma'am, I wasn't being rude. I just don't like discussing that topic."

"Then that is what you should say, instead, you want to poke your chest out Mr. Man! You know I don't tolerate that."

"Sorry Ma."

"Yes, you sure are." Martha said. She looked over at Lynn and winked her eye then smiled jokingly. Lynn placed her hand over her mouth to muffle her chuckles. The ladies began to laugh and Willam said nothing, he just continued eating.

After the meal was finished, Willam sat in the living room and talked to Lynn for a short while before calling her a cab. With his car still impounded, Willam couldn't drive her home. They stood out front and talked until the cab pulled up. Willam walked his girlfriend to the cab and opened the rear passenger door. He gave her a kiss on the lips and she climbed in. "Call me later Will, before you go to bed tonight okay?" Will nodded and shut the door. He watched as the car vanished down the hill of F Street.

Willam returned inside the house and stopped in the dining room where Martha was now resting. He opened up the top drawer of the mahogany buffet cabinet and retrieved a pen and a small pad of paper. "What are you doing?" Martha asked.

"I need to make some notes. I just can't sit here and leave my life in somebody else's hands. I've got to do something."

"Do what?"

"I don't know, but I've got to at least try to figure this thing out." Willam returned to the living room and started writing on the pad. He continued this for over an hour until the knock came at the door. He got up and opened it and there stood Uncle Ray.

"I heard you were home, that's great."

"Yeah, I don't know what's next but I'm gonna do some digging of my own."

"Son, you've got to be careful because you can bet that you are being watched constantly and who knows, whoever is behind this might have you in his sights as well."

"I can't worry about that. I need to know who's doing this and try to make sure that this doesn't happen again."

"I did some checking into your buddy you were screaming about, Ralph. It seems he actually did enlist in the Marine Corps, but was later discharged on a Medical. After that, the trail went cold."

"My thinking is that old Ralph isn't too far."

Willam and Uncle Ray continued to talk for hours about his friends and school mates from high school and college, but couldn't come up with anyone who would have motive. It didn't make any sense at all. Uncle Ray took some notes and gathered up his things in preparation of his departure. Martha had gone upstairs earlier and was getting ready for bed.

After walking Uncle Ray out, Willam returned to his notes. He couldn't come up with anything. He got tired and decided to turn in. He walked into Martha's room before he went to bed. He leaned over her and gave her a kiss on her forehead. "Thanks Mom, thanks for everything."

Martha mumbled some garbled remark then drifted back to sleep.

The room was lit brightly. Willam squinted his eyes as the sun poured in through his bedroom window. Willam got up and walked to the bathroom. He relieved himself, brushed his teeth and washed up before returning to his room to slip into his jeans and sweatshirt. He sat on the side of the bed and leaned forward and grabbed the pad from off of his dresser. After reading through the first two pages, he tossed it back on the dresser then picked his socks up off the floor and pulled them up on his feet. He stuck his feet into his shoes and tied them. He placed the pad in his back pocket and picked up his metal bush pick and pulled it through his hair. After making his way down the hall, he set his path for the living room. Taking two steps at a time, he jumped down onto the living room floor and snatched his jacket from off the chair next to the closet door.

"Is that you Will? Are you hungry?" Martha yelled from the kitchen.

"Yes, it's me Ma. No, I don't want anything right now. I'm gonna run down the street for a second, I'll be right back."

"Okay."

Willam left out of the front door and walked around the side of the house. He walked through the rear gate and across the alley to Ralph's grandmother's house.

"Will! Willam! Where are you going?" Martha yelled, but Willam could not hear her. He walked around to the front door and began to knock. He continued to knock until the door slowly opened.

"Who is it?" The lady asked.

"Ms. Jordan, it's me Will, Willam from across the alley. I've been trying to find Ralph. Can you tell me where I can find him?"

"Why, why are you looking for Ralph?"

"I just need to talk to him, that's all."

"I'm sorry, come on in, where are my manners? How's your mother? Tell her I said hello."

"She's doing fine and I sure will. Do you know where I can find Ralph?"

"I'm not sure. You know he doesn't really come around here much anymore. He was in the service, but then after he found out about his daddy, he started having problems and he eventually got discharged."

"His daddy, what about his daddy, he moved away right?"

"Oh no, we just told Ralph that because we knew he would have been devastated finding out that his father was sent to prison. Would you like something to drink? How about some milk and cookies?"

"No thanks ma'am. I didn't know that he had been sent to prison. What was he sent for?"

"Oh, he was a jealous man you know. Yes he was. We should have seen it coming. We knew how crazy he got and how his temper was. All and all, I guess you could say that he went to prison for jealousy."

"Jealousy? I don't understand."

"He thought that she was having an affair with her employer, so he used to follow her."

"Follow who?"

"My precious little girl, Lord, rest her soul. He would follow her everywhere she went and she knew it, too."

"He went up to her job and waited. He claimed that he saw her and that man kissing. She would have never done that, for as crazy as he was, for some strange reason she loved that fool. His jealousy got the better of him so he killed her. He killed my baby and now he's paying for it." She sat at the table and looked out the window for a moment. "When Ralph found out about it, he was devastated. Poor Ralph, no one had ever told him what happened. I'm still not sure how he found out but he's never been the same since the day that he did. He started getting into all kinds of trouble with the military. Then when his girlfriend couldn't take it any longer, she left him while she was carrying his child. He really flipped after that. Said he couldn't take anymore and that's when he tried to commit suicide. That boy scared us to death. He's been going to his therapy sessions. Well, I guess he's still going, I'm just not sure anymore."

"And you don't know where he is now?"

"No, he calls me from time to time, but I have no idea where he's staying."

She went back to staring out the window and Willam stood watching her for a moment then casually headed for the door. Willam looked back at Mrs. Jordan to thank her. She now sat looking sad and lifeless.

"You take care, Mrs. Jordan. If you need anything, you'll let me know?" She didn't answer. Instead, she continued to concentrate on the small spot on the wall just in front of her. Willam walked to the door and looked back once more. He turned the button on the door knob and walked out slamming the door securely behind him. Willam now realized that Ralph could possibly be the person possible for everything that was happening to him more than ever. Hearing about how unstable he was assured him that Ralph was somehow involved. He walked

142

around the neighborhood as he thought of his next move, stopping for a moment to jot down some notes for Uncle Ray. Before he realized it, he was standing in front of Rusty's. How he missed his buddy.

"Hey man, looks like you're a big celebrity now, huh? I saw you on the news. You looked bigger. Hey, you want a hit? I know you need one, huh?"

Willam walked over to where the guys sat and smoked. He didn't want any of the funny smelling cigarettes that they inhaled so deeply. He just wanted to sit with them for old times sake, wanting to feel associated with somebody, hoping to eliminate the empty feeling that he still had embedded in his soul. The guys were engrossed in a conversation about which cartoon character was the most attractive, Wilma Flintstone or Betty Rubble. They continued trying to pass him the hand rolled cigarettes and Willam continued to decline. Willam placed his arm on Joe's shoulder. "Man, I really miss your crazy brother. I'll be glad when he comes back home. When is the next time he's on leave?"

"Leave? I don't know nothing about no leave, but he should be home at his usual time I guess, about 9:30 tonight."

"What are talking about Joe? Has that weed blown your mind or something? Your brother's gone man and after he's finished his 'A' school, aint no telling where they're going to send him."

"What man? What in the hell are you talking about? 'A' school, who? Send him where? Hey, be honest, doesn't Wilma have a nicer body?"

"Wilma, Wilma who?"

"Flintstone, fool!"

"Rusty, your brother, you do remember him don't you, he's in the Navy remember?"

"Navy, what Navy?"

"You know as in the United States Navy? Uh, hello in there, is anybody home? You miss him too, huh?"

"Miss who, Rusty? Where has he gone? Do you really think that my little piss ant of a brother would join the Navy? Hell no you don't. Hell, that boy's scared to take a bath in too much water let alone join some Navy. Y'all hear this fool? My clown brother in the Navy, yeah right!"

"Wait, so you're telling me that Rusty's not in the Navy? What happened, did they send him home?"

"That fool hasn't been anywhere and why do you keep saying that? You're making me confused man. You're blowing my high. As for the Navy, well let's say, if Westingate Security is part of the Navy, then he's enlisted and if that's the case he goes on leave every night about 9:00 pm and stays at this barracks until the next day."

"Rusty's a security guard, but I thought…"

"That's right, from 1:00 pm to 9:00 pm at night. Then after that he's just a pain in the ass."

The guys on the wall started laughing then quickly turned their attention to the slow creeping white van that pulled up on the opposite side of the street. They continued to stare at the vehicle as the doors slowly opened. Joe mashed his twisted cigarette against the brick wall on which he sat. After the fire was extinguished, he returned his focus on the van. The two figures stepped out of the van and walked over to the guys on the wall.

"Hey Will, what's happening man? What are you doing here, thought you were…." It was Blue and Ronnie. Just as Blue began his questioning, he was cut off abruptly by Ronnie.

"So what's going on with you?"

Willam couldn't help but to notice how strange they acted toward him. "Uh, things are fine with me. I'm just trying to keep my head on, that's all."

"So what are you doing, waiting for Rusty to get off?" Blue asked

"You guys knew that he wasn't in the Navy, too?"

"The Navy, what made you think that he was in the Navy?"

"He told me that, I have no idea why though."

Ronnie looked over at Blue again, with a strange look then gestured to him with just a slight nod of his head. He started heading back toward the van, "Come on man, we need to be going. Catch you later Will."

"Yeah, catch you guys later."

Willam still could not figure out why these two were acting so oddly until something popped into his mind. He remembered the white van that slowly pulled away from the dorm at Livingstone the night he found Debra. He stood up and walked over to the brown station wagon parked in front of the house and pulled out his pad. He scribbled down more notes then retuned to the wall.

"Man, what are you writing over there?"

"Nothing, just taking some notes."

"Those two are pretty weird man, you need to note that! That's all they do is ride around in that damn van. Blue's dad sends them down to Richmond a lot now. They must have girlfriends down there or something because sometimes they are down there for days. Actually, I take that back because I have never seen either one of them with a girl. They used to come hang out every once in a while, but now they just stay to themselves," said Joe.

Willam sat with the guys for a little while longer. After getting tired of refusing the burning twisted sticks each time a new one was lit, he headed for home.

Martha, just heading out for work, waited for Willam to reach the top of the stairs where she stood. She was wearing her white nurse's uniform with white stockings and shoes. She also had, pinned neatly to the top of her head, a white nurse's cap. Willam loved her in that uniform. He especially loved that nurse's cap. Martha stepped down on the step where Willam stood and took him by the hand. "I left you some bacon and eggs in the oven, it should still be warm. I'll be home as soon as I can and remember, don't have anyone in the house while I'm at work." Willam knew his mother was talking about Lynn. The brakes squeaked as the car slowed. Short quick blasts of the horn was just enough to take Martha's attention off Willam. She leaned toward her son and gave him a peck on his lips.

Willam kissed his mom back and watched her as she rushed to the awaiting car. "Call me if you need me, the number is still taped to the refrigerator door." Willam smiled and waved as the car sped off. He stepped inside and proceeded to the kitchen where he found his breakfast sitting comfortably on the top rack of the oven covered with aluminum foil. He took the meal from the still warm oven and placed it on the counter. Laying beside his meal was a white envelope. It had been turned over and there was writing on the reverse side. Willam picked up the envelope then rested himself against the refrigerator and began to read. It was a note that Martha had left there before leaving for work. It read:

"Willy, try to get some rest.
I love you,
Mom"

Willam dropped the envelope in the trashcan which sat next to the refrigerator. He grabbed a fork from the small kitchen drawer next to the stove then took his plate into the dining room, sat down and began devouring the pile of food. After finishing his meal, Willam went back inside the kitchen. He opened the refrigerator and pulled out the carton of milk. He pushed the "V" shaped sides of the top of the container apart then pulled the waxy feeling seal outward to reveal the white liquid. He pressed his lips against the carton then tilted it upward pouring the contents into his mouth. He gulped down most of the milk before closing the carton and returning it from where it came. Martha hated when he did that, but she wasn't home. Willam poked around in the fridge for a second longer. He soon found hiding far in the back, almost wedged behind the crisper bin was what he was searching for, the small resealed Coke bottle.

Ever since he could remember, his mother would have a Coke or ginger ale bottle stashed somewhere in the refrigerator. It didn't contain a soft drink beverage though. Well not completely. It would always have a mixture of either rum and Coke or gin and ginger ale. Willam was just a young boy when he first discovered the camouflaged beverage. It was on a morning after Mr. Daniels had stopped by. He had always noticed that no matter when Mr. Daniels stopped by, his mom would always have one of the two soft drinks for him. There was never a Coke for Willam and he loved Coke. He liked the way it would burn his nose when he sipped too much too quickly.

One particular morning, while Martha was still asleep, Willam was determined to have his nose burned by the dark fizzy drink. He tiptoed downstairs to search for the cold sweet beverage. When he opened the refrigerator, it was in plain sight. It was half full, cold and calling out to him. He tipped back into the living room and listened for Martha. He could still hear the heavy breathing of her slumber. He rushed back into the kitchen and opened the door of the refrigerator and pulled out the bottle of Coke. He struggle with the cap trying to remove it. It had been sealed tightly. He tilted the bottom slightly and gripped onto the cap and turned as hard as he could, but it would not budge. Then he remembered what his mom would always do when she had problems opening jars and such.

He walked over to the kitchen sink and snatched the dish cloth that was draped over the faucet. It was still slightly damp from the night before. Willam wanted to run some hot water over the cap first because he had seen his mother do that so many times, but he did not want to take the chance of waking his mother. He wrapped the cloth around the cap, balled up his tongue, gripped the cap as tight as he could then twisted. After he heard the first short blast of the air escaping from the bottle, he knew he was home free. He was rejoicing in his mind. He leaned back beyond the wall and peeked for Martha. No visual and no sounds from upstairs. He quickly removed the cap, turned the bottle up to his mouth and took a giant gulp. "Blah!" Willam didn't know that the cold bottle not only contained the sweet cola, but also Jamaican rum. Willam spit all of the contents of his mouth onto the floor then rushed over to the sink and began drenching his mouth with water. He reached up and grabbed a cup from the cabinet and filled it with water and gulped it down.

"Willy, what are you doing?" It was Martha heading down the steps. Willam dropped the cup into the sink and snatched the coke bottle from the counter. He replaced the cap and shoved it back on the shelf in the refrigerator. He picked up the dish cloth and wiped the liquid off the floor and draped it back across the faucet.

"I said, what are you doing down here by yourself this time in the morning?"

"Nothing."

That was always his standard answer. Martha never did find out about that incident and he never told her. If she had caught him that day, she would have given him the beating of a lifetime. Probably close to the beating that he received when she caught him stealing her Katydids from the bottom of the can. Oh yeah, Willam was pretty sneaky but sometimes never quite sneaky enough.

Willam pondered on that episode for a second more, smiling before snatching the soda bottled from its hiding place and removing its lid. It made a loud fizzing sound. He licked his lips and placed the bottle to his mouth. He took a few sips, each one causing his face to frown up. He burped then took one more sip before wedging it back behind the bin. Will closed the refrigerator, placed his dishes in the sink and went upstairs.

He lay across his bed with his television volume turn down pondering the day and all the new information that he had discovered that day. He smiled to himself when thought about Ralph's dad rotting away in a prison. After all, he had struck Willam's mother, his favorite girl and he never forgave him for that, not even after all these years. Willam did feel bad for Ralph though. He knew what it was like to never see your father again, even though when his dad Jimmy was killed, he had been too young to remember him. Now Ralph had lost both of his parents.

Willam rolled over onto his back and stared at the ceiling. He thought and thought but still could not make any sense out of Rusty's Navy story. "Why would he say that?" he thought, but nothing reasonable would come to mind. He continued to lie and think until he dozed off.

The rusty metal of the round faced contraption was mounted securely on the shiny handlebars of the fast moving tricycle. Willam's son was peddling as fast as he could down the alley and pulling the tab on the round bell. It would ring longer than most, but was not very loud. He sped by the yard giggling and waving to Martha and Jimmy. Jimmy didn't look anything like he did in his photos. Each time the child drove by, both of Willam's parents would wave to their grandson then embrace and kiss each other. Willam rushed over to the grill and began turning the hamburgers over. The bell was beginning to increase in volume. His son was getting closer but he could not see him. The ringing grew even louder but still no sign of his son. Willam walked up to the fence and looked down the alley. He could see the tricycle rushing toward him. The bell was ringing in loud repeated blasts. As it neared, Willam noticed that his son was no longer mounted on the seat of the tricycle. It passed by the yard quickly.

The bell rang, this time louder than ever. Willam jumped up and ran into Martha's room. He grabbed the black handle and with a dry, raspy voice spoke into the receiver, "Hello".

"Hello Will, are you alright?" It was Martha.

"Yes ma'am, I kinda dozed off for a while."

"I was on my lunch break and thought I'd check on you. Good, you're getting some rest. There's some chicken in the refrigerator if you get hungry."

"Yes ma'am. I'm getting ready to run back down to Rusty's, I heard he was home."

"Oh that's great Willam. I'm sure he'll be glad to see you. I've got to go now and I'll see you when I get home."

"Ok Ma, be careful and I'll see you later."

"Ok, see you son and love you."

"Love you, too."

Willam did not have the heart to tell his mother that Rusty had lied to her, but one thing's for sure, she could never have been more wrong. Rusty was not going to be glad to see Willam and he was going to find out why tonight. Willam walked into the bathroom and washed his face. He snatched his jacket off the rail as he ran down the steps and out the front door. He trotted down to the now smoke free wall and sat back down with the guys. They were not smoking now, not with Joe's mother home. Willam sat and talked with his still high buddies about any and everything. They still hadn't decided which fictitious, now in color, diva from the Stone Age was the most attractive, but they were leaning heavily on Betty Rubble. Most of it made no sense, but he tolerated their deep and animated discussions. He was just biding his time; he was waiting for Rusty. Willam watched as the headlights of each vehicle passed. He stared up Hilltop Terrace then down F Street. He stared and waited. He was in deep concentration now, formulating his questions for Rusty when he felt the slight tugging of his shirt.

"How 'bout it Will, what do you think?" Steve asked.

"Uh, think, think about what?"

Joe slid over closer to the steps and began to chuckle, "This fool thinks that if dogs could speak, they would all speak English. I keep trying to tell this fool that German Shepherds are from where? Germany, thank you very much."

"Nah man, they were brought over here like slaves. They lost their language a long time ago. Now you might find a few of the very old shepherds that can still speak their old language, but they're like the immigrant dogs that really haven't lost a sense of their roots." Steve added.

"What do you think Willy?" Joe asked.

Willam looked around at all of the glassy eyes. They were sitting on the edge of their seats awaiting his answer. They were actually debating a topic this crazy and farfetched. Willam sat and tried to think of an answer that could end the debate and make some kind of sense. After several seconds, he leaned forward and spoke the words that none of the guys had anticipated.

"I don't know."

A dead silence covered the wall for only a short while before Joe blared out. "Damn, with all that college, you still don't know nothin'."

The lights skimmed quickly across the sides of the parked cars, Willam's eyes followed both of the bright beams of light as they neared. The squeaky brakes whined as the car slowed down and eventually stopped in front of the house where they sat. Willam lowered himself and sat closer to Steve to screen himself from Rusty's view. The back door of the car opened and Rusty climbed out. "Have a good one." He yelled to the driver as he slammed the car door. He walked toward the wall where the guys sat quietly.

"Hey, what's happening y'all? What's wrong, you all look like you just seen a ghost or something."

The guys said nothing. Rusty walked up the steps and toward the door.

"How was 'A' school or should I say the guard training academy? Is that the new Navy uniform?"

Rusty slowly turned. He peered into the darkness where the group sat. "Oh you're funny. At least I have a job. Who said that anyway?"

Willam stood up. He took a few short steps to the end of the wall and ran up the steps leading to where Rusty stood. "I said it. You got an answer?"

"An answer to what?"

"Why did you lie to me, man? I don't get it. Why would you tell me something like that and lie to my mother, too? Then you hide out down here so she doesn't see you. How long did you think that you could get away with this lie?"

Rusty, shocked to see Willam, remained silent. He looked down trying hard to muster up the appropriate reply but could not. Finally, he raised his head up and looked at Willam in shame. "I'm sorry man."

"You lied for nothing man, I just don't get it," Willam started in.

Rusty stepped toward Willam. His look of shame no longer appeared on his face, he now produced a look of anger. "For nothing, how do you think I felt when you left huh? You were the guy who got the good grades, you were the guy that had the nice job driving a big Caddy all over town, it was you who had the nice girlfriend and you who left and went on to the big time college, and where was I? I was here. That's right, it was you, it always has been Willam, Willam, Willam."

"What was I supposed to do? It wasn't my fault that you had poor SAT scores. It was you who goofed off instead of studying, not me."

"Ok, I'll accept that, but what about the job and girlfriend? That was when you pushed me aside. I mean, we were boys and all. That's not how you treat your boy! If you hadn't been running around sniffing after Kathy, maybe you could have encouraged me to study, but it all boils down to one thing....you didn't care. You cared about her and she didn't care about you. She used to hang around the dry cleaners with the guy who worked there. She was there almost everyday that you were working. You didn't know that did you, and I didn't say a word. As a matter of fact, I was glad that she was cheating on you. You thought that she was so precious, and she was nothing but a whore."

The mumbling from the wall ceased. Willam stared at Rusty. He was enraged. He fought with the idea of bashing in Rusty's face. He had no idea that Rusty had felt that way. He gritted his teeth and spoke through them. "Man, you're acting just like a jealous woman. As far as I'm concerned, you're where you are because that's where you want to be. Quite frankly, I'm surprised that you have a job at all. Rusty, your problem is that as you get older, you get lazier. You think that everything is supposed to be about fun all the time. Hard work are two words that irritate you. You don't want anybody to have anymore than you have. If you were really my friend, truly 'my boy', you would have been happy for me.

I'm going through hell right now, fighting for my life and all you can think of is how pissed you are at me because I decided to grow up. Oh yeah, and by the way, I knew about the guy at the dry cleaners, that was Tony. He was Kathy's cousin, she used to go down and keep him company until I got off, so as always, you wouldn't know what a whore looked like if you lived with her. This is our last discussion Rusty, I finally see what kind of so called friend you are."

Willam turned and walked down the stairs past the guys who were now sitting still and quiet. Rusty rushed up to the top step and began to yell at the departing Willam. "Friends, that's your problem, we were never friends. I'm glad that they're gonna lock you up, and I hope they throw away the key! That's right run on back to your Mama."

"Come on man, why don't you ease up on the boy. The man's going through a rough time, he doesn't need to hear that crap from you and besides, he's right. You are acting like a jealous woman." Joe said.

"Yeah, that was some foul shit that you did man." Steve added.

"Again, everybody likes Willam." Rusty turned and headed for the front door. As he grabbed the handle of the screen door, he turned and watched Willam's shadow dissolve into the darkness.

Chapter 9 - Tribulations

Eleven months had come and gone so rapidly. Willam's big day now loomed darkly before him. Yes, his trial was tomorrow. He stood in the front doorway and watched the cars pass by while he wondered about the trial, his life, and perhaps, even his fate. Eleven months had passed and still he was no closer to proving his innocence. He had kept to himself and trusted no one, no one except his precious Martha, and maybe Mr. Daniels. He was his friend and Willam knew that his concern was genuine.

The day seemed to pass quite quickly. Before he knew it, the sunlight was beginning to fade and the dim shadows that were cast from the parked cars were now growing larger and darker as the departing sun was replaced by the artificial light from the street lamps. Willam returned to the kitchen. He rummaged through the refrigerator looking for something to satisfy his growling stomach. He had tried to eat earlier, but his stomach was too queasy from being so nervous. He pulled the large jar of grape jelly from the fridge then walked over to the cabinet that was located just above the microwave oven. He reached up and removed the jar of Jiff peanut butter from the cabinet and grabbed the remaining loaf of bread from the bread box.

After collecting everything needed for the preparation of what he now thought could possibly be his last home meal, he made his sandwich and poured himself a glass of milk. He sat down at the dining room table and began to say Grace. His grace became a long prayer. He prayed that his day in court would be an easy one. That whoever did these terrible things to the women that he knew and cared for so much, would step forward and accept their punishment. He prayed hard and long as the tears streamed down both sides of his face. As he slowly opened his eyes, and while reaching for his sandwich, he noticed her.

Martha stood before him in the dining room smiling. "Don't worry son, I've put a word in with The Man upstairs too and He always answers prayers. I know you're afraid, but there's no need. Just leave it in God's hands and He'll make it alright. He'll bring all those who have done wrong doings to justice, His justice."

Willam never spoke a word. He lowered his head and stared at his sandwich. Martha stood there for a few minutes more smiling, then left her son alone to think and perhaps pray some more. Spending most of his life in church did teach him a few things about waiting on God and believing that He would make a way. Willam sat and pondered for over an hour, after which he looked down at his plate and noticed that only two bites had been taken from his sandwich and the milk had not been touched. He still had no appetite. He gathered his plate and glass and placed the remains of the sandwich in the trashcan and the dishes in the empty sink. He turned off the kitchen light and headed upstairs to his room. While he lay across his bed, he continued to think.

Daybreak had not quite arrived before Willam had showered and partially dressed himself. He had not been able to sleep at all that night. He had gotten out of his bed at 4:30 am that morning and began preparing himself for this most important but not anticipated day. He picked up the small photo of Lynn and stared at it for a moment. It had been nine months since he had seen her. Her parents were so afraid for her, that only after a couple of months, she was no longer allowed to visit him nor could he see her. He stood for a few moments thinking of her face and her smile before placing the photo into the inside pocket of his black suit jacket.

It was now 5:45 am. Willam, with jacket in hand, marched down the steps leading to the living room. He sat on the couch thumbing through the small pad of notes that he had collected during his stay at home. He could hear Martha walking upstairs. He heard her footsteps moving toward his room then back over to the upstairs banister.

"Willy, Willy, are you down there?"

"Yeah Ma, I'm in the living room."

"Well what are you doing?"

"Nothing, go ahead and get dressed, Mr. D. said he'd be here by 7:00. We've got to be there by 8:00 to go over things with Mr. Fisher. The trial begins at 9:00."

"What are you doing up so early, you okay?"

"Yeah, I'm okay, just couldn't sleep is all."

"Are you hungry, you want some breakfast?"

"No ma'am how about you, are you hungry? I can fix you something."

"No, I'm okay. I could stand a cup of coffee though. Can you put some water on for me?"

"Sure thing, Ma." Willam got up from the couch and walked into the kitchen and put on a pot of water. He glanced out of the back door window over at Mrs. Jordan's house. He noticed that the back door was wide opened. Willam stared at the house and could now see a figure moving from the kitchen then back to the dining room. He could now see the silhouette of the large figure now moving back into the kitchen. Willam opened the curtains wider to get a better look.

"Willy, Willy!"

Willam closed the curtains and turned to his mother. "Yes Ma'am?"

"Where's my coffee? I thought you were making it?"

"Coming right up."

Martha sat down at the dining room table and began looking through the newspaper. Willam pulled a coffee cup and saucer from the cabinet. He picked up the jar of instant Maxwell House coffee from on top of the microwave oven and a spoon from the drawer underneath. He removed the top from the jar of coffee and dipped in the spoon. He turned, with the jar of coffee in hand, and using his right elbow, Willam slid the right side of the backdoor curtains over and peered back at the house of Ms. Jordan. He saw a figure standing at the kitchen sink. The figure turned and walked toward the kitchen door. Willam couldn't move. He knew that it had to be Ralph. As the figure drew nearer, he could see the face. It was Ms. Jordan standing in her bathrobe and hairnet.

"Willy? Are you okay? Uh coffee, remember?"

"Oh, sorry Ma, guess I just got caught up in thought."

Willam served Martha the coffee and she drank while he sat at the table with her talking about family members that he hadn't seen in a while and places they'd like to go and visit. They talked about everything, everything but the trial. She was trying to keep his mind off of it until he walked inside the courtroom.

At 7:00 am on the dot, Mr. Daniels pulled up; not a second after. Martha grabbed her purse and Willy snatched his jacket from the arm of the living room couch. He held the door for his mother. After she had exited the house, Willam slammed the door tightly and off they went down the front steps to the waiting double parked Cadillac.

"You want to drive Willam?" Mr. Daniels asked.

"Nah, I really don't feel up to it today Mr. D."

Willam helped Martha into the passenger side of the vehicle then jumped in the back seat. Mr. Daniels started the car then slowly drove down F Street.

The waving microphones and flashing lights from the cameras met the approaching car at the curb in front of the courthouse. The police officers had roped off the area leading to the court entrance but the reporters and photographers were still very aggressive.

"Mr. Trent, Mr. Trent, over here!"

Willam looked over in the short, bald man's direction. He had a very kind and gentle look about him. He stuck out his handheld mini tape recorder in Willam's direction. "Mr. Trent, is it true that you killed these women because you hate your mother? Is it true that you have had sexual relations with your mother? The people deserve to know! Mr. Trent!"

Willam frown up his face and yelled over to the man, "That's sick! You're sick in your head!" He looked over to his mother who didn't seem to be bothered by the bald man's comments.

"Willam, Willam over here!" It was Mr. Fisher. He was standing in the entranceway of the building waving them toward him. Willam and his mom rushed past the yelling crowd to the awaiting Mr. Fisher.

"Good morning. It's a mad house out there. Let's go somewhere where we can talk, we still have some time." Mr. Fisher led Willam and his mother to a small room near the courtroom where his trial was to be conducted. They discussed the case and went over every detail; the same details that they had discussed over and over already on several occasions. Mr. Fisher went over some of the trial procedures and etiquette. Willam was receptive to all of his information and instruction. At 8:30 am, Mr. Fisher gathered his papers, placed them back into his brief-case and they marched into the courtroom.

Willam and Mr. Fisher passed through the opening be-tween the oak railings and sat down behind the large shiny wood-en table while Martha slid by the row of seats of the front until she was positioned directly behind Willam. The State's Attorney and two of his assistants sat at an identical table across from them.

At 8:58 am, the door located just off to the side of the judge's bench opened. Twelve people were led into the court-room. Seven men and five women climbed up the steps to their seats. After they were situated, the bailiff, who had just intro-duced himself to Willam and Mr. Fisher, began brushing and straightening his uniform. As the door to the judge's chamber opened, the bailiff stepped forward, "All rise. The Prince George's County Court of Justice is now in session, the Honora-ble Judge James Dunn presiding." Everyone in the courtroom stood as the small thin man dressed in a black robe and eyeglasses stepped upon the bench then sat. The bailiff continued, "You may be seated."

After everyone had taken their seats, the bailiff continued. "The case before the court, Case Number 82160 in the matter concerning murder in the first degree: The people of the State of Maryland versus Willam Xavier Trent."

The courtroom became silent. Willam looked back at Mar-tha and she smiled and nodded her head. The judge shuffled through some papers on the desk while bumping against the microphone. He cleared his throat before leaning closer to the microphone.

"Counselors are you prepared to give your opening statements?"

"Yes we are," said the State's Attorney.

"We're prepared Your Honor," Mr. Fisher affirmed.

Judge Dunn looked over the rim of his glasses and held out his hand toward Mr. Fisher, "You may begin your statements."

Mr. Fisher rose from his seat and walked over toward the twelve members of the jury and began addressing them.

"Ladies and gentlemen, this young man before you today has never been in any trouble a day in his life. He has spent more time in church than most of us today. He has been an upstanding member of society and his community and is currently attending college to further better himself. He takes care of his mother and the elderly neighbors next door.

We will prove that this young man is not what the State is accusing him to be. In fact, he is the complete opposite. He is a model for other young men his age. We will prove that it was impossible for him to be at the scene of the crime when it occurred and that there is not one shred of evidence that could possibly link this young man to that crime in any way! Thank you."

Mr. Fisher returned to his seat and the State's Attorney, Mr. Price rose to his feet while buttoning the buttons of his suit jacket. He walked over to where the jury sat and leaned against the wooden railing running the length of their seats and cleared his throat.

"Ladies and gentlemen of the jury, the State will prove beyond a shadow of a doubt that the defendant was in fact the only person with Ms. Clark at the time of her murder. He was the only person who had the keys to his car; the only person whom she trusted. We will prove that the defendant wanted an intimate relationship with Ms. Clark and when she refused, he became enraged. We will prove that the defendant's rage, did in fact, lead to Ms. Clark's demise."

Mr. Price walked back over to his seat and sat down. He leaned over to one of the young men who sat at the table with him and whispered something in his ear. The young man nodded while scribbling on a large pad.

Judge Dunn removed his glasses from his face and pointed them to Mr. Price, "Is the State ready to call its first witness?"

"Yes we are, Your Honor. The State calls Mrs. Olivia Davis."

Mrs. Davis rose from one of the first three rows in the front of the courtroom. She walked down past the wooden railings and stepped up onto the witness stand. An older man in a faded brown suit walked over and picked up the large Bible from a wooden stand. "Please raise your right hand and place your left hand on the Bible and state your name."

Mrs. Davis followed the man's instructions and he continued, "Do you swear to tell the whole truth and nothing but the truth in this court of law, so help you God?"

Mrs. Davis nodded her head, "I do."

Mr. Price walked over to the witness stand and placed his hand on a part of the surrounding railing. He smiled at Mrs. Davis and she returned the gesture.

"Mrs. Davis, I know that this is very difficult for you. I know that you too, not too long ago, lost a loved one, your daughter."

"Yes. Yes I have."

"Do you know the defendant?"

"Yes."

"How do you know him?"

"He used to date my daughter, Kathy."

"Where is your daughter now?"

"OBJECTION!" Mr. Fisher yelled out.

Mr. Price walked over to the judge's bench. "Your Honor, I'm just trying to touch on one of Willam's past relationships and it's relevance to this trail. I believe it can help depict how the defendant was viewed by a person in a previous relationship with him."

"The witness was not in a relationship with my client Your Honor."

"Objection sustained," said Judge Dunn.

Mr. Price walked back over to Mrs. Davis. "Mrs. Davis, did your daughter seem happy with Willam? I mean, they were dating right?"

"Yes, they were dating and they seemed to be doing fine. They went to the same school and saw each other every day."

"They went to the movies and on walks, that sort of thing?"

"Well my husband, Mr. Davis kept Kathy on a pretty tight leash if you know what I mean. He was pretty strict. No movies, but he did let Willam sit on the porch with her and occasionally walk her to the store as long as they were coming right back."

"So what about after they graduated? They went to different schools right? How did Kathy feel about him then?"

"Objection Your Honor, the witness could not know how or what her daughter felt at any certain time," said Mr. Fisher.

"Sustained," the judge said.

"I'll rephrase the question Your Honor. Mrs. Davis, did your daughter say anything to you about the change in the defendant's behavior after they graduated from high school?"

"Yes, yes she did. She said that he always acted suspicious and was starting to accuse her of seeing other boys while she was at college. She told me that he once told her..."

"Told her what Mrs. Davis?"

Mrs. Davis opened her purse and pulled out a white handkerchief, wiped her eyes, and then continued. "She once told me that he said that if he ever found out that she had been cheating on him, he'd kill her."

The courtroom erupted in a quiet uproar. The entire courtroom was noisy from everyone's outbursts. Judge Dunn slammed his gavel down and yelled for order in the courtroom. Mr. Fisher leaned over and whispered to Willam then leaned back in his seat. Mr. Price walked back over to the D.A.'s table and Judge Dunn looked over to Mr. Fisher. "Your witness."

Mr. Fisher rose quickly and walked up to the witness stand. "Mrs. Davis, have you ever seen Mr. Trent touch your daughter inappropriately, or speak to her in a disrespectful way?"

"Well no, I can't say that I have, and besides Willam knew that Mr. Davis would never stand for that," she said while smiling and looking at her husband.

"In fact, Mrs. Davis, as far as you know, Willam Trent treated your daughter with the utmost respect. Did you know that your daughter approached this young man stating that she was ready to have sex? Were you aware of that?"

Mrs. Davis looked at Willam, then over to her husband and shook her head. "No, I didn't."

"Do you know what this man did? The young man who you believe to have wronged your daughter in the worst way, what do you think he did?"

Mrs. Davis lowered her head and answered quietly. "I don't know."

"I'll tell you what he did. The man that you think is so cruel and evil told your daughter that she was too pure and precious to give herself to anybody before the time was right and that they should wait. Is that the actions of a jealous, controlling young man? If he was so afraid of some other man being with her, it would seem to me that he would want to be the first man that she had been with. Wouldn't you agree?"

"I guess."

"Please answer yes or no Mrs. Davis," said Judge Dunn.

"Yes, I would agree."

"No further questions, Your Honor."

The D.A. next called Diane Martin to the stand. Diane approached the witness stand and was sworn in. As she sat, Mr. Price walked up to her smiling.

"Can you state your name for the courtroom please?" asked Mr. Price

"My name is Diane, Diane Martin," the young lady replied.

"Ms. Martin, how did you know Ms. Clark?"

The young lady looked around the courtroom before answering. "Beverly and I have been friends since high school."

"So you two were pretty close wouldn't you say?"

"Yes, Bev and I were very close, we did everything together."

"Did Ms. Clark ever talk to you about the defendant?"

"Yes, many times. She liked Will, everybody knew that."

"So she just talked about how she admired him?"

"Yeah, pretty much."

"Did she tell you anything else, anything about his behavior?"

"Objection, Your Honor. Council is leading the witness." Mr. Fisher yelled out in a monotone voice.

"Sustained."

Mr. Price raised his hand in acceptance of the judge's decision before leaning on the railing of the witness stand. "Ms. Martin, did Ms. Clark ever speak badly of the defendant?"

"Sometimes she did. Sometimes she would say that he was evil. She said that he seemed so sweet and innocent on the exterior, but he had a serious mean streak in him."

"You also worked with the defendant, isn't that correct?"

"Yes sir, we worked the evening shift together at the warehouse."

"That's the Dart Drug Warehouse, is that correct?"

"Yes sir."

"Was he cordial at work?"

"Sometimes."

"What do you mean, sometimes?"

"Well, he was always pretty quiet. Some days he would speak and smile and then other days he wouldn't speak to you even if you spoke to him first. It was as if he had two personalities. I've even caught him on several occasions talking to himself. I'm not sure what Bev saw in him, but he was creepy to me. I told Bev several times that I thought he was weird and that she should leave him alone, but she just had a thing for him."

"I object! The witness is not a doctor in the field of mental health Your Honor. How can she state if my client has two personalities?"

Judge Dunn leaned forward and looked over his glasses. "Sustained. The statement concerning multiple personalities of the defendant is to be stricken from the record."

"Thank you Your Honor," replied Mr. Fisher.

Mr. Price continued. "Ms. Martin, can you tell the court your recollection of the day in question?"

"Yes sir. We were working our usual shift, Bev and I. Will was working over in receiving, that's where he worked. He was acting strange that day, you know, it was one of those days that he didn't talk to anyone. Bev had a message for Will that she had gotten from the front desk. She walked over to his area to give it to him. I stood at the top of the stairs and waited for her. I saw her open the slip of paper as she walked in his direction. Will was operating his fork lift, you know, moving skids of merchandise around to make room for the incoming shipment. After finally noticing her standing there waiting, he turned the lift off and turned and just stared at Bev. She began talking to him. I couldn't make out what she was saying. She opened the slip of paper and read from it and smiled at Will. He said nothing. He just stared at her. I watched her smile slowly disappear as he turned his back to her.

Later that evening she walked over to the snack room and got her lunch then headed for the back exit. I saw her stop by Will's area. She spoke briefly to him and he nodded before once again turning his back to her. She smiled and walked out of the door. I couldn't take my eyes off of him. He seemed so strange that day. He sat at his work desk looking at his box cutter for what I considered a long time before going back to completing his inventory slips. I watched him for a while longer then I saw him look up at our station. I pretended to place items on the shelves then walked back over to the work table. I had a bad feeling after looking into his eyes. I decided to go find Beverly. Just as I was leaving the station phone rang. I rushed over to the phone and answered it. The voice on the other end of the phone was asking about a sku number for a particular wristwatch, a Timex. I walked over to the merchandise catalog computer printout to look it up. It was taking a long time to find it, too long. I gave up and returned to the phone to let the person know that the item did not exist. The phone was dead. I rushed over to the stairs and looked down into the receiving area, but did not see Will.

I knew that if Beverly kept pressing him about going out with her that he would probably yell at her or possibly hit her. I had no idea that he would kill her!"

"OBJECTION, Your Honor, witness is drawing her own conclusion!" yelled Mr. Fisher.

"Sustained."

The D.A. looked over at Mr. Fisher, "Your witness."

Mr. Fisher rose from his chair but remained behind the table. "Ms. Martin, have you ever heard the defendant say anything harmful to Ms. Clark? And please answer yes or no."

"No."

"Have you ever seen the defendant do any bodily harm to Ms. Clark at any time?"

Diane paused. She stared at Willam as she answered, "No, I haven't but...."

"That's all Ms. Martin. No further questions Your Honor."

"You may step down Ms. Martin," said Judge Dunn. Diane climbed out of the witness stand and stared at Willam as she walked back to her seat.

"You may call your next witness Mr. Prosecutor," said the judge and Mr. Price called for Mr. Paul Robinson. Willam looked back into the courtroom and watched as Rusty made his way down the aisle and up to the witness stand. He got sworn in, sat comfortably in the chair and pulled the microphone closer to his mouth while clearing his throat. Mr. Price walked up to him and folded his arms. "Please state your name for the court."

Rusty leaned forward closer to the microphone and spoke loudly making the microphone squeal, "My name is Paul Robinson."

"And where do you reside Mr. Robinson?"

"I live at 545 Hilltop Terrace, S.E. Washington."

"How do you know the defendant?"

"We grew up together."

"So you two are pretty close, good buddies?"

"No, not really."

"Wait, you grew up together, you did say that? You went to the same schools and played together right?"

"Yeah, we went to the same schools and grew up in the same neighborhood and all, but that doesn't make us close, he's too weird!"

"Why do you say he's weird?"

"Will has always been weird. He's weird because he tries to hide the fact that he hates everybody. Actually, I believe he hates everything. He thinks everybody's out to get him. He thinks that everybody is stupid but him and he doesn't trust anybody but his mother. He's pretty strange and has a really bad temper."

"Why do you say he has a bad temper?"

"Heck, everybody knows that. He once beat up this guy just for saying that he could ride his bike faster than him. Pretty stupid reason huh? He was always getting into fights. And when he wasn't fighting he was doing other crazy things like cutting off the heads of poor innocent birds."

"Cutting off the heads of birds? That sounds like a pretty strange hobby."

"Objection!" Mr. Fisher shouted once again.

"Sustained, Counselor don't try me in my courtroom, are we clear?" said Judge Dunn as he pointed at Mr. Price.

"Sorry, Your Honor."

The judge continued, "Your personal opinion is of no interest, nor does it have any merit in this courtroom."

"Yes Your Honor."

"You may proceed." The judge grunted.

Mr. Price walked around to the side of the witness box and rested his arm against the railing. He placed his opposite hand in his pant pocket before continuing. "So Mr. Robinson you say that Mr. Trent was occasionally getting into altercations with the other boys in the neighborhood?"

Rusty looked at Mr. Price strangely for a second before answering. "Altercation, well if that means fighting than the answer is YES! Well, it was mainly when we were younger. Guys used to tease him about his mother. I didn't though, she was a nice lady."

"What about his mother?

"Well, a long time ago somebody started the rumor that Ms. Trent used to be a prostitute. I think it was only because she was so pretty. Willam couldn't stand for anybody to even ask about her. He always made it out to be something, even when it wasn't. He hit Andre on his hand with a baseball bat and broke his thumb just because he had asked how his mother was doing. Andre had heard from his mom that Mrs. Trent had fainted at work due to the heat and he was genuinely concerned. Oh no, you couldn't be nice to Willy."

"So you're saying that the defendant was an angry and aggressive person…."

"Objection, prosecutor is leading the witness Your Honor."

"Sustained," said the judge.

"No further questions," said Mr. Price as he walked back to the long wooden table.

The judge looked over at Mr. Fisher, who was now conferring with Willam. They whispered back and forth to each other before being interrupted by Judge Dunn, "Your witness Counselor."

Mr. Fisher looked up at Rusty who was looking directly at him. He looked down at his legal pad that sat before him then back at Judge Dunn, "No questions Your Honor."

The D.A. then called a multitude of witnesses one after the other. He called other neighborhood friends of Willam's, people who worked with him and people who studied with him in school. They all basically said the same thing. They testified that Willam was quiet and stayed to himself. It wasn't until Mr. Price called the next witness that Willam appeared to be a little nervous. Mr. Price stood and called Mr. Alfonso Baxter to the stand.

Alfonso walked down the aisle, brushing off his slacks and making sure that everything was in place. After being sworn in, he sat down, adjusted his hair and crossed his legs. Mr. Price walked up to the witness stand and adjusted his jacket as well.

"Mr. Baxter."

"You can call me Alfonso."

Mr. Price smiled. "Alright, Alfonso. You were the defendant's roommate at Livingstone College, correct?"

"Oh yes sir, we were roommates, that's about it."

"What kind of roommate was he?"

"He was quiet most of the time, kept to himself, you know."

"You said most of the time? What do you mean by that?"

"Well you know how it is, we were in college. Every now and then we'd have a little sip of something. Will couldn't handle alcohol. He was a totally different person after he started drinking. He was a wild man!" Alfonso said while laughing.

"What did he do as a result of the alcohol?"

"Oh you mean what kind of crazy things did he do?"

"Yes, if you could elaborate."

"Ah man, Will would get drunk and do just about anything. Nobody bothered him then because they knew that he would pound them in a heart beat. I remember once he was pissed...Oh I'm sorry, can I say that?"

Mr. Price smiled and asked Alfonso to continue.

"I remember when Will was upset at one of his professors for giving him a bad grade on a paper. He had a few drinks and went to his professor's class and broke out every window. He even tried to break into the building so he could get inside the classroom. We finally convinced him to go and sleep it off. Oh yeah, Willy was a wild one, except for the ladies."

"The ladies? What do you mean by that? Have you ever seen him mistreat a woman?"

"Nah, not Willy, I'm not sure if he was afraid of women or just dedicated to the one he had at the other school. He just never said much to any of them. I mean, I was hitting my fair share, but it never bothered Willy at all. I would be doing my thing and I know he could hear us but he never complained. Sometimes though, he would look at some of them as if he hated them, but it was probably because we kept him up so long. Now that I think about, he looked at all of them like that."

"No further questions." Mr. Price said as he returned to the table.

Mr. Fisher stood and walked over to the stand. "Mr. Baxter…"

"Alfonso."

The snickers bounced throughout the courtroom in somewhat of a sporadic pattern. "Excuse me. Alfonso, have you ever seen the defendant be physically abusive to anyone, male or female?"

"Well no, I can't say that I have."

"No further questions Your Honor."

Alfonso was instructed to step down and return to his seat. The judge called for a short recess then exited through the side door.

Mumbling filled the courtroom air, then without warning, "all rise" rang out. Judge Dunn had returned to the courtroom after the brief but needed recess.

During the short break Martha had a moment to speak to Willam. She reinforced her position with The Man upstairs and told Willam not to worry. After Judge Dunn had finished reshuffling his papers and readjusting the microphone, he asked Mr. Price to call his next witness.

Mr. Price rose from his seat while buttoning the middle button of his suit jacket. "Your Honor, I call Ms. Martha Trent to the stand."

The mumbling and whispering began once again as Martha rose from her seat and slid along the wooden banister across the aisle. She walked up to the witness stand and waited for the elderly gentleman to make his way over to her with the large bible. After he stood before her, he extended the book and recited once again, what he had recited numerous times during his tenure. "Do you promise to tell the truth and nothing but the truth so help you God?"

With her left hand resting on the Bible and her right hand raised, Martha calmly answered, "I do."

"State your full name, please."

"Martha Elizabeth Trent."

"You may be seated."

Martha sat down on the hard, uncomfortable chair and leaned on her side as she crossed one leg over the other. She seemed very serene. She looked over at Willam and smiled, trying to further boost his confidence. Mr. Price walked up to the witness stand. He had his eyeglasses in one hand and an off-white manila folder in the other. He rested his right arm upon the banister which partially surrounded the witness stand while looking at the document. He slipped on his eyeglasses and continued to thumb through the folder. After removing his glasses, he placed one hand on the banister and spoke to Martha in a very calm voice. "Ms. Trent, you are the mother of the defendant, is that correct?"

"Yes, yes I am."

"And you are his only parent, correct?"

"Yes sir."

"Willam's father was murdered shortly after he was born, correct?"

"Unfortunately, yes."

"I see." Mr. Price opened the folder and pulled out one of the documents then placed his eyeglasses back on his face. "Ms. Trent, here in my hand, I am holding a copy of the certificate of birth for Willam Xavier Trent. On this certificate of birth it states that James Trent is the father and Martha Trent is the mother. Am I reading this correctly?"

"Sir, apparently your eyewear is working just fine."

Light chuckles fill the courtroom once again and Judge Dunn quickly tapped his gavel and asked for order in the courtroom. Mr. Price walked over to the table where the elderly gentleman sat. "Your Honor, I'd like to enter this document, the birth certificate of Willam Trent into evidence." He then handed copies of the document to the elderly man who in turn logged them in and provided both Judge Dunn and Mr. Fisher with copies. Mr. Price walked back over to the witness stand and continued. "Mrs. Trent, may I ask what your blood type is?"

"I'm 'A' positive."

"And your son?"

"I'm not sure."

"You're a nurse, surely you know your own son's blood type?"

"Objection Your Honor, Counsel is badgering the witness," Mr. Fisher yelled out.

"Sustained," replied the judge.

Mr. Price continued. "Well Mrs. Trent if you don't know, let me tell you. Your son's blood type is 'AB' positive. And what was your late husband's?"

Martha looked over to Willam. Her confident smile had disappeared. She uncrossed her legs and placed both of her hands on the arms of the chair in which she sat before answering. "I don't know, I don't know what Jimmy's blood type was."

"Well let's see, I believe that too is in here. Yes, here it is. Your husband's blood type was 'B' negative."

"So?"

"That was my next question Nurse Trent. So?"

"I don't know what you're getting at."

"Well, should I call my expert laboratory doctor up and then recall you or shall we just spare the court some time?"

Mr. Fisher yelled out his objection once again with his reasons, which were once again sustained by Judge Dunn, but that meant nothing. Martha knew that she was on Mr. Price's hook and he was just moments from reeling her in.

Martha stared at the floor for a moment then over to Willam. "Jimmy wasn't his daddy, ok. Now do you feel proud of yourself Mr. Price?"

"Do you? You lied to your son for years and for what? Do you realize that you've committed perjury in this courtroom today and that charges can be filed against you for that?"

"Yes."

"You won't be warned again Mrs. Trent. So, if James Trent is not the defendant's father, who is? Who is Willam Xavier Trent's father?"

Martha paused. She stared into Willam's eyes then slowly turned to Mr. Price. "I don't know."

"And why is it you don't Mrs. Trent? Is it because during the defendant's childhood you were a prostitute, turning tricks in your own home while your son was there?"

The tears began to stream down Martha's face. She tried to hold them in but her heart was broken after witnessing the sadness on her son's face. "It was hard. Being alone trying to make ends meet and having to feed and clothe a child."

"Ms. Trent, has the defendant ever been present in the house with you while you were prostituting?"

Martha looked at Willam shaking her head. She whispered to him as he sat in his chair with the pain of his life painted over his face, "sorry baby". She looked up at the judge and he nodded. Martha forced the words through her sealed lips, "Yes."

"Ms. Trent, do you think that you somehow instilled the wrong values in your son?"

"Objection!" Mr. Fisher yelled.

"Sustained. Be very careful Counselor."

"Sorry Your Honor, I'll rephrase." Mr. Price continued. "Ms. Trent, do you think that with all that your son has seen, do you think that he is capable of a crime such as murder?

Martha placed her face inside her hands and began to cry again. "I don't know, I just don't know. What have I done?"

"It's alright Mama! It's ok, I still love you!" Willam yelled out. His eyes were full of tears.

"Order! Order young man! Council will instruct your client to refrain from such outbursts in the courtroom," Judge Dunn demanded.

Martha sat crying as Mr. Price mumbled, "No further questions."

"Your witness, Mr. Fisher."

Mr. Fisher quickly rose from his seat. He walked up to Martha and handed her his handkerchief. She gently pulled it from his hand and began wiping her eyes.

"Do you need a minute?" Mr. Fisher asked. Martha shook her head slowly and Mr. Fisher started. "Ms. Trent, I know sometimes we have to do what we need to make it in life. I know during those times, somebody like Mr. Price wasn't just going to walk up to you and say, 'Hey young lady, you look like you're having a hard time, here's some money to help you out.' Sometimes we have to do whatever it takes to provide for our young and to just stay alive."

"Objection Your Honor, the counselor is suggesting that committing a crime is something just. He's glorifying a crime sir." Mr. Price interrupted.

"Your Honor, I'm just simply trying to show the court how things are not always plain vanilla, and that people have to make sacrifices sometimes and it costs."

"Objection overruled."

"Ms. Trent, you raised a good son," Mr. Fisher continued. "A son who always not only cut the grass at home, but would cut the grass and wash the car of your next door neighbors. He never would ask for money, he was just happy to help them out."

"Yes, Willam is a good son. He's always had a good heart."

"So I ask you without any shame, without any guilt, and because you know what kind of son you raised, do you truly believe that your son Willam could have done anything like this? Do you think that he could have harmed anyone?"

Martha looked back over to Willam, wiping her tears and smiling, she answered proudly. "No, no I don't."

"Thank you." Mr. Fisher nodded his head and smiled at Martha, "No further questions."

Martha was instructed to step down from the witness stand. She slowly walked back to her seat looking at Willam the entire time. They never lost eye contact until she was seated. Willam reached back and placed his hand on top of hers which now rested on the wooden rail, and smiled to her but she could only manage to press her lips tightly together and nod.

Meanwhile, Mr. Price had called his next witness. He called Ms. Olynthia Lawrence to the stand. Willam looked over his right shoulder looking for her. Martha looked puzzled. Only knowing her by "Lynn", she had no idea who the D.A. had just called on to testify against her son. The small figure rose from the back row of the courtroom. Lynn walked down the aisle and Willam watched as she stepped into the witness box and placed her hand on the Bible. After answering the elderly man's only question, she was seated.

Mr. Price immediately advanced from behind the table and began his questioning. "Ms. Lawrence, how do you know the defendant?" Mr. Price asked while extending his hand in Willam's direction.

"He was, I mean, he's my boyfriend."

"Your boyfriend, and this means that you what, go to the movies and take walks together....what?"

"It means that we're a couple, we hang out, talk on the phone, we enjoy each other's company. Haven't you ever had a girlfriend?"

More outbursts of laughter again filled the courtroom and the judge once again called for order. Mr. Price smiled at Lynn and then continued. "Ms. Lawrence, have you ever been to the Dart Drug Warehouse and had lunch with the defendant?"

"Yes, several times."

"Is it true that not only one week before the night in question, the defendant became enraged and pushed you up against his car and put his hand to your throat?"

"Well…..no…I mean, he was upset!"

"And why was he upset, Ms. Lawrence?"

Lynn paused as she looked over at Willam. He looked away from her and down at the floor. He remembered that night. Lynn looked back at Mr. Price, then she too, began to find herself lost in the vague beige swirl designs of the courtroom marble flooring, but it wasn't a safe haven, she still had to answer the question. "It was just a little misunderstanding, that's all it was."

"What kind of misunderstanding Ms. Lawrence?"

Lynn paused even longer this time. Drowning herself in the beige swirls with no desire to come up for air.

"Please answer the question, Ms. Lawrence," Judge Dunn demanded.

"We were sitting in Will's car like we did every night that I brought his lunch. I had asked him about him and me, you know, how serious we had gotten. I asked him if he felt the same way that I did and he said that he did. So, I asked him if he thought that it was time, you know, time to do it. He was nice at first, but I guess I pushed a little too hard, I do that sometimes. He was beginning to get angry, and then finally he asked me if I was some kind of slut or something. I got angry too, and asked him if he was some kind of faggot or something and that's when he told me to get out. He told me that I was just like the rest of the whores that he had dealt with. I got out of the car and he got out, too. He tried to apologize, but I was too mad. I told him that if he didn't want me, someone else would, that's when he put his hand on my throat, but he didn't do it hard, he just placed it there. I guess he was just trying to scare me."

Mr. Price looked at the jury then back at Lynn. "What did he say to you? What did he say to you while he had his hand to your throat?"

Lynn looked at Will again then slowly back to the sea of beige and mumbled just loud enough for Mr. Price to hear, "I'll kill you."

"I'm sorry Ms. Lawrence can you please speak up for the court?"

"He said I'll kill you."

The spew of chatter saturated the room. Judge Dunn yelled for order repeatedly until the courtroom was silent. Mr. Price looked over at the jury members before returning to his table. "No further questions for this witness Your Honor." He sat down and began to write on his pad.

Mr. Fisher rose from his seat and proceeded to where Lynn sat. He buttoned his jacket and produced a caring smile. "Ms. Lawrence, do you still care for Mr. Trent?"

"Yes, yes I do sir. Very much."

"I noticed that when Mr. Price asked you about your relationship with Mr. Trent you first said 'he was' then you changed that to 'he is my boyfriend'. Now unlike the prosecution, I have had a girlfriend before."

Snickers and little chuckles could be heard throughout the courtroom.

"Objection!" Mr. Price yelled.

"Sorry, Your Honor." Mr. Fisher said while raising his hand to Judge Dunn. "Ms. Lawrence, why do you seem to be unsure of what kind of relationship you have with Mr. Trent?"

"Because he said that he didn't think we should see each other anymore. He said he didn't want people looking at me and saying bad things about me because of him, but I don't care about that stuff. I'm still his girl."

"So, after everything that has happened, everything that he has been accused of, you still feel safe around him?"

"Yes, Willy wouldn't hurt anybody."

"No further questions."

Mr. Price called several more witnesses which Mr. Fisher cross examined. They all stated the same basic fact; Willam was quiet and strange and was raised by a prostitute mother and thought that his secret was unknown to anyone else. Mr. Price called his first expert witness to the stand, a forensic expert from the Prince George's County Police Department. A scrawny little fellow wearing a brown suit and a bowtie bounced his way down the aisle. After being seated in the chair he adjusted his wire framed square lens eyeglasses and brushed back his salt and pepper gray hair. He sat pompously in the chair and seemed almost excited about giving his expert opinion on matters. Mr. Price advanced and appeared more professional with the man. "Mr. Krazchek, you have worked in the area of forensic science for how long?"

The small framed man looked around the courtroom proudly then spoke directly into the microphone. "I have worked in the field of forensics for over twenty-five years."

"That's very impressive. And out of those twenty-five years, what is the percentage of crimes that are solved using forensic science?"

"Oh, I would say about eighty percent of crimes today are solved using forensic science."

"Could you tell the courtroom a little about the science of forensics?"

"Forensic science is the method of taking and using evidence from a crime scene such as blood, fabric particles, hair samples and so on to link or identify persons who were in contact with a victim. It goes much deeper, but that's pretty much it in a nutshell."

"So you use whatever was left behind to help I.D. other individuals who were present at a particular crime scene?"

"Yes, you'd be surprised at just how much information is collected from a crime scene. Crime scenes talk, actually, they yell out to us with information, if you will."

Mr. Price nodded his head several times, then returned to the table. He picked up a white sheet of paper with bold black letters inscribed on the top which read, "Forensic Report for:" followed by some typed written words and the date. He stepped up to the witness stand and showed the form to the forensic official. "Is this your signature Mr. Krazchek?"

The scrawny man pushed his eyeglasses up tightly against his face and peered at the bottom of the form. "Yes, yes that's my signature."

"Your Honor, this is exhibit 'A' which was presented into evidence prior to trial. Both you and the defense currently have a copy of this document, Sir."

Judge Dunn nodded while retrieving the form from his stack of papers. He looked over at Mr. Fisher who had also been presented with the document and nodded in concurrence. Judge Dunn looked back over to Mr. Price, "You may continue Counselor."

Mr. Price turned back toward Mr. Krazchek. "If you please sir, could you tell the Court what this document is and explain to us its content?"

"Why yes," Mr. Krazchek continued to look the document up and down then sat the paper on his lap. "This is our standard forensic report that is filled out for every crime scene analyzed by our team. It lists and describes every shred of forensic evidence found by us at that scene."

"And what does this report tell us?"

Mr. Krazchek raised the document from his lap and glanced over it for a short moment then sat back comfortably in the chair. He raised his chin and produced the most important look that he could before speaking. All of his arrogance flowed between each syllable that he spoke. "Well Mr. Prosecutor, this report states that the defendant was at the crime. Fragments......"

"Your Honor, objection," Mr. Fisher shouted. "Everyone knows that the defendant was at the scene of the crime. He was the one yelling for help for the victim for crying out loud!"

"Objection overruled Counselor. Mr. Krazchek is an expert witness and is presenting facts from an official document. And Counselor, random outbursts are clearly not the same as an objection, understood?"

Mr. Fisher dropped his ballpoint pen on top of his pad and sat back in his chair and clasped his fingers together and crossed his legs. His expression was that of a scolded child. "Yes, Your Honor," he replied.

Judge Dunn looked at Mr. Krazchek and calmly said, "Please continue sir."

Mr. Krazchek looked over at Mr. Fisher for a brief moment then turned to Mr. Price as he continued. "Fragments of the defendant's clothing were found in the car....."

"Objection! Your Honor, it was the defendant's car, surely particles from his clothing would be inside of it, along with his fingerprints and a host of other things."

Judge Dunn tapped on his pad with his ink pen. What Mr. Fisher said did make sense. He looked at him then responded, "It is in the report, I'll allow it. Overruled!"

Mr. Fisher, now very upset, shouted, "Exception!"

"Noted," responded the judge. "Please continue sir."

Mr. Krazchek continued describing and explaining what was reported by the forensic team. He read about the skin fragments of Willam's found under Beverly's fingernails. He explained how close a person had to be to another person to have clothing particles embedded in the clothing of a victim such as in this case and how Willam's clothing particles were found on the side of Beverly's face. He talked about how pieces of the victim's hair, was found on the Willam's clothing. He went on for over twenty minutes describing undisputable evidence linking Willam to Beverly Clark's murder.

When Mr. Krazchek had finished, Mr. Price gave him a confident smile and a nod, "Thank you sir and no further questions Your Honor."

Judge Dunn looked over at Mr. Fisher who at this time was whispering to Willam. "Counselor, your witness."

Mr. Fisher looked at the skinny arrogant man for a second. He looked down at his scribbling on his pad then slowly rose to his feet. "Mr. Krazchek, you stated earlier that eighty percent of crimes are solved by forensics correct?"

"Yes."

"May I ask where you got this number from, I mean, is it in some official report somewhere that I can find?"

"Well yes, I believe I read it in a publication. You know it's not just some number that I made up."

"No sir, I don't know. Where can I find this eighty percent?"

"Well…I'm sure if given some time, I could dig it up for you."

"Sir, that's what we don't have is time. We're talking about a young man's life here and you're throwing out random numbers only to sound important and nothing else!"

"Objection!" shouted Mr. Price.

"I'll withdraw, Your Honor," Mr. Fisher quickly stated. "So, Mr. Krazchek, let's say your eighty percent is correct. How many innocent men and women has forensics sent to prison that make up a part of the twenty percent?"

"We just list what we find."

"What if I was on a bus and I just happened to brush up against the arm of another guy on that same bus, then somebody stabs him. Now, unknowing that the guy has been stabbed, he falls up against me then falls to the ground, scratching my neck as he falls. Someone yells, 'Oh my God, you killed him.' A police officer just so happens to be right there and rushes in. I am arrested AND going by what you just told the court, forensics would confirm that I was the perpetrator, correct?"

"Well, that sounds pretty farfetched Counselor, but to answer your question, forensics would only prove that you were in contact with the victim. You would have just been at the wrong place at the wrong time in that fairy tale."

"My thoughts exactly sir, your science would have only proved that I had been in contact with the victim. If I had worked with him, I would have been in contact with him probably several times that day before he had left to catch that bus. So, with that said, isn't it true that the defendant could have been with the victim prior to the incident and provided the same types of fragments, particles and anything else that is shown in your report on the victim?"

"Well yes, that is….everything except for the victim's blood."

"And that's true, BUT the blood, in this case, could have been absorbed into his clothing while he was trying to help the victim. Is this correct?"

"Well yes, I suppose so."

"No further questions, Your Honor."

Mr. Fisher returned to his table and gives Martha a smile of confidence. As he sat down, he placed his left hand on Willam's shoulder and nodded at him with assurance. Mr. Krazchek stepped down from the witness stand and returned to his seat. Next, Detective Lindsey was called to the stand. He immediately walked briskly to the witness stand and assumed the position to be sworn in. After which he sat upright and erect in the chair awaiting his questioning. Mr. Price did just that. Without hesitation, he began questioning the detective.

"Detective, how would you describe the scene in the parking lot of the Dart Drug Warehouse on the day in question?"

"Well sir, I'll put it to you like this. I've seen a lot of things in my day while being on the force, but this rattled me. The victim had been traumatized and her throat was slit from ear to ear. We're not sure what type of blunt object was used to strike the victim in the back of the head, but it had to be something made of metal or wood."

Everyone expected Fisher to object here, but he didn't. He knew that the pictures of the crime scene were to follow and it would have been just a waste of time and would make the pictures even more grotesque by removing the image. Mr. Price continued.

"Detective, was there any evidence that the defendant was at the scene of the crime?"

"Yes sir, his finger prints were all over the place amongst other pieces of evidence as described by Mr. Krazchek."

"When you approached and questioned the defendant, what kind of state of mind was he in? I mean if it was me, finding my friend in my car with her head bashed in and throat slit....."

"Objection, Your Honor." Mr. Fisher couldn't let him continue down that road. He was trying to paint the scene even more grotesque than the pictures would display.

"Sustained," the judge replied.

"So how was the defendant's appearance?" Mr. Price asked.

"He seemed pretty shaken up. He appeared to be in shock. He was taken to the hospital for observation. My partner and I questioned him the next day, and he spoke with us briefly, but he seemed calm then."

"Wow, you'd have to be pretty unemotional to stay that calm. No further questions."

Mr. Fisher waved from the table to the judge, "No questions Your Honor."

Mr. Price shuffled through his papers while conferring with his assistants. Judge Dunn tilted his head, strangely looking at Mr. Price in all of his confusion. "Counselor, do you have another witness?"

Mr. Price stopped shuffling just long enough to stand and address the judge. He still had a look of confusion on his face. Just then, one of his assistants handed him a sheet of paper. Mr. Price glanced at it then cleared his throat.

"Yes Sir, we do Your Honor. The people of the State of Maryland call Mr. Wallace Cotton to the stand."

Cotton rose from his seat and slid past those that blocked his path to the aisle. While passing the last person that sat on his row, he tripped over the young lady's foot into the aisle. He looked around the courtroom, adjusted his jacket then strutted down the carpet onto the marble flooring of the oval center opening to the witness stand. He placed his hand on the bible, listened for a second then gave the elderly gentleman his "I do." Immediately afterwards, he alternated the yanking of his cufflinks then was seated.

Mr. Price, without hesitation, quickly began his questioning. "Good day Mr. Cotton, nice suit."

"Thanks, thanks a lot man. I got it in New York."

"Very nice. Now, Mr. Cotton can you please state your name for the court?"

"Yeah, my name is Wallace Cotton, but uh…everybody just calls me Cotton."

"Mr. Cotton, can you tell us your relationship to the defendant?"

"Well, we really didn't have a relationship if you know what I mean. We just worked at the warehouse together. I used to toss him a loan here and there, that kind of thing."

"Tossed him a loan, what exactly does that mean?"

"You know, sometimes people at work don't have enough for lunch snacks or whatever. They come to me and I float 'em a loan, twenty-five cents on the dollar."

"Did the defendant always pay his loans back?"

"Yeah mostly all, except for this one time. Man, this one time I loaned him a twenty. He said he'd pay the twenty-five on payday. When payday rolled around, I came looking for him. I asked him what was up and he told me that something came up and he'd have to catch me next payday. At that point, I didn't worry about it because he had been pretty reliable at paying his debts. When the next payday hit I checked my books and headed back over to his area. He was stacking some merchandise. I ask him about my bread and he told me next payday again. I tell him that I needed my dough now. He turned and looked at me and mind you I grew up in The Bronx and I've seen some shi...I mean some stuff out there on the street. That look that he gave me. That was a look that was like no other. He said nothing, but his look said it all. His look said that he wouldn't hesitate to gut me like a pi......"

"Objection, Your Honor. How can the witness know what the defendant was even thinking without verbally stating so?" yelled, Mr. Fisher.

"Objection sustained. Please strike the last portion of the witness's statement from the record," the Judge said to the stenographer.

Mr. Price continued. "Mr. Cotton, can you tell us what you saw on the night in question?"

"Yeah sure, I was working in my area and I saw someone down in the truck bay area. One of the loading dock doors was open, but that's not unusual because they open them early sometimes when they are expecting a delivery..."

"When you say they open the doors, who would 'they' be?"

"The guys in receiving."

"Did the defendant work in receiving?"

"Yeah."

"Please continue."

"Anyway, I keep on working then I remember that fat Greg told me to stop by and pick up some money that he owed me, so I head down to his shop. While I'm heading down his way, I see this guy running back in from the truck drop-off. He's panting, huffing and puffing, sweatin' and all. So I figure it was somebody stealing something so I walk back to see if I could dig my nails in, you know, tell 'em I'd snitch if they didn't give me a cut. But when I saw who it was, I left it alone. Like I said, this cat gave me the chills. About a half hour later I hear him yelling and Bev is dead. I don't know."

"The man you saw, is he here in this courtroom now and if so, can you point to him?"

"Yeah sure, that's him right over there."

"Let the record show that the witness is pointing to the defendant, Willam Trent."

"Mr. Cotton, have you ever seen the defendant with Beverly Clark?"

"Yeah, all the time. I told Bev and Diane not to be around him, I said 'you two don't need to be hangin' with that cat, he's bad news.' I guess they didn't believe me. I sense these kinds of things."

"No further questions."

Mr. Fisher popped up from his chair and rushed over to the witness stand. "Mr. Cotton, you say you worked with Mr. Trent at the Dart Drug Warehouse?"

"Yeah, I'm not sure how long, but yeah."

"Are you still employed by Dart Drug?"

"Well uh…no…not at this present time."

"And why are you no longer employed there sir?"

"Well…they kind of let me go."

"And why is that Mr. Cotton?"

"They say I was stealing, but they got no proof."

"Stealing? How could you be accused of stealing? Don't they have a security guard at the front and back entrance?"

"Yeah, they say I was taking stuff through the bay doors."

"So you're saying that more than just the receivers had the access codes to the doors?"

"I mean you could get the codes"

"You didn't answer my question. Yes or no, could anybody else have those codes?"

"Yes."

"Now Mr. Cotton, you stated that you saw the defendant run back in the bay door panting and perspiring, correct?"

"Yeah, I saw him."

"Now correct me if I'm wrong. This was at night, correct?"

"Yeah."

"How many lights does the bay area have?"

"I'm not sure."

"Well let me tell you…..none. So if it was dark and the only light you had was the parking lot lights that are over one hundred feet away and the light from the moon, how could you see the defendant's face so clearly?"

"I don't know, maybe it was a full moon or something. It was him, who else could it be, he was the only one working receiving that night."

"Didn't you just tell me that anyone could get the access codes to those doors?"

"Yeah sure, but…"

"Let me remind you that perjury is a serious crime. Now let me ask you again, can you unequivocally say that the defendant was who you saw run back through that bay door?"

"Well no, I guess I can't but……"

"A simple yes or no will suffice."

"Well then no." Cotton said sarcastically.

"No more questions Your Honor."

Cotton was given the approval to step down from the stand, which he gladly did.

"This court will recess until 9:00 am tomorrow morning," said Judge Dunn.

"All rise!" shouted the voice of the bailiff. Every person in the courtroom stood to their feet and the judge disappeared through the side door. Mr. Price gathered his papers while glancing over to Mr. Fisher who was talking to his client with confidence. Martha stood behind them smiling and Willam watched as Lynn waved to him as she exited with her mother. The courtroom cleared rather quickly and they all left to an awaiting group of reporters.

Morning seemed to have bypassed the night, that's how it seemed to Willam anyway. After all the commotion that followed the long grueling day, Willam was both mentally and emotionally exhausted. His mind had finally lost the race that it obviously had been competing in for most of the day. After he had showered and settled in, he lay across his bed and closed his eyes. After what had seemed to be only a brief moment, he opened his eyes to a sunlit room. Time had passed without warning, without a hint.

The new day had arrived to greet his old problems. Willam draped his legs over the bed and eventually pushed himself up to a sitting position. He looked out the window and up at the cloud filled sky then closed his eyes to pray. After he was done with his quiet time, he headed down the hallway and was greeted by the scent of bacon. Martha was making breakfast. Willam quickly showered and dressed. He sat down with Martha and had breakfast. They hadn't spoken much since the trial. In fact, the ride home was traveled in complete silence. The two finished their breakfast and Martha went upstairs to gather her last minute necessities while Willam stacked the dishes in the sink. Soon after, Mr. Daniels was blowing his horn outside. Willam trailed behind his mom as they rushed out the door and into the awaiting automobile.

The media crowd didn't seem as large as yesterday's, but still, they were ever so aggressive. Today, everyone knew what to do to avoid them. They climbed out of the car and rushed inside. Willam began to feel nervous again. He could feel his breakfast roiling in his stomach. Mr. Fisher had met them at the entrance of the court building and insisted on meeting briefly before entering the courtroom. The small group followed behind the quick paced defender. Just as they approached the small room, it hit. His neck extended outward and with his mouth forced opened as wide as it could, the lumpy fluid erupted. Willam continued this for several moments until he strained out the last remains of partially digested breakfast.

Willam rushed off to the men's room and Mr. Fisher followed. While Willam cleaned himself, Fisher talked. William, standing staring at himself, realized at that moment, that Mr. Fisher was nervous about the trial. His strong and confident manner seemed to have abandoned him. He appeared nervous and unsure. Willam was now truly worried. All morning, he had nothing else on his mind but the trial, and now this. He dried his shirt with brown paper towels and walked out of the men's room leaving Mr. Fisher behind. He did not return to their meeting room. He walked into the courtroom and took his seat behind the large table.

Chapter 10 - Verdict

"They hate me." Willam thought to himself as he looked around the courtroom. He looked at each juror then at the spectators throughout the room. "The jurors appear so insensitive. Actually, most of them seem pretty nonchalant to be making a decision about the future of another person's life. Look at that guy, he's not even fully awake yet, yawning. These fools are who my life depend on, I can't believe this. How did I get here?"

Mr. Fisher tapped Willam on his shoulder and motioned for him to stand as the judge entered the room. With thoughts of what his future could be racing through his mind, Willam failed to hear the bailiff bring the courtroom to their feet for the judge's entrance. Willam was still in his trance. With his stomach now empty and his mouth dry and still filled with the stench of vomit, he squinted and frowned before lowering himself back into his seat. "Blah...blah...blah, blah...blah...blah...." Was all that Willam's mind had picked up from the bailiff's announcements; he was still deep in thought.

"They think I did it, all of them think I killed her. They don't care about who I am or how quiet and polite I've been to everybody in my youth. They only see the bastard son of a whore before them. They think I hate women because my mother was a whore. They want to condemn me for cutting the head off of a damn bird and for taking up for my so called friend. Who are they? They don't know me. They don't know anything about me except for what's been said in this room. THEY DON'T KNOW ME!!!!" Willam screamed out in his mind. "Wait, did she just smile at me? The lady juror just smiled at me. Maybe they do see. Maybe they do understand what my mom had to do and that it doesn't matter to me. Maybe they can see the love that we have for each other and maybe… They can't find me guilty. There's absolutely no evidence. So what if I cut the head off of a bird, that's hardly a viable comparison to a human being. And Rusty, well, I'm sure they could see just what kind of clown he really is. Nah, no way, they couldn't possibly think that I did it. No way!"

Willam's mind drift was interrupted by the commotion in the courtroom. He had been unaware that it was directed at him until he witnessed the fear on his mother's face. Kathy's cousin Tony rushed into the courtroom yelling that Willam should be condemned to death for killing both Beverly and Kathy. He was charging toward Willam while he made angry threats at him. Tony was quickly subdued and taken out of the courtroom. Willam looked over at his mom and smiled, hoping that would assist in calming her down. Mr. Daniels sat calmly while patting her hand. Once the courtroom had calmed down, it was Mr. Fisher's show and Willam knew that his life was now in his hands.

Mr. Fisher stood slowly and called his first witness, Mr. Paul Robinson. The tall skinny young man walked back down to the witness stand and dropped into the wooden seat. "I must remind you Mr. Robinson, you're still under oath." Judge Dunn said.

Rusty nodded his head then looked over at Willam. Mr. Fisher started in quickly. "Mr. Robinson, you stated in your testimony earlier that Mr. Trent was, in your own words, 'weird'."

"Yeah, I said that."

"And do you really believe that Mr. Robinson? Do you really believe that Mr. Trent is weird?"

Rusty sat there and looked at Willam for a few seconds before answering, "Yes, I do."

"Well Mr. Robinson, I find that hard to believe. For the last five years or so, you were always with him. Both of you were planning to go to the same school. As a matter of fact, you two were going to be roommates. Are we to believe that you were going to do all of this with a guy that you thought was so weird? No Mr. Robinson, you don't think he's so weird, not at all. In fact, you believe Mr. Trent to be a good guy, a guy that everybody likes; a guy that has a bright future, a future brighter than yours and you couldn't stand it!"

"Objection Your Honor, defense is speaking for the witness!" Mr. Price yelled.

"Sustained," said the judge.

"Sorry Your Honor," mumbled Mr. Fisher. "So Mr. Robinson, would you please tell the Court just why on earth you would hang out and be by this weird young man's side for all of those years?"

"Will was cool."

"Cool meaning good?"

"Yeah, he was cool, but he thought he was better than everybody else." Rusty looked over at Willam and yelled, "You're not better than me!"

"So when you say better, what, you mean in sports or was he just better than you in everything?"

"I said he wasn't better than me! I could have gotten into that stupid college and could have had a nice girlfriend like him too, but he always had to try to make me look bad just so he could look good to them. That's what he always did. Ridin' around in that big fancy car and all, and dressing better than us.

He thinks he's better, but he isn't and that's why he's sittin' over there right now. He's sittin' over there sweatin' and hopin' I'll say somethin' nice about him, but I won't. So when I say he's weird, I mean it in the sense where you never know what he's gonna say or do. He cut the head off of a poor defenseless bird for cryin' out loud! It's like he could have a split personality or something. That's what you should do, you should give him a psycho test or something. Look at him, he's crazy! "

"Now Mr. Robinson, I'm not a psychiatrist or anything along those lines, but this sounds to me like a pure and simple case of top notch jealousy, sir. This sounds like the type of jealousy that would cause a man to do everything he could to bring down those that he is jealous of. I mean the type of jealousy where one would make a person do anything to get at somebody, including murder!"

"Objection!"

"Withdrawn. Just one last question, Your Honor. Mr. Robinson, have you ever killed a fly or a mouse or anything at all?"

"Of course I've killed a fly and insects and those kinds of things."

"So you are capable of killing?"

"Objection Your Honor," came the low baritone voice from the prosecution's table.

"No further questions Your Honor," said Mr. Fisher as he returned to the table.

Mr. Price declined to question Rusty again, and he was ordered to step down from the witness stand. Mr. Fisher called other witnesses who only confirmed that Willam was a nice, but quiet boy. Weeks had passed between the prosecution and the defense questioning and Willam had grown tired of court and everyone affiliated with it. Just as Mr. Fisher was about to call his last witness, he looked over at Martha. She looked down at the floor then lifted her eyes and made contact with the defense attorney who seemed to be awaiting her approval. Martha nodded her head while it remained close to her bosom.

Mr. Fisher focused in on Willam who then too turned his sights to his mom, who continued only to stare at the marble floor. He looked back over to Mr. Fisher who was now looking just off to the right of Martha. He turned and looked in the same direction. Moments later, Willam raised his hand slightly from the table as he slowly returned his attention to Mr. Fisher. With a stunned look on his face, he waved his hand just enough to get the attention of Mr. Fisher. Mr. Fisher returned his focus back over to Willam only to see him slowly shake his head while whispering, "No." He did not want to hear what he had already realized from the moment he looked into his mother's eyes. He knew, after setting his sights to his mom's side what Mr. Fisher was about to do. Realizing that Mr. Fisher had ignored his gesture, Willam slammed his fist down forcefully against the wood table causing an exploding sound. The entire courtroom's attention was now drawn to Willam. He looked at Mr. Fisher coldly then lowered his head.

Mr. Fisher stared at Willam for a moment before returning to the table. He looked back at Martha, but kept his focus forward. He then cleared his throat and adjusted his suit jacket. He stood tall and erect then spoke loudly and clearly to the judge, "Your Honor, the defense rest."

The sound of garbled voices carried over the courtroom. Judge Dunn scribbled on a pad of paper and looked through a small document before tapping his gavel and calling for order. Once the courtroom was again silent, Judge Dunn removed his eyeglasses and looked at Mr. Fisher oddly. He couldn't believe that the defense had not built a better case. He looked out over the courtroom then spoke loudly, "This Court will be adjourned until Monday morning 9:00 am. We will hear closing statements at that time from both the defense and the prosecution. Court is adjourned."

The courtroom emptied slowly. Willam sat slumped over and remained motionless at the table with Mr. Fisher. With his arms draped across his thighs and his head hung over, he stared at the shiny table top and said nothing. Once the room's acoustics were filled with silence, in a very calm and quiet voice, Willam spoke.

"How come you never told me?"

Martha leaned forward and placed her hand on her son's shoulder. She lowered her head then after a few moments had passed, she apologetically whispered, "I'm sorry Will. I'm so sorry that you had to find out this way, I just didn't want to hurt you. I didn't want people saying things about you. I was just trying to protect you."

"And you?"

Willam could hear the deep voice over his left shoulder mumble, "I wanted to, but...."

"But what, you were ashamed? Afraid that people would know that you weren't just the great friend that you pretended to be? That you weren't the great guy who was helping out the widow and her poor son out of the kindness of your heart? That you were sleeping with a whore and she bore a son by you or was it that your wife would find out and your other children would hate you for sleeping around with a whore, which is it?" Willam sat up in the chair and turned to Mr. Daniels. Looking him directly in the eyes, he asked, "Is that why you've always been so nice to me? You both should be ashamed. And what about Jimmy Trent, did he know that I wasn't his son?"

"Willam, I know you're hurt and angry but you're still going to show some respect. After everything I've done and been through for you!" Martha whispered.

"Respect, how much respect did you show me? I've walked around all these years thinking that my father was dead but he was sitting right beside me and I was driving him all around town the entire time. You still didn't answer my question mother, did James Trent know that I wasn't his?"

"Yes. He knew that you were not his son, but he loved you Will. You know that he loved you. I told him that I didn't know who the father was and he asked me to marry him before I could finish my sentence. When you were born, he was so proud and he never looked at you any other way."

"It sounds like he was a very special man. He sounds like a man that I would be proud to be the son of, but instead I am the son of a two bit hustler and a prostitute. It also sounds like you knew that he would marry you if you told him you were pregnant. That's why you went to him, isn't it? If you knew who my father was, why didn't you tell him?"

Martha said nothing for a moment. Finally she answered, "I couldn't. I just couldn't."

"You set him up! A nice guy with a job, that's all he was to you, a meal ticket." Willam stared at Martha then over at Mr. Daniels. "No wonder I'm so screwed up. I'm in church sitting beside my mother on Sunday morning and by Sunday night she's upstairs screwing a John. I drive my dad all around town to run his numbers but can't show up at his house because someone may suspect that we're related." Willam broke out into laughter. "Maybe they're right! Maybe I am weird and just don't know it. Maybe I did hurt those girls and just don't remember, and maybe I deserve to go to jail for the rest of my life. It's probably better than dealing with you two."

"Don't you say that Willam Trent! Don't you ever say that! Now I may have done some things that I am not proud of, but it was all for you. It has always been for you. I've always done what I thought would be best for you. I wanted to tell you so many times about your father, but I just couldn't. Especially the way you looked up to him. I was afraid that if you found out that he was really your daddy, you'd be devastated and hurt. I was just looking out for you Will, just like I always have."

"You know, what he said was true don't you?"

"Who, what who said?"

"Rusty. He said that I really didn't like women and I believe him. I like their company and all, but….I just don't like for them to touch me in that way, and I believe it's because of you mother. You have my head so screwed up. I feel like Norman Bates. Is this how you've protected me? You've made me into some sick individual who thinks that sex is filthy. You always told me about dirty little girls when I was just a young kid, and how they can give you diseases and I guess I never forgot that. How could you say that? How could you talk about someone being dirty when you were sleeping with all of those men? You think that I enjoyed hearing you at night or watching them leave our house after they were done with you? You talk about dirty, little girls. What about dirty, big mamas?"

"I'm sorry Will but I wasn't ever gonna let that happen to you. None of those little fast hussies meant you any good. They were just fast little girls with nothing on their minds but sex. You didn't need to have anything to do with any of that, not at your age. Next thing you know, you'd be a daddy. You'd have to get a job, a real job. And your college education would be right out the window. Not you, nobody was going to do that to you. That's why I told you how those nasty little girls could be. Look where it got me. I was young with a baby, no husband, and trying to make ends meet however I could. I wasn't going to let that happen to you."

"So is that why you treated every girl that I ever cared about like they were less than respectable?"

"That's exactly why. They weren't good enough for you Will. They weren't young ladies, none of them."

"Who are you to say that Ma? If you are their judge, then who is yours?"

"You just don't understand son."

"I understand perfectly."

Willam clammed back up. Both Martha and Mr. Daniels tried to talk to him, but he would not answer. He was in deep thought once again. He sat without speaking for about twenty minutes before he stood and walked out of the courtroom followed by everyone who had remained with him. Willam was speechless for the rest of the day.

The following Monday morning was not very different for Willam. He sat in the courtroom presenting a face of stone. He said nothing to his mother or to his newly declared father. Mr. Fisher conferred with him and he merely nodded or shook his head to answer. The jury watched, as they saw, not the young attentive face of a worried boy, but the cold, calloused glare of a "could be" murderer. Judge Dunn had called the counsels up to the bench. Both Mr. Price and Mr. Fisher quickly approached the judge's bench. Judge Dunn covered the microphone with his hand and they mumbled to one another before both men returned to their perspective tables. "Prosecution will now begin its closing statement," the judge announced.

Mr. Price, already standing, began to tug on his suit jacket and unbuttoned the last button at the bottom of his vest. He placed two of his fingers into the small right pocket of his vest as if he were digging for a pocket watch. It was clear to everyone that there was nothing inside this shallow vest pocket but nevertheless, he continued with his digging motion. It made him feel distinguished or more of a scholar. Every eye was on him during that time. He walked over to the jurors' box same as when he gave his opening argument. Standing silently for just a brief moment, he took in a deep breath and shook his head slowly as he released the wind from his lungs. He exhaled slow and long.

"What is this world coming to? I must ask this question. We have heard two things during this entire proceeding. One, the defendant has had a more than abnormal childhood. From watching his mother having sex with dozens of strange men, could quite possibly have affected his mental state causing introverted type behavior. Two, the defendant seems like a good, young man, but kind of strange acting. That is the only defense his lawyer could come up with. He's begging you to look at his innocence.

Lee Harvey Oswald looked like the boy next door, but was captured for the assassination of one of the greatest presidents of all time. So I ask you again, what is this world coming to? When someone thinks that looks and looks alone are enough to make society turn their heads the other way. You must ask yourself, can I ignore the facts and let my emotions or my beliefs set a murderer free? And what happens if he kills again? That's blood on all of our hands, mine for not doing a better job of presenting you with the facts, and yours for avoiding and shielding your eyes from the truth which prevents you from making a fair judgment. You've heard all of the facts. You've heard that the defendant had befriended Ms. Clark. You've heard from a forensics expert that a multitude of evidence was found at the scene of the crime which matched that of the defendant. Hair, skin samples, fabrics from his clothing to name a few, all belonged to the defendant.

Ms. Clark was found in the defendant's car for heaven's sake. Witnesses saw the defendant running back from the crime scene and the defendant was the only person with a key to his car. There were eye witnesses testifying that they saw the defendant crying out for help and drenched in Ms. Clark's blood. Wouldn't you be upset if you had taken somebody's life? And why were there no other fingerprints or any other evidence linking anyone else to the crime scene? I'll tell you why because no one else had been in that car with Ms. Clark, nobody but the defendant.

Why did he do such an evil, terrible thing to this young woman, somebody's child, somebody's sister, somebody's dear friend? I'll tell you why, because she liked him, nothing more. She just wanted to be with him. She wanted to have sex with him and he thought that it was dirty. He looked at her as something that he hated, something that he watched for most of his life, a whore. So he felt that the world would be just a little nicer or maybe just a little cleaner without her in it. So he killed her. He killed somebody's daughter, sister, aunt, or somebody's best friend.

He judged her, passed sentence on her, and took what we hold so precious and sacred. He took her life. Don't listen to me, listen to the facts. Don't listen to your hearts or your emotions, listen to the facts. Let's tell him and others like him that you can't hide behind your innocent looks any longer. You are and will be accountable for what you have done. Let him know that he can't get away with this, not on your watch!

When you return to this box after your deliberation, return with your heart satisfied and your conscience clear, return with a verdict filled with the truth. A verdict filled with real justice, a verdict of guilty. Thank you."

Mr. Price returned to the table from which he came. His colleagues leaned over and whispered to him as soon as he was seated. He leaned back in his chair and looked over at Mr. Fisher who still remained seated.

"Counselor," Judge Dunn called.

Mr. Fisher remained in his seat. He reached for the stainless steel pitcher of water and filled his glass. He placed the pitcher back on to the large square mat then lifted his glass to his mouth. He drank half of the glass of water then cleared his throat. He sat the glass down on the mat and stood. He buttoned his suit jacket and looked down at Willam and placed his hand on his shoulder. He walked over to the jurors stand and smiled to them.

"That was pretty impressive, huh? It's like magic isn't it? That's what the prosecution is trying to lead you to believe. He wants you to believe that my client could be in a confined surrounding, that of an automobile and commit a bloody and vile crime and walk away without one fingerprint or any traces of his DNA on the victim. He also wants you to believe that my client thinks of his mother as the devil, the same woman whom he waits up for every night to make sure she arrives home safely from her night job. The same woman whom he prepares dinner for night after night so that she'll have something to eat as soon as she gets home from work. The exact woman he cherishes to this day.

He talks about listening to the facts. Have you heard any real facts in this courtroom during this case? No, you've heard allegations. You've seen more smoke and mirrors in this courtroom than at a David Copperfield show. This young man has a life; don't take it away from him because of all the flash that has been put in front of you. The so called forensics expert, as you found out was not an expert at all. All of the prosecutions eyewitnesses all stated that they could not be certain about anything that they saw. You can't take away a young man's future for what somebody thought that they saw.

And yes, Miss Clark was someone's daughter, sister, and friend, but doesn't that same statement hold true for Mr. Trent. We can't save Beverly Clark's life today, but you can save this young man's by not putting him away for a crime that he did not commit. It's just that plain and simple. You must be certain without a shadow of a doubt, but do the facts reflect that? No. There's one thing that the prosecution and I agree on and that is that you must do the right thing. When you return, return here with a verdict of not guilty. Save this young man's life and let's send him home. He's already been through more than he should have. Enough is enough already. Please send him home. Thank you."

As Mr. Fisher returned to the table, Willam looked up at the faces of the jury. As he polled their faces, he stopped on the face of the little woman who had once smiled at him. She no longer smiled, but looked at him as if she had no feeling. He could feel her unsympathetic gaze even after he had turned away.

Judge Dunn removed his glasses and directed his next statement to the jury. "Members of the Jury, it is now my duty to instruct you on the rules of law that you must follow and apply in deciding this case. When I have finished you will go to the jury room and begin your discussions -- what we call your deliberations. It will be your duty to decide whether the state has proved beyond a reasonable doubt the specific facts necessary to find the defendant guilty of the crime charged. You must make your decision only on the basis of the testimony and other evidence presented here during the trial; and you must not be influenced in any way by either sympathy or prejudice for or against the defendant or the State of Maryland.

The State of Maryland has the burden of proving the defendant guilty beyond a reasonable doubt, and if it fails to do so you must find the defendant not guilty as to that count. If you are convinced that the defendant has been proved guilty beyond a reasonable doubt, say so. If you are not convinced, say so. As stated earlier you must consider only the evidence that I have admitted in the case.

You have heard the testimony of Mr. Thad Krazchek, an expert regarding the science of forensics. An expert witness has special knowledge or experience that allows the witness to give an opinion. You do not have to accept an expert's opinion. In deciding how much weight to give it, you should consider the witness's qualifications and how he reached his conclusions. Remember that you alone decide how much of a witness's testimony to believe, and how much weight it deserves.

The defendant has pleaded not guilty to the charges of this case. This plea puts in issue each of the essential elements of the offenses described in these instructions and imposes upon the State of Maryland the burden of establishing each of these elements by proof beyond a reasonable doubt. Are there any questions?"

The blank glare of each jury member indicated that there were no questions. The jury was then escorted out of the courtroom and the court was adjourned until the completion of the jury's deliberations. Willam and Mr. Fisher were lead to the waiting area followed by Martha and Mr. Daniels. Lynn later joined the foursome. She came in and walked over to Willam. She gave him the biggest hug that she could and he hugged her back. He wouldn't let go of her. This was the first time ever that he had even touched a female in front of his mother. Martha felt very uneasy with it too, but said nothing.

Willam looked over at Mr. Fisher. "So what do you think?"

"Think about what?" Fisher replied.

"Do you think they're gonna let me off?"

"Let's hope so."

"How long do they usually take to decide?"

"It depends"

"I heard if they take longer than four hours, things don't normally go in your favor. Is that true?"

"Well, you hear all sorts of things, but don't you worry."

"Don't worry Will, I've been praying and God answers prayers." Martha said proudly.

"Do you think that God is going to answer one of your prayers? I doubt it."

Martha turned and walked over to the long bench in the room and sat down. Willam was still upset with her and she didn't want to upset him anymore. She sat and remained quiet for the duration.

"Mr. Fisher, if they find me guilty, do you think they'll give me the death penalty?" Willam asked.

"No Willam, they don't have the death penalty in Maryland, and besides they're not going to find you guilty. You'll be home before you know it." Mr. Fisher summoned up the closest thing he could to a smile and displayed it. It wasn't very convincing though. Willam sank down into the leather wing back chair in which he was now sitting and closed his eyes.

Three hours had passed before there was a knock on the door. Mr. Fisher looked over at Willam. "See, less than your four hours," he said while smiling.

He opened the door and was greeted by a bailiff. "Jury's going to reconvene at 8:00 am tomorrow morning."

"Ok, thanks." Fisher closed the door and conveyed the message. "We'd all better go and get some rest for tomorrow. I don't know how long this thing is going to linger on." Everyone concurred, then began gathering up their belongings and headed out for another night of anticipation.

Willam looked tired and worn out; he hadn't gotten a bit of sleep the previous night. Martha could see his worry upon his face and would try to uplift him as best as she could, but he still provided no response to her. She continued to remind him how she knew that her prayers would be answered and God would bring the unjust to their punishment. Willam, still hurt and angry from what he considered to be the biggest betrayal of his life, kept ignoring her.

The call came shortly after 1 pm that afternoon. The jury had reached a verdict. They had deliberated for over seven hours.

The courtroom was swarming with all sorts this morning. Spectators, friends and family had arrived early. Though cameras were not allowed inside, reporters had filled the entire left side of the huge room. Everyone was there to bear witness to the fate of Willam Xavier Trent. Willam sat at the table with his hands clasped together and his eyes closed. He was saying his last prayer before hearing from the twelve strangers.

The judge sat patiently, allowing the low hum of conversation as the jury was preparing to enter. After Willam had completed his request with The Man upstairs, he looked behind him. She was there as always, still smiling. Willam's head dropped in shame then his eyes slowly returned to her face. With a slight whisper he uttered the only words that he could manage to get out, "I'm sorry."

Martha smiled at her son and pressed her hand firmly against her mouth as she so desperately tried to hold back her tears. And with a quiet cracked voice, she whispered back to him, "Me too, but there's nothing to forgive."

That was all Willam needed, he turned around and sat calmly in his seat with his hands resting in his lap. He suddenly felt reassured. For some reason he knew that the jury would not find him guilty of any wrong doings. He could feel himself breathing more calmly. And even though they were complete strangers, he knew that they would see him for who he really was. Despite his abnormal childhood and up bringing, he was not a menace to society nor was he the monster that the prosecutor made him out to be.

They walked through the door one by one. Each one seemed to look over at Willam as they walked up the short stairway to the juror's booth. Once seated, each juror avoided eye contact with Willam. Their stern faces were directed to Judge Dunn only. All but one, the lady. The lady that once smiled at him now had an apologetic look on her face. She looked at Willam sadly, inhaled deeply then she too painted on a stone look. The courtroom was quiet and still. The only sound Willam could hear was his own heart beating. Fisher placed his hand on Willam's shoulder and nodded to him. "Don't worry, it's going to be alright."

Willam only smiled back at him. He still felt confident and was so ready to get this day over with and go back to his life. He still couldn't believe how calm he was. His mind was not even there. It had gone elsewhere. He was having thoughts of pancakes for dinner and making things right with Rusty. He thought about Lynn and how he was never going to leave her alone. He thought about everything except where he was. He was off in another world until he felt Mr. Fisher tapping him on the arm. The judge had just read the verdict and passed it back over to the bailiff to give back to the head juror.

"Will the defendant please rise." Judge Dunn ordered. "In the charge of Case Number 82160, murder in the first degree, Jury what say you?"

Willam could hear his mother breathing deeply and the tapping sound of her high heel shoe tapping on the shiny marble flooring. He looked back at her and smiled once more.

"Don't worry Mother dear, it's going to be alright. I'll be home with you soon and things will be alright." Willam thought to himself.

There was dead silence in the courtroom. The fat, balding man wearing a cheap, tan suit with a plaid shirt rose from the juror's box. He adjusted his dark brown tie then reopened the small piece of paper that the judge had returned to him. He looked at Willam then back at the judge.

"Your Honor, We, the jury, on the charge of murder in the first degree, Case Number 82160, for our verdict say: We find the defendant, Willam Xavier Trent, as to murder in the first degree, Not Guilty!"

"Thank you Jesus!" Martha yelled. The entire courtroom erupted. The judge called for order and dismissed the case. The jury was dismissed and the reporters rushed out to phone in their stories. You could hear the whispers of the unsatisfied as they left the courtroom. Mr. and Mrs. Davis left with solemn looks fixed upon their faces. As the jury filed out, the lady that once smiled at Willam turned just before she departed the courtroom and smiled once again. He nodded in return before he was rushed by all of his family and friends.

Martha ran up to him screaming, "I told you my prayers would be answered. He knew if they had locked you up, I would have surely died. Hallelujah!"

"You were right Ma, I'm sorry that I ever doubted you."

Willam could see his "out of place look" through the crowd. He made his way through the group to him and embraced him. "I'm truly happy for you Willam." Mr. Daniels said.

"Well, just don't expect me to start calling you Daddy now." Willam replied. The two laughed and hugged and of course, Martha continued to cry. It was truly an exciting day for Willam and he basked in it for as long as he could. He was as happy as he ever had been in all of his days.

The flashes of light were somewhat blinding, but for once it didn't matter to Willam. He stood in front of the cameras with his mother and Mr. Fisher and listened as Mr. Fisher answered the reporters' questions.

"Mr. Fisher, were you ever worried about the verdict?" One of the reporters shouted.

"You're always worried about a verdict. It only takes one person to change or convince the views of others. I'm just glad things turned out the way they did. Now this young man can return to his life and start putting things back together."

"How about you Willam, how do you feel now that this ordeal is over?"

"Wow, I can't find the words. If it wasn't for The Man upstairs and this guy here, let's just say we'd be having a different conversation altogether. I just hope that the law finds and brings whoever is responsible for this crime to justice. And now, I've got to go. We're going home to celebrate."

E.L. RHODES

Chapter 11 - Truth

The music could be heard from blocks away as neighbors, friends and relatives gathered at the Trent house to celebrate Willam's victory. Everyone brought food and drinks to assist with the festivities. Willam was having the time of his life. Even Mr. Fisher stopped by. He too, was the man of the hour and everyone showed their gratitude. Mr. Daniels stopped by with his daughter and one of his sons. He introduced them to Willam as their brother and to Willam's surprise, they accepted and embraced him. Willam danced and laughed for hours before his still shadowed but present reality kicked back in.

Through all the commotion and excitement, he had managed to place the murders of the young ladies up on a shelf somewhere in the back of his mind. Suddenly, he was no longer in the party mood. Quickly, his mind shifted gears. His happy and celebratory mood was extinguished and replaced with suspicion and paranoia. He stared into the faces of all those who approached him to offer their congratulations. Everyone was a suspect. Willam stood quiet and alone, as he made everyone who stopped to speak with him feel very uncomfortable with his gazing.

"Everybody! Can I have your attention please? Somebody turn the music down! Everybody please, I'd like to just say how happy I am that my son has made it through that terrible ordeal. I want to thank you all for joining us in this celebration. I'd also like to thank this man here, Mr. Fisher. He worked so hard to prove that Will was innocent. He told us in the very beginning not to worry and that everything would work out, and it did and I thank you for all that you have done. But it just wasn't you in that courtroom Mr. Fisher, oh no, you were just His instrument. God has delivered my boy home to me and He will deal with those responsible for the evil that has plagued the families of those precious young ladies!"

"Amen, sister, Amen!" a voice yelled from the crowd.

Everyone started clapping and yelling. Mr. Fisher, although appearing to be so comfortable in front of all of the cameras and microphones while addressing the media in front of the courthouse, seemed to be a bit shy in front of the small group of supporters at the Trent house.

"Willam?" Martha called out. Willam looked over to his mother then walked toward her and Mr. Fisher. "Don't you want to say anything?" she continued.

Willam stopped after he had reached the center of the crowd. While clearing his throat he scanned the faces of the people that surrounded him. He placed his hand on Mr. Fisher's shoulder while looking at his mom. He smiled and quickly shifted his focus to Mr. Fisher. "You still never said if you believed me."

Mr. Fisher looked at Willam oddly.

"You still never said if you think that I did it or not. Do you? Do you think that I am innocent? You said to me that it didn't matter what you thought, but it does. Do you believe me?"

"Willam, it's over. You were found not guilty, is that not enough?" Mr. Fisher replied.

"No, it's not enough. Not if I told you every intimate detail of my life and my relationships with those women and you still have doubts. What do you think that these people standing here right now could be thinking?"

"I think they're happy for you. I think that they're relieved that things turned out in your favor. They're thinking about how blessed you and your mom are."

"Willy, why are you acting this way?" asked Martha.

"I'm sorry Ma. I guess I'm tired. Sorry, Mr. Fisher I didn't mean to......."

"I do believe you Will. I know you didn't do anything wrong and I believe everything that I said in that courtroom to be true. I'm sure that you'll put your life back on track and make us all proud."

Mr. Fisher placed his arm around Willam but Willam's expression remained blank and earnest. "Well I just hope that I'll never let you down, none of you. You've done a good thing for us and we appreciate it," Willam stated.

As the crowd, already geared up in celebration, resumed dancing and singing, Willam eased his way through the crowd up to his room and to his awaiting bed. He lay across his bed once again, in deep thought.

He thought about each of the young ladies whose lives were taken. Their only commonality was their association with him. Was that the reason? Were they taken because of him? After all this time, he still couldn't figure it out. One question was persistent and constantly repeating itself in his mind, where is Ralph? Somehow he knew that he was involved in this.

The music died down and the conversation of only a few people bounced from the walls of the hallway. Willam knew that the celebration was winding down and the house was soon to be vacant of guests. Shortly after hearing the last of the celebrants exit the house to their automobiles, Willam removed his shirt and trousers and climbed into bed. His exhaustion caused him to quickly fall into a deep slumber.

As he slept, he dreamt of Kathy, Debra, and Beverly. In the distance, they all walked toward him. He could see the blood filled slashes of each of their throats and their garbled voices were incomprehensible and screeching as they drew near him. Their blood shot eyes sank deeply into the sockets in which they were seated and thick pulsing veins protruded from their heads. Their pace was extremely slow but steady and somehow Willam found himself surrounded by them. He placed his hands over his face but continued to look at them. Suddenly, one by one, each gory faced woman ripped open and pulled blood soaked blond haired embryos from their wombs. All of the embryos resembled Ralph.

Willam jumped from his slumber screaming and terrified. He sat on the side of his bed, drenched from perspiration and trembling. He tried to make sense of his dream but could not. Willam slowly climbed back onto his mattress. He looked around his room then closed his eyes.

The familiar voice that had awakened him so many mornings before forced him into the new day earlier than he had expected. As he opened his eyes, he could see him sitting at the foot of his bed. "If you're going to sleep all day, just let me know and I'm outta here." It was Rusty. He had come by early, just as he used to do. "Look man, I came to apologize. I feel like a real ass for everything that I said to you. I guess I made you look pretty bad in court too with all that I said. Anyway, I'm glad that the jury didn't pay any attention to my dumb assed statement. I don't blame you if you don't ever want to speak to me again or if you hate me and all. I just wanted to get this off my chest."

Willam remained silent. Rusty looked down then pressed both of his hands down onto the soft mattress and pushed himself up and stood over Willam. Willam still did not speak. He just stared out of the window as if Rusty was not there. "Well I guess I'd better get going." Rusty mumbled. "I'll see you around sometime."

"You mean you're not going to stay for breakfast? You never turn down my mom's breakfast." Willam calmly said while smiling at him.

Rusty looked down at Willam and smiled. "You know, you really are weird."

"I must be, I hang out with you don't I?" The boys laughed and Willam climbed out of bed. They wrestled around playfully then Willam got dressed and the two headed downstairs. After making their way into the living room, Willam noticed a small envelope resting on the coffee table. It was addressed to him. It had no stamp or return address on it.

"I found it in the mailbox with the other mail this morning." Martha said as she greeted the boys with their plates. Willam picked up the envelope, carried it into the dining room and placed it on the table. He and Rusty enjoyed the perfectly prepared meal and talked about old times. They agreed to get together later and Rusty left. Willam remained close to home for most of the day.

After he had showered, he put on his clothes and helped his mother with chores around the house.

"Got any plans this evening Mr. Free Man?" Martha asked jokingly.

Willam smiled. "I just plan on hanging out with Rusty for a while that's all."

"Well, call Lynn, she misses you and maybe she can come over and keep you company for a while."

"Are you sure that's alright with you?"

"Yes, It's alright, I trust you. It's her I don't trust!" she said smiling. "I've been a selfish mother to a good son. I hope someday you can forgive me for what I've done."

"Well, today is 'someday', and there's nothing to forgive. I know you were just trying to be the best mother you could."

Later that evening, Willam walked Martha out to her ride as she prepared for her part-time job. He watched her as she drove off with her co-worker. Willam returned inside and headed for the kitchen. As he passed through the dining room, he noticed the envelope resting against the salt and pepper shakers. He picked it up and ripped it open. He pulled the small piece of paper from the envelope and began to read. His mouth flung open and his eyes grew large as he read the contents.

Willam rushed into the kitchen and picked up the phone and called Uncle Ray. Uncle Ray's first instinct was to calm Will down. He wanted to help but could not make out exactly what Willam was trying to tell him. He was in a panic.

"Will, slow down, slow down. Now, what's going on? Are you alright? Is your mom alright?"

"He's says that he's going to kill her!"

"Kill who? Who said that they were going to kill somebody?"

"Ralph, I mean the killer. He says that he's going to kill her. He left a note."

"Wait right there, don't move, I'll be right over."

The phone went dead. Willam stood there for a moment with the handset of the phone still pressed against his ear. He hung up the phone then immediately yanked the handset from the base to place another call. He pressed the buttons as quickly as he could and listened for a voice, any voice to answer. By the third ring, Willam felt even more of a panic attack coming on. He couldn't just stand there any longer. He had to get to her. He had to warn her. Seven rings and still there was no answer.

Willam rushed toward the front door. He couldn't wait, not for someone to hurt her. He promised her that he would protect her. He stopped at the door then turned and ran as fast as he possibly could up the steps and down the hall to his room. Snatching his keys from off the top of his dresser, he turned and darted back down the stairs to the awaiting police officer standing at the front door. It was Uncle Ray.

"We've got to get over there. We've got to go now!" Willam shouted.

"Where, go where?"

Willam reached in his pant pocket and yanked the paper out and slapped it into Uncle Ray's hand. "Read it!"

Uncle Ray read the scribbling on the paper then looked at Willam. "Did you call her?"

"I tried but didn't get an answer."

"Let's go, I'll drive and you tell me how to get there."

Uncle Ray rushed to the kitchen and made a quick call to the station. The men jumped into the car and quickly sped off. They drove through Fort Dupont Park at unbelievable speed. They turned onto Minnesota Avenue without slowing. They did not stop for traffic lights nor stop signs, not even at one of the busiest intersections in the city, Minnesota and Pennsylvania Avenues.

They crossed over Pennsylvania Avenue leaving only the scent of burnt tire rubber behind them from avoiding automobiles. Cars swerved and honked as they passed by driving on the opposite side of the road heading up to Young Street. As they continued on, they hardly noticed a trailing squad car following with flashing lights.

Both cars pulled up to the house and all of the men pounced onto the pavement in full stride. Rushing up to the door, it slowly opened. Standing before them is the small framed woman that Willam knew well.

"Is she here?" Willam asked.

"No, she's not here." The lady replied. "What's wrong? Oh dear, is she in trouble?"

"Do you know where she went?"

"No, I just got here not to......."

Before the woman could complete her statement, they heard the sound of her voice from the walk. "Will, what's going on? Why are you here, and why is the police here?"

Willam rushed down to her. He threw his arms around her and held her close to him. "I thought...."

"You thought what? Tell me, what's going on?"

"We have reason to believe that a direct threat has been made against you. We will have some one here around the clock until we have this person in our custody or we prove otherwise." Uncle Ray interjected.

"Why me?" Lynn asked nervously.

Willam looked into her terrified eyes then put his arm back around her shoulder, "Because of me, Lynn."

Willam walked Lynn inside. He sat down with her, her mom and Uncle Ray and explained everything. He didn't mention the note. He just said that they heard rumors from a source. They talked for hours before the brown sedan pulled up in front of the house. Two men in suits walked up to the front door and were greeted by Uncle Ray. They were two detectives from the station. They stepped into the house then followed Uncle Ray to the kitchen where they talked. Soon after, another squad car parked in front of the house and two more policemen soon entered the house. They joined the others in the kitchen.

Thirty minutes had passed before the men returned to the living room. Uncle Ray waved Willam over.

"Let's go, we need to talk. They can handle things from here. They'll have someone posted here all night."

Willam looked over at Lynn and she smiled and nodded. He walked over and gave her a hug before leaving. "Go ahead Will, we'll be alright," Lynn said with a trembling voice.

"I won't let anything happen to you, I promise. I'm so sorry to have you go through all of this Lynn. I don't know why or who, I just don't understand any of it, still."

Willam and Uncle Ray made their departure, leaving the remaining officers behind with Lynn and her mother.

Once Willam and Uncle Ray entered the car they began discussing school and people at Willam's job once more. He was looking for anything that might have gotten overlooked during the other several times that Willam had gone through the drill. He asked about his friends old and new, but Willam could not come up with any possible enemies or motives that he knew of.

Three days had passed. Still, there were no signs of any attempted contact or harm to Lynn. Willam went to her house everyday with Uncle Ray after Martha left for work. They would talk and play cards for most of the night before Willam would return home. He would always hug her before he left and she would squeeze him as if it were the last time she would ever see him.

From the front door, the large gap between the two parked cars seemed odd without the presence of the blue and white squad car. The 24 hour guardian commitment had expired. The police captain would only allow three days of overtime. Of course, Uncle Ray and Willam continued with their visits and were planning to stay with the ladies for the entire night. They had discussed alternating shifts during the week and Uncle Ray had spoken to some of his friends who worked that beat and they agreed to drive by as often as they could.

That night, during their normal game of cards, Lynn jokingly accused Willam of cheating. They laughed as Willam pretended to pull cards from under his shirt and Uncle Ray joked about him hiding cards in his socks.

"See, you are a cheater!" Lynn laughed out.

Willam laughed. "Now you know I'd never cheat on my favorite girl."

"Wait a minute. Favorite girl? Not me. That would be your mother," she replied smiling. "At least that's what you told me you used to call her all of the time, 'your favorite girl'!"

Willam and Uncle Ray exchanged looks and jumped up from their seats.

"How could I have forgotten?" Will stammered.

Willam and Uncle Ray ran toward the door.

"What?" Lynn yelled out. "What did I say?"

"We've got to hurry!" Willam called out.

Lynn grabbed her jacket and followed the men outside. They quickly piled into the car and without hesitation, they sped off.

The car sped down the vacant street. It was 2:15 am. The only vehicles visible on the dimly lit street were motionless and silent. Without warning, rain began to pour from the dark and starless sky. Still, the vehicle moved swiftly across the asphalt. It was as if it hydroplaned across the inflexible surface. Uncle Ray hugged the corners of the road like an experienced NASCAR driver. He mashed the gas pedal as far to the floor as it could go and zoomed through the park. They sped through the red light and crossed over Ridge Road on to Texas Avenue. The tires smoked as Uncle Ray slammed on the brakes to make the sharp turn onto F Street.

Flooring the pedal once more, they soared up the hill and within seconds were in front of the house. Willam and Uncle Ray immediately jumped out of the car into the downpour.

"Wait here," Uncle Ray whispered to Lynn.

The men rushed up the front stairs and onto the porch. Willam's heart sank when he found the front door ajar and the house completely dark. The men entered the dark house. Willam rushed into the living room while Uncle Ray headed up the dark staircase.

Meanwhile, Lynn sat nervously in the car. Still not quite sure of what was actually going on she realized that she was alone. Shaking and scared, she began looking through each of the car windows scanning the surrounding area. She was terrified. She slowly leaned across the front seat and pressed the black vinyl latch down to lock the car doors. That's when she saw it. The small piece of paper was lying on the front seat just beneath her. She bent over and picked it up. She unfolded it and slid back, low in the rear seat to make use of the glimmer of light from the street lamps. The note read:

> *"Congratulations to you!*
> *They're all gone and you have avoided punishment for yourself.*
> *This is unacceptable to me.*
> *Let's see how much you'll miss your FAVORITE GIRL!"*

Lynn quickly unlocked her car door and rushed out into the pouring rain. She ran up the stairs and slowly opened the front door. Cautiously, she entered the house. After reading the note, she knew exactly to whom the note referred. She had heard Willam refer to his mother as his "Favorite Girl" many times before. She looked around the room only to find Willam down on his knees, bent over his mother's motionless body. Blood oozed from the back of her head onto the carpet.

Uncle Ray had just come up from the basement and paused for a moment in the kitchen to place a call. As he exited the kitchen, Lynn noticed that he held a flashlight in one of his hands and his firearm in the other. She realized that whoever had done this to Martha could still be in the house. She froze. Suddenly, the screen door slammed open. The soaking wet figure stood in the faint light cast from the outside street lamps. Uncle Ray pointed both his flashlight and weapon at the unexpected intruder.

"What's going on?" Asked the dark figure.

"Paul?" Uncle Ray shouted.

"Yeah, I saw you speeding up the street from the window. I thought something was wrong."

"Fool, you almost got your head blown off running in here like that. What are you doing up this time of night anyway?"

Rusty said nothing. He walked over to where Martha's body lay still and lifeless. "Oh no." He too, then kneeled down beside her next to Willam.

Uncle Ray looked down at both of the young men. "Whoever was here probably ran off when they saw us pull up. I've checked all the floors. They must have cut the main power, too. I've already called for an ambulance and backup. We'll have the place dusted to see if they've left any prints behind.

"Is she...?" Lynn started to ask with her voice trembling.

The sound of the slow dripping water caught both Uncle Ray and Rusty's attention. Just as Uncle Ray stepped into the living room the figure appeared from behind the front door. In his rush through the house, he failed to do the first thing that he had learned at police academy training years ago. He didn't look behind the partially opened door. A dark figure wearing a floppy rain hat and a wide, dark rain coat still wet from the drenching rain, quickly stepped behind Lynn. The thin razor sharp blade was placed across the jugular vein of Willam's girlfriend. Her arm was yanked behind her back and held firmly. Uncle Ray pointed his revolver at the shadowy figure, but it remained still. Willam and Rusty slowly rose to their feet.

"Look, please don't hurt her. It's me you want. Take me!" Willam pleaded.

The figure slowly backed toward the entrance and kicked the screen door open. The blade was slowly slid across Lynn's throat leaving only a fine line that slowly opened to release the deep red blood which it had once contained. As quickly as it had appeared, it had vanished. The figure stepped through the door and out into the rainy night. Rusty rushed over to tend to Lynn while Uncle Ray took off in pursuit.

The blood squirted from her veins in massive amounts. It flowed down her collar bones and shoulders in both directions, leaving only another section of the cheap living room carpet soaked in blood. Rusty clasped both of his hands together and pressed firmly against her severed skin. "Hold on Lynn, help's on the way." He said to her as she lay trembling.

Willam stood there frozen like a statue, not much different than before. It was the same as with Beverly. He couldn't move. Uncle Ray ran to the side of the house. There he saw the two dark images as they wrestled on the water soaked lawn. Finally, one of the figures turned over and mounted the other. He began pounding his adversary beneath him. One after another, his huge fists pounded into the other's flesh.

"Freeze!" He yelled.

The man continued to beat the now still body. He raised his fist high to deliver another possibly deadly blow but was interrupted once more.

"Freeze! This is your last warning. Move and I'll blow your damn head off!" Uncle Ray yelled in a stern voice. The man did not move. He looked over at Uncle Ray then fell over onto the ground.

Uncle Ray could now see the flashing lights of the squad cars off in the distance. Within seconds, several officers were storming into the yard. They rushed over to the two limp bodies and rolled them over face down and handcuffed them both. The paramedics pulled up to the house shortly after and were directed into the house by one of the newly arriving officers, only to find Rusty kneeling beside Lynn's blood covered body. He was sobbing and pounding his thigh with his fist. Willam was kneeling on the other side of her holding her limp hand. He looked up at one of the paramedics and said with a shaky voice, "I heard her take her last breath. This is my fault. It's all my fault. I should have never let her come here."

One of the paramedics began checking her vital signs while the other walked over and knelt down beside Martha. He pressed two of his fingers on the side of her neck before looking at his partner. "I've got a pulse over here!"

Willam looked over in surprise as he had thought that his mother was now holding the hand of God. He watched as both men worked on the two women that he loved. The paramedic who tended to Martha worked diligently to bring her back into consciousness, but was unsuccessful. He placed the clear oxygen mask over her nose and mouth then began applying a solution to the wound on her head. "She's ready for transport. D.C. General is waiting."

The siren blared as a second ambulance raced up the hill of F. Street. One of the paramedics jumped out and headed for the door. He was greeted by the paramedic that was tending to Lynn. He spoke to him briefly and directed him to the side of the house. After returning to Lynn's side, the paramedic closed up his bag and walked over to assist his partner with Martha. It was too late for Lynn, she was dead.

The paramedics prepared Martha for transport to the hospital. "I'll ride with you." Willam said. "I'm not leaving her side."

Martha was still unconscious, but alive. He looked down at Lynn and began to weep uncontrollably. Rusty placed his arm around Willam to console him but he too needed consoling. Willam could hear one of the paramedics on the porch talking into his walkie-talkie.

"It appears that they have apprehended the person responsible." Upon hearing that, Willam ran outside to the side of the house. The rain had stopped. The police were crowded around the handcuffed but injured bodies as the paramedics tended to their wounds.

Willam walked up to the crowd and looked down at the man's face. "Ralph, I should have known."

The weak and bloody man managed to raise his head just barely high enough to witness the face of his accuser. He spoke in a low voice to Willam. "I saw him on the side of the house from the window. I saw the lights go out. I knew something wasn't right. Something just wasn't right. I came over here to make sure your mom was alright. That's when I saw you pull up. I waited. I waited right here, and watched from the window. I saw him cut her throat and run out. I stopped him. I had to stop him." Ralph slumped over.

"He's lost a lot of blood." The paramedic said. "His cut is pretty deep. We need to get him to the hospital."

Willam looked at the other muddy body lying face down in handcuffs. "Turn him over." Willam yelled.

The police officer pulled the limp body up to its feet. Willam snatched off the wide rim rain hat and stared surprisingly into the face of the person who had caused him so much despair, the face of a woman. He looked even more puzzled than ever. He did not recognize this woman's face and could not make any reference or connection to her. She was a heavyset woman with a short boyish haircut. She wore all black underneath her rain gear, black pants and a black turtleneck as if she were a burglar. Willam knew she was no burglar. She was a killer.

Suddenly, Rusty pushed his way through the small crowd. He took one look into the face of the woman and mumbled, "Well I'll be damned! Colette?" The woman looked up at Rusty then over to Willam who was now staring at her face.

"Blame yourself." She said. "Blame yourself Will for all that's happened to you."

Willam said nothing, he only looked down at the wet earth.

"How does it feel?" she continued. "How does it feel to have your life turned upside down? That's exactly what you did to me. That's exactly what you did to my life that night. You remember that night don't you? Yes, you remember, the night you followed Ralph down to meet me by the tunnel. The night you watched as I pleaded with him to take me back. The night he said goodbye to me because I had given myself to somebody else. Tell them what you did Will, tell them! Tell them how you watched us from the darkness, just as I did you. How you watched me take off my clothes to give myself to him but he didn't want me. How you watched as Ralph left me standing there crying. Tell them how you suddenly appeared and because I didn't want to be with you, you called me those names! Tell them how you beat me. Tell them. Tell them how you took me and then urinated on me like I was nothing. You were supposed to be protecting me! You were like a big brother to me! HOW COULD YOU HAVE DONE THAT TO ME, HOW?!!"

Then with a very calm voice, Colette whispered her last words to him. "Tell them how you slit my throat and smiled as you watched me bleed."

Willam looked at Colette with sadness in his eyes. He could barely speak, but manage to utter only two words. "I'm sorry."

"Take her away," said Uncle Ray.

Rusty looked over at Willam. "You alright?"

"They're all gone. They're all gone because of me."

"She's crazy man, just plain crazy." Rusty said.

Uncle Ray stepped up beside Willam and placed his hand on his shoulder. "Will, I've waved the ambulance on. They're taking her to the hospital. They said she'll be fine. I'll let you know as soon as I hear anything."

Willam nodded. Uncle Ray pulled out his handcuffs and placed Willam's arms behind his back and attached the metal bracelets around his wrists. He walked Willam to the car past the swarm of policemen and detectives and placed his hand over Willam's head as he lowered him into the back seat of the squad car.

Willam sat in the back seat of the car with a blank stare upon his face, singing in a low and strangely muffled voice. "We've come this faaaaaaar by faith, leaning on the Loooooord."

PREVIEW OF THE UPCOMING

NOVEL BY E.L. RHODES

E.L. RHODES

THE MEETING PLACE

Chapter 1 - Viola

Her hand, small and petite, covered by the soft blue thick cotton glove gripped the metal pole as she stood still waiting impatiently. The icy cold of the metal pole cut deeply and painfully, piercing through her glove like the blade of a razor-sharp knife. She quickly removed her hand and wrapped her arm around her body. Her other hand was wrapped firmly around the thick rope handle of the shopping tote bag which contained her precious items. Barely moving, she stood as if she had already been frozen solid by old man winter himself. Staring in the same direction for over twenty minutes, she wanted only to see just a glimpse of its nose peeking over the horizon. Now swaying from side to side, she remained focused on its expected sight. She was at its mercy. The bitter cold made her seek its refuge and she was now longing to snuggle comfortably in its warm bosom.

The cold wet bead of moisture crept slowly from the corner of her eye down the front of her face as the frigid wind forced its way through her layered garments chilling her small bones. She wiped her face then tightly folded her arms together and

3

tapped her feet against the cold pavement in an alternating succession.

Finally, creeping slowly toward her from off in the distance was the vision of that which satisfied her desire. Her anticipation grew stronger as it advanced nearer. Now upon her, after slowly settling to a complete stop, the doors of the #4 bus opened. It had just completed its run through Main Street. The thin small woman hurried aboard.

"Morning Vy!" Greeted the driver while looking out at her from under the brim of his hat.

The young woman quickly dug into the pocket of her coat. Just as fast as she retrieved it from her pocket, she dropped the coins into the small oblong glass encased receptacle. She then sashayed down the aisle without uttering a word. As she maneuvered toward a seat, the heads of the other passengers turned and the faint whispers began. She held firmly on to her bag while keeping her nose pointed toward the ceiling of the now moving transport. Just as she was about to slide onto the blue vinyl bench seat, she turned and placed herself on display for the snobby and snide remarking spectators.

"Take a picture why don't ya?" She declared loudly. She looked at all of them with her sassy but angry look then turned and faced the back of the bus. She reached around to the bottom of her blue and gray plaid coat and not only did she pull up her coat, she raised her coat and dress high above her waist. She bent over and smacked her bottom while yelling as loud as she could, "YOU ALL CAN JUST GO STRAIGHT TO HELL AND KISS THIS ON YOUR WAY DOWN!"

The rude stares and snide remarks were what she had to contend with daily; ever since everyone in her small town of

Emporia, Virginia found out that she had been impregnated by none other than Willy Sims. Willy Sims, also known as the Honorable Reverend Sims, was the pastor of The Mount Calvary Baptist Church of Emporia. This tidbit was the talk of the town and everyone has something to say about it. Everywhere she turned the words whore, harlot, or home-wrecker was whispered from the lips of some self righteous sinner masquerading as a holy saint.

After adjusting her clothing, she placed her large bag on the seat and cautiously lowered herself down. She grabbed onto the chrome bar that was attached to the seat directly in front of her before leaning back against the backrest. The heat blew from the small holes along the bottom of the windows. It wasn't cozy, but just warm enough to help take the chill out of the air. She folded her arms and closed her eyes. She was tired; tired and cold. If it wasn't for her son who had taken ill with the flu, she would have never left the house. He needed to be cared for and they were running out of food and medicine. She would have walked to town if she had to for him.

After resting her head and closing her eyes for a quick nap, her small pleasure was quickly interrupted.

"Vy! Hey Vy!" The voice whispered.

She ignored the voice and continued with her resting.

"Viola!" The voice whispered once again.

"What in the hell do you want? Don't you see me trying to get some rest?"

"Does Jessie know?"

"Does Jessie know what?"

"Does he know about the baby? I mean, it being the Pastor's and all."

Without opening her eyes or turning her head, she answered. "Why do you want to know about me and Jessie's business? So you can only have more rumors to spread around town about me? I'll tell you what, I'm gonna answer your question but only after I bust you in your big loud gossip tellin' mouth so you can't spread no more of your filth!"

A cold dead silence rushed throughout the bus cabin. Viola piled all of her belongings snugly against the wall then rose from her seat and turned toward the woman who was now looking terrified. She removed her high heeled shoes and balled up her hands into two little fists. She stood up tall and erect then inched toward the back door of the bus. Moments after, the vehicle slowed and then came to a stop.

"Viola, now you settle down back there. We'll be havin' none of that today. You leave Miss Thelma alone. Miss Thelma, you go on now, this here is your stop. Leave her be Viola, you just leaver her be. I won't have to call the sheriff again will I?" yelled the big husky bus driver from his seat.

With that, Viola relaxed her hands and lowered her head. Thelma having realized the impact of the bus driver's statement, noticed the affect that it had on Viola. She slowly rose up from her seat all the while never taking her eyes off of Viola. She inched between the angry little woman and the seat closest to the rear exit then hesitantly started down the steps to the double doors.

"Go on Miss. Thelma, she ain't goin' to harm you none." Once again the bus driver reassured the trembling woman. Thelma reached for the long chrome handle of the doors and began to push. As she turned to exit she looked back at Viola and produced a snobbish smirk over her face. She turned up her nose then mumbled under her breath, "Just shameless."

Viola's hands once again returned to their balled position. As Thelma turned to lower herself down on the last step to exit, Viola quickly took hold of the shiny bar secured tightly to the back of the seat in front of the exit doors and the long vertical chrome pole that was located just at the top of the steps. Bracing herself, Viola pulled herself off the floor and raised her foot.

"Viola no!" Yelled the bus driver.

The unsuspecting snobby Thelma looked over at the driver who had now risen from his seat. He was waving his arms and gesturing like a policeman stopping traffic. Just as Thelma began to turn toward Viola, she could feel the hard boney heel of the little woman's small foot wedge between her shoulder blades.

"Noooooooooooo Viola!" Yelled the driver.

It was too late and Thelma knew it. Without warning the tiny woman delivered a powerful jolt to Thelma's back. The passengers could hear her yell out loudly as they watched her head whip back toward her shoulder blades.

"Iiiiiiiiiieeeeeeeeeemmmmmmmmmm!" Thelma screamed. Before she knew it, Thelma felt herself lifted up and out of both of her high heeled shoes then soaring through the air. As her body began to crash through the rear double doors, her head wasn't as lucky. During her short flight, her head was quickly greeted by the metal threshold just above the doors. The top of her forehead scraped against the metal during her forced exit. As she was spit from the exit-way every item in her handbag scattered through the air as the bag itself took flight. Her knees made impact with the awaiting ground after which she slid about four feet across the cold pavement. With her hands down by her sides, her nylons ripped down to her ankles, scratches across her forehead and shoeless, she swayed forward then slowly to the rear before slamming face first to the pavement. As she lay on the cold concrete covered with earth she uttered the remaining half of her statement, "Sor-ry" then passed out.

"Now smirk at that you self-righteous hypocrite! If it wasn't so cold out there I'd come and whup you some more!" Viola yelled as Thelma lay face down on the pavement.

Everyone on the bus rushed off to Thelma's aid.

"Yal better get back on this bus for you all get left. She'll be alright. I gotta get home so let's get movin'. I got a sick boy at home so come on now. I said she'll be alright. She'll have a headache and maybe a mild case of 'next time I'll just shut the hell up' but other than that she'll be alright, so let's get goin'." Viola said.

The crowd didn't budge. They ignored Viola as they continued assisting the young woman who was still sprawled out on the cold pavement. The bus driver had even joined in with the revival of poor Thelma.

"Ben, now you get back on this bus so I can get home. Anybody else who wants to stay can just get left!" Viola screamed.

Still, everyone remained focused and tended to Thelma. Angry and frustrated even more now, viola walked up to the driver's seat and pulled the metal switch down to the "close" position. The doors to the bus closed. The group of passengers all rushed over to the door yelling for Viola to let them back on board. Ben, the driver rushed through the crowd and began banging his hand against the glass of the door.

"Viola, now you open these doors, right now!"

Viola just sat quietly, looking around at all the different controls. "You goin' to take me home then?" Viola asked calmly.

"If you open the door, sure." Ben replied.

Viola pushed the switch back to the "open" position. As the doors began to open, Viola immediately pulled the switch back down and the doors re-closed. She stood, while leaving the crowd standing in front of the door. Thelma had managed to pull herself up and was now sitting on the freezing curb. Viola walked across the aisle and lowered one of the windows. She leaned her head out and yelled as loud as she could. "Thelma, you'd better get your nosey ass up off that cold ground pretending to be more hurt than you really are before I come out there and turn that pretend into reality! You'd better be up by the time I get there or else!"

Viola stared at the woman for a moment before closing the window. Before she could make her way to the back door, Thelma jumped up and staggered as fast as she could down the sidewalk. After slamming the window shut, Viola walked back over to the driver's seat and once again pushed the switch to open the doors. The driver and all of the angry passengers rushed back on to the warmth of the transport. As they returned to their seats, Ben picked up the handset of his two-way-radio. He looked back at Viola angrily as she slowly sashayed back to her seat still mumbling to herself.

9

"Viola, I'm afraid I'm gonna have to ask you to leave the bus!"

Viola, now lowering herself in her seat, calmly replied. "Well, I guess I'm afraid that I'm gonna have to ask you to kiss my ass Ben."

"Now Viola, don't make me have to call the sheriff. Come on now, let's go!"

Viola slowly raised her head and continued to speak in her calm voice. "Now Ben, why you wanna go and do that? Aint no cause for you to call the Sheriff now is it? You know that busy body Thelma was instigating me. Now I don't want no trouble Ben, but you know I aint scaret! And besides, it'll be pretty hard drivin' this here bus with only one eye to see out of. How many days will you have to take off from your job before your vision comes back, huh? So ask yourself, is it really worth it? Besides, you wouldn't want me to call and tell Luke that you called the sheriff on his dearest and most favorite cousin now would you? He'll ram his foot so far up your ass your farts will smell like shoe leather for six weeks!"

Luke was Viola's first cousin. He, like Viola was as mean as a snake, maybe even meaner. He was so mean that he once beat a man to near death just for touching his new car after Luke had just run him over. That's right, after he had hit the man with his car. The young man was only crossing the street with his bag of groceries; Luke drove up and failed to stop at the stop sign at the intersection. He struck the man and knocked him to the ground. The poor guy's groceries flew in every direction. Luke remained in his car waiting for the man to collect himself and remove himself and all of his belongings from out of his path so that he could continue on his way. He revved his engine as the man struggled to pull himself up from the ground. Having become more agitated, Luke began yelling at the man to move while blowing his horn at him.

Spectators stood and watched but said nothing as the man helplessly tried to maneuver himself to an upright position. No one said a word to Luke for they all knew how crazy he was. Two of the male spectators finally walked over to assist the young man. As they lifted him to his feet it appeared that the leg that was struck by Luke's car was broken. Not able to apply any pressure on the leg, the young man lost his balance and before either man could catch him, the young man placed his hand on the top of the hood of Luke's new car in an effort to steady himself. This infuriated Luke.

"Hey, get off the car!" Luke shouted at the man. He climbed out of his car and rushed around to where the young man stood wincing.

One of the spectators assisting the young man backed away slowly from the car while the other held firmly on to the young man's arm for support. Luke walked up and slapped the young man's only crutch. The Good Samaritan let go of the young man's arm and held the side of his face. He looked at the young man and said, "You're on you own!" and then ran off.

Luke stepped closer to the young man who now was balancing himself on one leg. Without saying a word, Luke slammed the young man to the ground and beat him for over five minutes. When he was done, he walked back around to the driver side of his car, climbed in and sped off running over whatever groceries that remained in the brown paper sack.

Yes, Luke was crazy and none of the residents of Emporia wanted any dealings with him. The only person that he had any respect for other than his father was Viola. His father was just as mean as he was and as for Viola, well she was the only other person ever to have whipped him. He never forgot when Viola laid into him. She hurt him pretty bad. That was when he, as she had put it, "took part of my virgin."

Viola had injured Luke so intensely that he walked with a slight limp from that day forward. Luke rained down havoc and hell on all of Emporia. Nope, Ben wanted no part of Luke, not in this lifetime. He wanted only to drive the bus for another day and he knew if Viola called her crazy cousin and told him that Ben had given her a hard time on the bus that Luke would come calling. As Ben returned from his deep thought he could still hear Viola's voice in the distance.

"How much money will you loose for not being able to work 'cause you know Luke's gonna tear your ass up?! You'll be walking around with a tin can and cane by the time he's done with you." Viola then became silent as she slowly rose to her feet once more. Once again her hands transformed into little tightly balled fists. "Now why don't you just put that radio back in that cradle Ben?"

Viola inched closer and closer to where the big burly man sat. He slowly placed the handset of the radio back into the cradle and pulled the switch down to close the doors. He looked at the little lady in frustration. "You know, you're more trouble than you're worth. I'll be glad when Jessie gets back home. Somebody needs to settle you down."

"Well it won't be you, so just drive FAT BOY!"

THE MEETING PLACE

READER'S NOTES

E.L. RHODES

www.ingramcontent.com/pod-product-compliance
Lightning Source LLC
Chambersburg PA
CBHW022011010726
47494CB00003B/997